Lauren Wilkinson grew up in New York City and lives in the Lower East Side. She earned her MFA in Fiction and Literary Translation from Columbia University and has taught writing at Columbia and the Fashion Institute of Technology. She has received writing fellowships from the Center for Fiction and the MacDowell Colony, and her fiction has appeared in Granta.

LAUREN WILKINSON

AMERICAN SPY

dialogue
books

DIALOGUE BOOKS

First published in the United States in 2019 by Random House,
an imprint and division of Penguin Random House LLC, New York.
First published in Great Britain in 2019 by Dialogue Books

10 9 8 7 6 5 4 3 2 1

A CIP catalogue record for this book is available from the British Library.

Hardback ISBN 978-0-349-70100-4
Trade Paperback ISBN 978-0-349-70099-1

Printed and bound in Great Britain by Clays Ltd, Elcograf S.p.A.

Papers used by Dialogue Books are from well-managed forests
and other responsible sources.

Dialogue Books
An imprint of
Little, Brown Book Group
Carmelite House
50 Victoria Embankment
London EC4Y 0DZ

An Hachette UK Company
www.hachette.co.uk

www.littlebrown.co.uk

For my mother, Linda Perry

Son, after I'm gone I want you to keep up the good fight. I never told you, but our life is a war and I have been a traitor all my born days, a spy in the enemy's country ever since I give up my gun back in the Reconstruction. Live with your head in the lion's mouth. I want you to overcome 'em with yeses, undermine 'em with grins, agree 'em to death and destruction, let 'em swoller you till they vomit or bust wide open.

Ralph Ellison, *Invisible Man*

PART ONE

1

Iunlocked the safe beneath my desk, grabbed my old service automatic, and crept toward my bedroom doorway, stealthy until I was brought to grief by a Lego Duplo that stung the sole of my foot. I hobbled the rest of the way to the door and crouched behind it.

A few moments passed, just enough time for me to feel ridiculous. I told myself that what I'd heard was the house settling. That was always what it wound up being.

The room was still and dark; the only light was from the moon. Poochini, our German shepherd mix, was closed in your bedroom with you. He let out a single, cautious bark. I heard the whoosh of tires on asphalt—a car passing on the Boston Post Road, which was hidden just behind the tangle of woods at the back of our small house. Then it was quiet again.

That night I'd been up late working on a translation at the desk in my room, so it was after two when I'd finally shut off the light and climbed into bed. I hadn't been able to sleep. As I was staring at the ceiling, I'd thought I'd heard a floorboard creak in the hall. Instinctively, I'd climbed out of bed and gone for my gun.

Your room was across from my own. I pictured you both asleep, and told myself I was being irrational. I told myself we were safe.

Then a man appeared in my bedroom, and my heart picked up speed as I watched him approach my bed. I lunged low at him from behind, toppling him to the floor with a crash. His gun thudded against the hardwood and disappeared into the darkness. He tried to stand, but I climbed on him, pinned him down. His lean, hard body bucked beneath mine. He shoved me off and my back collided with the bedside table. My lamp clattered to the floor. I'd lost my gun too. I tried to get to my feet, but he grabbed a handful of my hair and yanked me back down. He rolled on top of me and his hands searched for my neck. They found my mouth instead, and I bit him so hard he screamed. Spat out an expletive that was the first word uttered by either of us. I clawed the skin I could get at—his face, his arms—and struggled against his weight. He went for my neck again, and as he started to squeeze I reached behind me, flailing my arms, hoping to find the fallen lamp in the dark; instead my fingers curled around a 9mm that didn't belong to me. I lifted it to the man's temple. Squeezed the trigger.

The sound of the shot exploded through our quiet house. He crumpled and his weight pressed me down against the hardwood, suffocating me. I heard Poochini race into the room and your footsteps in the hall. Gasping, I struggled to push the heavy body off me, then went to turn on the overhead light and lock the door so you couldn't see inside my room. My breath came hard and fast as I looked at the body.

"Maman?" one of you called from the hall.

"Stay there," I barely managed to choke out, still coughing. My voice was raw and constricted from the violence done to my throat. And my senses were surreally sharp, the effect of the adrenaline coursing through me. I felt like I could see more clearly than I ever had before, and smell more keenly: The tangy scent of his blood and sweat in the air were oppressively strong. I looked at his face. Much of it was missing, but I didn't think I recognized him. Poochini watched me check his pockets for ID, but found none. It didn't matter—I knew who'd sent him.

"I'm coming right now," I called to you two as I searched for my gun. I locked it back in the safe, and took the man's with me. Poochini followed me out of the bedroom and tracked bloody dog prints all over the wood floor. I pulled the door closed behind me.

William, you were there blinking against the bright light; Tommy, you were peeking out from your room, half hidden behind the door-frame. I realized the phone was ringing.

"Blood," you said, William, and pointed at my face.

"It's okay," I said. "I'm okay." I sped down the hall, crossed the living room to the front door, and stepped outside. Peered out into the dark, but didn't see anyone or any unfamiliar cars. I went back inside. You'd followed and were standing in the foyer. Tommy, you were crying. I wanted to pick you up but didn't because of the blood on my clothes.

"We're safe," I said, hoping to soothe you as I made a circuit around the living room, Poochini following in my wake as I looked for the man's point of entry.

I went back down the hall and into the bathroom. He'd come in through the window there. I stared at the broken glass, then looked at my reflection in the medicine cabinet. There was blood on my face and neck and T-shirt. The man had choked me so hard that he'd broken blood vessels in my cheek. I turned on the tap; as I was washing my face, the phone sounded again. I picked up the living room extension, as if in a trance. My neighbor Irena was on the line. She lived next door, close enough to have heard the shot.

"Marie! I've been calling. Thank god, you're all right." Because she was panicked, her Polish accent was especially pronounced. Irena was around my mother's age. I went to her house sometimes to sit at her kitchen table, sip coffee, and gossip. We were bonded as conspirators. Outsiders. Neither of us was the type to talk about our past, but I'd picked up on the little hints that suggested she'd seen mayhem in her life: There weren't many retirees in that sleepy town who could so confidently identify the sound of a gunshot in the middle of the night.

I told her I was fine, then hung up abruptly because I'd heard a siren approaching. Irena must've called the police. I ushered you both back to your room, told you to wait there with Poochini. The bell rang.

"Marie Mitchell?" a cop called through the front door, and rapped on it once before kicking it open. As I was pulling your door closed, several sets of boots stomped through my living room. Three cops appeared at the mouth of the hall, trapping me. All three had their weapons drawn. Still holding the gun, I put up my hands.

Two of the cops stayed at the end of the hall while the third approached me. "Put the weapon down!" he ordered. "Put it down!"

"Listen, sir, my sons are in the house," I said as I bent to put the gun on the floor. You both were shrieking with fear.

"Do you have any other weapons on you?" he asked.

"They're behind this door. They're just little boys. They're four. Please don't—"

"Shut your mouth and answer the question," he barked. "Anything else on you that could be a danger to us?"

"No, sir."

The cop pressed me hard against the wall, and pain flashed through my bruised chest. As he searched me roughly, I stayed passive and compliant. He was twice my size, but if he'd shot me, they'd say in the report that it was because I posed a threat to him.

"What happened?"

Speaking as calmly as I could, not wanting to alarm him I said, "He's in my room, sir. He was going to kill me. I live here."

"Who is?"

"I don't know, sir. But he's dead." I added, "My father's a cop. His shield's in my purse." I kept a replica in a pouch with my insurance and registration, so if I ever got stopped in the car, I could casually flash it while handing over my documents.

The first cop glanced back to the other two. "She's clear."

As they holstered their guns, I asked if they wanted me to get the shield. The first cop shook his head. All three had finally started to relax.

"Which room's the body in? This one?" He had his hand on the knob to my bedroom door. I nodded quickly. He opened it and went inside.

"Can I go in my sons' room?" I asked one of the other cops, who nodded.

"Maman, I'm scared," you said, Tommy, and clung to me.

"I know." Not caring about the blood anymore, I crouched to put my arms around you both. I held you for as long as I could and kissed you. Then I quickly packed a backpack and shepherded the two of you and the dog out into the hall. You both tensed at the sight of the policeman. Tommy, I had to pick you up because you wouldn't walk.

"Don't go too far," one of the cops called after me as I was leaving. At Irena's house, she opened the door and threw her arms around me despite the state of my clothes. She was the only person living on our cul-de-sac that I genuinely liked.

"I have to go to the hospital."

She hugged me again; I must've sounded dazed. She said, "They can stay here as long as you need."

Before I left, I went to Irena's kitchen, to her bedroom, to each room of her house, assessing all the points of entry while everyone, Poochini included, followed quietly. You were more vulnerable there than I would've liked, but I didn't have much of a choice.

Once you realized I was leaving, you both started to cry again. As gently as I could, I had to unhook your arms from around my calves, and that was more painful to me than any of the damage done to my body. I promised I'd be back as soon as I could. I meant it.

Back at our house, a pair of EMTs had arrived. As one looked me over she told me what I already knew: My lip would need stitches. I said I'd drive myself to the hospital after the cops interviewed me, which I knew they needed to do.

The one who I'd felt most threatened by slipped on a falsely soothing posture that grated my nerves. He asked me if I needed anything, which I recognized as a prelude; he was testing the waters to see if I was ready to answer questions. I said, "Go ahead. Ask me anything you need to."

"Start from the beginning. What happened?"

"I was asleep in my room. It was three, maybe? I heard a noise in the hall and—"

"You were sleeping?"

"I was trying to sleep when I thought I heard something."

"Mm-hmm." The cop's eyes ran across my face. Heat flashed up into my cheeks, as I worried that my eagerness to be as truthful as possible made me sound like I was lying. Your grandfather was a career cop, which instilled a fear of authority in me that even my own time as a Fed couldn't cure.

The interview continued. Two coroners came through the open door. I waited around for everyone to clear out, then went to get my lip fixed. By the time I got back to our street, it was almost dawn. Next door, I looked in on you in Irena's den. You were lying on her pullout couch under a pile of blankets. Tommy, you're easy to miss when you're asleep. Your brother takes up a lot of space; he's all limbs, like a sweet little squid. But, Tommy, you curl into an impossibly tight ball.

Poochini came over to me, and I scratched him between the ears. I asked Irena in a whisper, "How were they?"

She shook her head. "It took them a long time to fall asleep."

I threw back a corner of one of the blankets and risked waking you to kiss your foreheads. Neither of you stirred. As Irena turned back to the hall, I wished her a good night, then sat on the arm of the sofa, and watched you sleep for a while, too wired to do so myself.

MARTINIQUE, TWO DAYS LATER

The man I'd killed had been an intruder in our home; I felt no legal obligation to the situation other than to submit to an interview as I'd done on the scene. But I wasn't sure the cops would see it the same way, so we'd left the United States on a set of fake passports that my father's friend Mr. Ali had prepared for me a few years earlier in case of an emergency. I hope that nothing about your adult lives will require you to be as paranoid as I was. The clerk at the Jumbo Car rental desk asked how my day was going, then looked up at me from his console. The smile slid from his face when he saw my stitches and the bruise in full bloom on my cheekbone.

I briefly took off my sunglasses so the clerk could compare my face to the one in the photo. The name on the license I gave the clerk matched my passport: Monica Williams. He used that name as he handed back my paperwork, and I glanced down at you two. Your French was good enough to have understood him, but you seemed oblivious to the new name.

Outside, you climbed into the backseat of a sporty-looking red Peugeot with Poochini; the clerk had given me a free upgrade to a larger car. I loaded our luggage into the trunk, then started up the engine.

Martinique's airport is in Le Lamentin, an industrial district, and as we sped along a factory-lined highway, I told you about the day you were born. That day we'd driven along the same road; I pointed out the window to the spot where my mother and I'd been forced to pull over when her old truck had run out of gas. We'd ended up having to hitch a ride to the maternity hospital, ten miles away. All that had happened because truck drivers for the oil refinery on the island had been on strike, refusing to deliver to any of the gas stations. *On strike*—it's a very French country. When they call it an overseas department they mean it.

On that road, I'd had the first intense contraction of my labor, one so overwhelmingly, violently painful that I'd wanted to put a pin in the whole situation and come back to it later, when I was a better person. You could call that kind of pain ineffable or transcendental, which I guess it was, but the problem with both words is their positive connotation. It wasn't pain that strengthened my character. Feeling like I was being atomized from the throat down did nothing to enhance my vision of myself. Don't get me wrong, I'm so glad to be your mother, and for the most part I enjoyed being pregnant with you. But the endgame could've used some improvement.

Martinique is a beautiful country. As we continued on in the Peugeot, through the countryside, through towns, coasting down steep inclines and around sharp curves, climbing switchbacked hills, I felt like I was in a movie, although that might have been more about my mental state than the lush scenery—the only way I'd managed to get through the last couple of days was to play everything at a distance.

Tired from the flight, you boys were quiet. Not Poochini, who rode with his head sticking out of the back window, barking and panting and so excited by all the new smells that I was worried he'd jump out of the car. He was one of those dogs who was a perennial runaway. I wish I knew what got into him, so I could break him of the habit. I'd taken far too many trips up and down our cul-de-sac in my bathrobe, screaming his name at the top of my lungs.

Agathe's farm was in Sainte-Anne, a commune at the very south of the country. As we approached a roundabout, I noticed a teenage hitchhiker waiting near it and stopped for him. He spoke to me in Creole; I answered in French that he should get in the passenger seat. *Auto-stop* was very common there, and Martinique was the only place on Earth where I'd pick up a hitchhiker. I owed a debt to the stranger who drove me to the hospital and wanted to pay it forward.

After I dropped the kid near a second roundabout, one closer to downtown, we continued south to the farm. The second I saw my mother's home in the distance, the tension in my jaw started to recede—I hadn't even been aware of the grip it had on me until I felt it diminish. We were almost to safety.

The property was split in two by the main road and enclosed on both sides by barbed wire. White cows dotted the pasture, which was brown and a little dry looking but still lovely. The farmhouse was at the top of a crest—one of my many reasons for going there. The sweeping vantage point would give me a strategic advantage if anyone came looking for me. I made the sharp turn and climbed up the driveway lined with large green aloe plants, the Peugeot's toy motor whining pitifully even in first gear. I parked beside my mother's same old truck, we got out and crossed toward the house. I let us inside.

Comfortingly, the living room was just as I remembered it: overrun by tropical plants and rattan. On the far wall were a pair of brown floor-to-ceiling plantation shutters, and a doorway that led to the kitchen. Your grandmother was in there, humming along to the radio. I could smell bacon. A pan clattered against the burner.

"Agathe," I called. She strode into the living room, rubbing her hands on her apron, and after I'd hugged her tightly she examined my bruises and lightly touched my cheek, her face knotted with worry.

"I know it looks bad," I said in French. "I tried to tell you."

She nodded. "You're my child. It hurts to see you all bruised up. Even with a warning."

It felt like I was being cruel by confronting her with the reality of what had happened. I wished I could've gone off somewhere to hide, to bear the burden of it alone. I wanted to protect her, as I wanted to protect you, and hated that I couldn't.

"Say hello," I said to you boys.

"I'm your grandma," she said, using the word *mémé*. She bent down, and you both gave her a perfunctory kiss on the cheek. Tommy, you seemed shy, as you always were with strangers. I didn't think either of you remembered her.

"They still speak French, right?" She stood. "They understood me?"

I nodded. "They're just exhausted. Especially William. His ears were hurting him on the plane. He couldn't sleep."

"No, I'm not," you said in French, William. "I'm not tired."

"How about you?" Agathe asked.

"I'm fine. I think." I was still feeling nothing at all.

She asked if you two were hungry and led you to the kitchen for breakfast. I sat on the sofa. Inhaled and exhaled slowly. At my mother's house, two thousand miles away from Connecticut, I finally felt like I was out of danger. I was suddenly exhausted. Unable to keep my eyes open, I lay down on the sofa.

When I woke up it was dark. I leaped to my feet, alarmed at having let my guard down, then followed your voices out to the back patio. Your grandmother was telling you a bedtime story. Poochini's tail thumped against the concrete as I stepped outside. You two were already in your pajamas, squeezed in together on the wicker sofa with Agathe.

"Maman!" Tommy called.

Looking at my watch, I was astonished to learn I'd slept for twelve hours. "Why didn't you wake me?"

"I'm surprised they didn't. They tore up the living room this afternoon. And you slept through a huge argument over absolutely nothing. I mean tears, screaming. The works."

I sat on the ground next to Poochini. "Sounds like you had fun today."

"You were dead to the world. You must've needed the rest." My mother sounded pleased as she added: "Their French is good!"

"We are French at home," you said, William.

"I try to get them to speak it with me so they retain it," I said.

"Does that work?"

"Sort of."

"Maman, what are stars?" Tommy, you asked this.

I looked up at the sky. I don't think you'd ever seen so many before. At night here, we could see more of them than I even knew to imagine when I was growing up in New York, and it made me feel good to think you had just a little more knowledge, a little more access to the world than I did when I was your age.

I started to explain, muddling something about them being big balls of gas and heat and light, that the sun was also a star, that the stars were like our sun but they looked small to us because they were so far away. By the time I'd finished, you were thoroughly confused.

"Mémé said—she says Daddy's a star. Now he is 'cause he died."

Tommy, you said this in that matter-of-fact way of yours. You added, "What star is he?"

I'd been anticipating questions about your father since you first learned to talk, but not that one. Annoyed, I looked at my mother. It had only taken her half a day to start filling your heads with her particular brand of spiritual hokum. She read my expression and gave me a small, apologetic smile. "They were asking what happens after you die. For obvious reasons."

"Is that bad man a star?" Tommy asked, apparently finding the logic in this more appealing than what I'd just told you.

"I don't know," I said pointedly to Agathe. "Mémé, is he?"

"No," she said. "If you're bad, you don't become one. You come back to Earth to try again to be good."

"Where's that photo album I gave you?" I asked. It was in her room.

"Let me show you a picture of your daddy before he became a star," I said when I returned to the porch, grudgingly endorsing my mother's fiction. I pulled a photo from the album, the one of my sister and a soldier in uniform. William, you're too quick for me. You slipped off the sofa and managed to pluck it from my hand. I watched as you brought it close to your face and inspected it in the lamplight.

"Be careful!" your brother scolded as he came over and tried to snatch the picture from you. I took it, told you to get on the sofa and sit nicely. Crouching in front of you, I held the photo out so you both could see. "That's him and Aunt Helene."

"Is she a star?" William asked. "She is," Agathe said.

"'Cause Daddy's a star why—umm . . ." William, you covered your upper lip with your tongue for a moment as you thought. "Why can't he come back?"

"You mean, after you die, why can't you come back and be alive again?"

You nodded.

"That's a hard one," I admitted. "Why'd he die?" William asked. "That's a hard one too."

The nature and quantity of the questions you ask are staggering. As

is how much the both of you talk. Until you came along, I hadn't realized how quiet my life had been. As I was trying to figure out what else
to tell you, Tommy, you put your hand on my cheek. "Maman?"

I looked down at your sweetly stern little face.

"Don't be sad."

I smiled at the seriousness of the command. It made me think of
how much like your father you are. You believe you can correct me, my
feelings, purely through the force of your will. That impulse at its most
essential is what your father understood love to be. And, William, you
are just as full of energy as he was. Just as fast. Just as impatient. Just as
generous. I wondered all the time what kind of men you'd be. I hoped
that if I could help you focus all that energy and will, you'd be as ex-
traordinary as your dad was.

"Okay. For you," I said, and kissed your cheek.

That was yesterday evening. Later, Tommy, you woke up from a
nightmare screaming and scared the hell out of your brother. I went to
your room to bring you water and rub your back, then lay at the foot of
the bed you're sharing until you both fell back asleep.

Now it's early in the morning. It's dark out, and the house is still.
Agathe is asleep in my uncle's old room because she insisted I stay in
hers, which is much larger and across the hall from yours. The furniture here is all oversized. Resting on the giant vanity is the only artifact
from our house in Queens, a framed photo that my father took during
his photography phase.

It's from Christmas 1962. I'd wanted our Airedale, Bunny, to wear
a Santa cap for the picture, so to please me, Helene is trying (and fail-
ing) to keep him from shaking it off his head. Bunny's a brown blur, and
she's glaring at him in openmouthed frustration. I'm grinning though.
Helene was like a little mother to me: always more dedicated to my
happiness than to her own. It's my favorite photo of us.

Last night on the porch, I told you your daddy died because he was
in a war, that he was in a plane and it got shot down. What I said cor-
responded with what I'd already told Agathe: Your father was an
American soldier who'd died in the line of duty, and his family wanted

nothing to do with us. I knew my mother didn't believe that cover, because I wouldn't have believed it. Every lie I'd told her about your father has come with a silent dare for her to call me on it. She never has.

I'd found the picture I showed you in one of the boxes of my sister's things that Pop was storing in her room.

In it she's in her backyard in North Carolina poised over a decrepit barbecue with tongs. The man in the photo is smiling and holding a beer and looking down at whatever's smoking on the grill. He's handsome. The only thing I know about him is his name. Ray. I'm a hypocrite. How can I be annoyed with your grandmother for telling you a fairy tale, then turn around and do the same thing?

I've pulled my mother's armchair up to the vanity, and I'm sitting here, trying to put as much of our story down on paper as possible before you wake up. While I can't explain why death is irreversible, I can explain why your father died. I can explain who he really was and what he meant to me. I can tell you who sent that man to our house and why. I'm writing this to give you honest answers to the questions I hazard to guess you'll ask while you're growing up. I'm writing it all down here just in case I'm not around to tell you.

2

I was a special agent in the FBI from 1983 to 1987, and in that time CIA hired me twice as a temporary contractor, the phrase they use for *spy*. That's how I met your father.

After my training at Quantico, I was assigned to the Indianapolis field office, where I had to put in two years as a first-office agent, the bureau's version of a rookie, before I could transfer. I chose New York, my hometown, as my officer preference, and was surprised to get it. I'd assumed it was popular, but as it turned out, New York was understaffed. Few agents wanted to be in the city because it was too expensive and because of the rumors that circulated through the other field offices about New York agents being mugged while working surveillance.

Our field office was the largest in the bureau. At the time, I was one of the more than twelve hundred agents in my department alone. I was a part of the Intelligence division, *intelligence* being a misnomer that the bureau has since corrected. Our division was actually concerned with counterintelligence; officially speaking we were supposed to be working to combat espionage, not engaging in it. On a personal note, I considered the name inaccurate because the division wasn't exactly a brain trust.

A sense of self-importance permeated the culture. So did machismo and knee-jerk conservatism. To get by, I told my colleagues that I didn't care about politics, which felt like a ridiculous thing to claim. They bought it though. Very few of those men understood having no choice about whether they were political or not: Unlike me, they weren't people who'd had their existence politicized on their behalf.

Although New York's Criminal division was better represented on film and in television, in the mid-eighties Intelligence was more active and better funded. One of the balms being applied to a Cold War–chafed public was a major influx in funding and support of the bureau's counterintelligence programs. DC's field office and our own got the lion's share of the money. We were stewards of the two regions that boasted, by leagues, the highest concentrations of suspected KGB agents in the country.

I started at the New York field office in 1985, which the newspapers called the "Year of the Spy." Eight major spy arrests had been made public that year. After each story broke, you'd watch interviews on the nightly news of people out in the middle of nowhere reacting to them. They'd talk about the precautions they were now taking, the suspicions they had of people who weren't like them. And of course it was crazy: What exactly would it earn the KGB to infiltrate Betty Johnson's prayer meeting in Great Falls, Montana? But the fear that it could happen was so present in so many minds that it dictated lives. It was an awe-inspiring thing. And more than a little frightening.

Don't let me suggest that I was completely immune to spy fever. I followed the Sharon Scranage case particularly closely because she was the only black woman among the eight, and it was the first time an American had been caught spying for an African intelligence outlet. The case suggested a broader and deeper scope to CIA's covert operations in West Africa than I'd ever considered before.

Scranage, who'd been a CIA clerk in Ghana, had been the target of a honeypot. Can you imagine? It was an absolutely wild, cinematic story that just so happened to be 100 percent true. She'd leaked the names of more than a half-dozen CIA employees and informants to her boyfriend, Michael Soussoudis, who turned out to be a Ghanaian intelligence officer. He was also related to the head of state, Jerry Rawlings, who'd assigned Soussoudis the operation because he believed CIA was trying to orchestrate a coup in the country. Looking back, it's hard to accuse Rawlings of baseless paranoia.

The field office was in the Jacob Javits building, which was located in an especially barren part of lower Manhattan, down near the Brooklyn Bridge and Tweed courthouse. As a kid I'd read something about the courthouse that has stuck with me my entire life: In the nineteenth century, Boss Tweed had used its construction as a pretext to embezzle millions from New York State. When they finally got around to trying him for that crime, they did it in the courthouse named after him. How hilarious an irony—here was a city government building celebrating one of the most corrupt members in its history. To be a New Yorker was to be assaulted from every possible angle by political double-dealing and corporate deception. It was quite literally built into the architecture of the place. In general, New Yorkers weren't afraid of outsiders—KGB agents—moving into town and betraying the public trust. Not when we had such a rich history of insiders doing it.

My division was on the twenty-sixth floor. I worked in a large, open-plan room scattered with chocolate-colored desks and busy with scurrying men in white shirts and black ties. Mr. Ali, my father's friend, had one of the few offices. My boss, the assistant special agent in charge—or ASAC—had another. Rick Gold was a squat, thick-necked man who looked like he might've been a high school athlete, maybe a wrestler, but had since let himself go to pot.

I didn't like him. During my first division meeting at the office, he'd interrupted himself during a briefing to ask me to run to the kitchen and get him a cup of coffee. Everyone in the room had laughed.

"I'll bring you back a mug of something, sir," I'd answered, tucking my anger as far into my chest as it would go. "But don't expect it all to be coffee."

There was a beat before Gold laughed at that. The rest of the men in the room joined in, and my training agent called out over the clamor: "Watch it, Ricky, that coffee's gonna come back looking yellow!"

I pretended to laugh too, compelled to prove that although I was a woman, I wasn't a killjoy. None of it was funny though, and I mean that as a statement of fact, not opinion: The basic premise of my training agent's joke didn't make sense, and Gold's was an embarrassing cliché.

My ASAC in Indianapolis had treated me well. In New York, Gold's behavior set a bad precedent in the office; my colleagues were emboldened by his obvious lack of respect for me. I was deliberately excluded from operational meetings and told it was because men were better at that kind of planning. I was left off certain surveillance squads, because agents "didn't feel safe" with me backing them up.

I'd fought my way into a few surveillance operations, but most of my work was concerned with recruiting informants. That and filling out oppressive amounts of paperwork—above all else the FBI is a sprawling, creaking bureaucracy.

Having Gold as a boss was stalling my career. But transferring out of New York would've felt like he'd won, and I was too competitive for that. So I was biding my time. I believed I would eventually get around Gold by outsmarting him.

It was late in the morning, but I was still home. I had plans to meet one of my informants at Pan Pan, a diner a few blocks north of my apartment, and head down to the field office in the afternoon.

Pan Pan was on the corner of 135th and Lenox, just a few blocks north of my apartment. I liked the place; the easy warmth of the women employed there and the food they served gave it a distinctly southern charm.

I walked in and sat at one of the U-shaped sienna tables. When the waitress approached to ask what I wanted, I ordered my usual lunch—a cup of coffee and a large fruit cup—then glanced out the wide windows. The day was warm and overcast; it looked like it was going to rain. There was still no sign of my snitch.

You might be surprised to learn how often I met my snitches in diners. The conversations we had looked (and generally were) boring, which I'd found was as good a security measure as total privacy.

In the two years that I'd been at the New York field office, I'd recruited a respectable number of informants and a couple of "hip pockets," guys I had no administrative file on but touched base with every once in a while. Aisha was the only woman. Actually, as far as I am aware, she was the only female informant developed by any agent in my division while I was there.

Aisha was my favorite snitch. She was a member of the Patrice Lumumba Coalition, a Pan-African organization based in Harlem with about a thousand members on its roster. Although the PLC's activities mostly revolved around protesting apartheid, we had them under investigation for two reasons. The first was because of their ties to the Communist Party USA. At the time, the CPUSA was receiving three million dollars annually from the USSR, so any organization with Communist members, no matter the size, was under our investigation.

The second was because its director, Aisha's uncle, had once been a Black Panther. More troublingly, he'd also briefly been associated with the Black Liberation Army—a violent, underground offshoot of the Panthers that had been active throughout the seventies. Before the FBI systematically disbanded the group, the BLA had been a domestic terrorist network responsible for the theft of millions of dollars and the murder of more than a dozen police officers.

When Aisha finally arrived, she was carrying a purse on her arm, a giant clear umbrella, a folded stroller, and her son, Marlon, who was two. As she dropped onto the bolted stool beside me, I said hello to Marlon, who promptly turned away from me and began to whine, pushing his face into the acne-scarred swath of skin exposed by Aisha's V-neck.

"He's tired," she said as an apology.

Aisha looked much younger than twenty. And like she'd dressed quickly, wearing a headscarf, a wrinkled white T-shirt, and jeans. I glanced up at the clock near the stainless steel order-up counter. "You're twenty minutes late."

She nodded and said she was sorry. I suppressed my irritation, not wanting it to be a contentious meeting because—as I'd already warned her—it would be our last. When the waitress came over, Aisha ordered an enormous amount of food: the chicken and waffles the restaurant was famous for, with a side of Georgia sausage. Once the waitress had gone, Aisha reached into her purse and handed me a sheaf of papers folded into thirds. As I looked over the first page of the report, she spoke sharply to Marlon, who was still whimpering.

I recognized her handwriting from my own youth. Some of the girls I'd passed notes with wrote their *a*'s and *o*'s in the same fat way, their *i*'s with large bubble dots. If there are regional variations in speech, I think it stands to reason that they also exist in handwriting, and I thought of Aisha's handwriting as the most prominent dialect of New York's black public schools. My own, as you've surely noticed by now, is quite sharp. I wonder what that says about my personality.

"Is it okay?" She was peering at me, insecure as usual about the quality of her writing.

"It's fine." The first page summarized the three PLC meetings she'd gone to over the last couple of months; what had happened and who had attended. The second detailed a protest they were planning in front of city hall. The group was hoping to put pressure on city government to divest from South Africa.

Her meal arrived, the waffles on a separate plate with a pat of Technicolor oleo on top. As she cut one into wedges, she said to Marlon, "You hungry?"

She held a wedge out toward him, but when he tried to snatch it, moved it out of his reach. "You gonna be good?"

He remained silent, passively resisting her terms. She sighed and put the waffle wedge in his fat hand anyway.

"How's his dad doing?" I asked.

"He's good."

A couple of years earlier, Marlon's father had gone up to Otisville on an assault charge. I didn't know the details, but something had compelled him to visit a comprehensive beating on a fellow inmate, which was technically a federal crime, Otisville being a federal prison. That second assault would've extended his bid by a few years, but I'd got those charges against him dropped. In exchange Aisha gave me intel. And on top of that I paid her. I thought she was getting the better end of the deal.

"Got his parole hearing coming up soon," she added, looking at me cannily. "But you knew that, didn't you."

I shook my head. "I've got no reason to be keepings tabs on him."

Of course we both knew that was a lie, as his status was my source of leverage with her. But recruiting and running informants was about cultivating their trust. To do that I found it worked best to lie frequently to them.

As Aisha ate, I asked her a few questions about the report she'd given me. Then I tried pressing her for information about the group's funding, but she said she hadn't seen the books lately. I valued this highly about her, the fact that if she didn't know something she said so directly. That was rarely the case with my male informants.

The waitress approached again. She spoke to Marlon and patted him on the head before beginning to clear Aisha's dishes. "You need anything else?"

"Just the bill," I said. She wrote quickly on the guest check, pulled it off the pad, and put it on the counter before strolling over to another customer.

I asked Aisha the same thing I always did to cap our meetings: "Is there anything else I should know that you haven't told me?"

She thought for a moment then shook her head. "No, ma'am."

She was telling the truth. At Quantico they'd taught us the so-called classic signals that someone was lying: if they glance up to the right before they speak, or if they won't look you in the eye. None of what I'd learned worked as well as listening to my instincts. I've always been good at ferreting out deception. I'm not entirely sure what my ability to detect a liar is based on—subtle cues maybe, subconscious awareness, an intuitive talent for reading microexpressions. I don't know, and I've found that the more I try to understand it the less effective I am. My ASAC in Indianapolis had taken full advantage of my skill and used me on a lot of cases. He called me his lie detector. Gold and I had never worked closely enough for him to have noticed my talent.

I fished a receipt from my purse and watched as she carefully signed her code name to it. She asked, "You really don't need me no more?"

I shook my head as I held a clean white envelope out to her. Inside were her usual bimonthly payment and a termination bonus: $350 in seven crisp $50 bills.

"Too bad. I got used to the extra cash." She was gathering her purse, her umbrella, her son.

"Well. See you around." I felt strangely sad, and it took me by surprise.

"Yeah." She hesitated, and then in a show of formality extended her hand to shake my own. It was such an uncharacteristic gesture that we both started to laugh.

I was nervous about firing her as I had, because I'd done so without my ASAC's permission, which meant the move was technically against bureau policy. But I couldn't continue to waste my career on developing informants. Participating in high-profile operations was the only way to get the recognition and promotion I wanted.

As Aisha left the restaurant, I gathered my own things. At the cashier stand I glanced out through the wall of windows into the rainy afternoon and saw Aisha under her clear umbrella, struggling to snap the stroller harness around Marlon, who was bawling. She was displaying Herculean patience in the face of his tantrum and in the bad weather. I felt a surge of fondness for her.

What I actually did for a living had long since inoculated me against any of the romantic ideas I'd once had about spies. Most of the ones I knew personally, or knew about, fell into one of two categories—they were either traitors like Scranage or snitches like my informants.

But she was the one informant for whom my contempt was mixed with something a little kinder. After all, she was snitching out of loyalty to her man, which was admirable from a certain perspective. My other informants only did it for the cash.

Plus, I could see something of myself in her. When I was just a little bit younger than she was, I started dating my first boyfriend, Robbie Young, whom I'd known since I was a kid. We'd go on to have an on-again, off-again relationship throughout my twenties.

Like Marlon's father, when Robbie was young, he'd been a guest of the state a few times (back then, to hear him tell it, a crime against property wasn't a real crime). I'd visit him occasionally, even during times when, strictly speaking, we weren't a couple.

Once, when he was up at Wallkill, he'd asked me to marry him. I remember looking around before I answered. The visitors' room had a distinctly family oriented atmosphere—there was a mural of the Manhattan skyline on one of the walls and a guard was gamely taking a photograph of a large family in front of it. An elderly inmate in a green jumpsuit and too-large, too-white dentures was at the very center and grinning for the camera.

I'd looked back at Robbie and shook my head. What would it have earned me to build a life and a family around a visitor's schedule? What would he have been to me but an albatross around my neck? I could never have made the choice Aisha did.

It's not romantic to be so loyal that you compromise your sense of yourself. I've been a lot of things, boys, including a spy, but I know who I am. And I'm not no snitch.

3

When your grandmother was twelve, her mother died suddenly, and she went to Saint-Pierre to live with her sister, Sido. A year passed before their father, Leon, got it into his head to send her to New York. His own sister, Agathe's aunt, had married an American serviceman in Paris and moved with him after the war. Leon was white. Agathe's in her sixties now and is still hearing rumors that so-and-so is probably a half sibling of hers. Aunt Sido is the only one with whom she shares both parents, out of maybe a dozen or so of his children. Sido believes that Leon loved Agathe the most because of her beauty and complexion, and that is why he sent her to New York. While that seems overly simple, I have no better explanation to offer.

Agathe's aunt strong-armed her into passing for white; I don't even think her uncle knew she was black until she married my father. Your grandmother characterizes her teenage years in New York as "nervous ones" (there's no one on this planet with her knack for understatement). She moved in and out of the New York places where Negroes were *interdits,* gathering her intelligence on the world that white people inhabited, always feeling like she was about to be made.

I can't say for certain what I would've done in Agathe's position, but most likely what I'd been told to. The thought alone is frightening. The privileges wouldn't have mitigated the risk, or the constant fear of a very dangerous type of exposure. Had I been subjected to that as an adolescent, I would've been permanently warped. In many ways, Agathe is much stronger than me.

I think Helene would've enjoyed tricking people she considered too stupid to really see her. She would've found pleasure in deceiving a particular type of fool: the one who looks at you and sees, not *you,* but whom he wants to see. As much as I loved her, she could be a little duplicitous.

My great-aunt's big oversight was letting your grandmother go to an integrated high school in Brooklyn, which was where she met your grandfather. One day, she left her lunch bag unattended for a moment and he scratched his name with a toothpick on the banana. When the scratches darkened into writing, the mystery of it and the cleverness made her ask around about who Bill was.

Pop had grown up in Harlem; his family had only recently moved to Brooklyn. He was the youngest of four siblings, and his father was a grocer. Color was the linchpin of my parents' relationship: My mother liked my father because he was dark, and my father liked my mother because she was light. He was Agathe's first and only boyfriend; their relationship was easy to keep secret because he was enlisted for much of it. They got married a few months after Pop returned from Korea. Agathe was eighteen. Helene was born seven months later. It still amuses me, the picture of this unknown white great-aunt furiously spluttering at the news of Agathe's marriage, the world she'd so carefully constructed for your grandmother falling down around them both.

Your grandfather started out as a beat cop, worked his way past sergeant then lieutenant, and eventually became deputy commissioner of community affairs. He was forced to retire a few years before you were born. Your grandmother is one of the few people I know who's never been impressed by his professional accomplishments.

My parents had nothing but their children in common. I've never known two people who were more poorly suited. They argued constantly, but what was even more oppressive were the lethally hostile silences that stretched between them for days, only occasionally punctuated by passive-aggressive sniping. Like once when Helene was nine and I was seven, and our family was planning to go somewhere— maybe to our grandfather's house for dinner. Pop noticed that Agathe was dressed smartly but wasn't wearing makeup. He'd frowned and commented on it.

"I don't feel like it," she said.

"See, that's your whole problem," he shot back. "You think you're fine the way you are."

I can understand what he thought he was saying. He was a person who believed you should never be satisfied with yourself. He thought there was always room for improvement. I can also understand what she heard, and why she muttered under her breath in French as she slipped on her wool coat.

"What's that?" he'd asked her, and when she didn't respond, he turned to Helene and me. "That's your mother for you. A beatnik right down to her core."

He spoke with a strained smile on his face, like he was joking, but we knew he wasn't. He'd first started calling her a beatnik after she got her hands on a copy of *Les Damnés de la Terre*—Frantz Fanon was Martinican too. The word became a catchall for all the things he didn't like about her. Then it became a way of commenting on—rejecting—who she was fundamentally, and once you get to that point in a marriage, it seems like there's little chance of bouncing back.

It was a tame enough insult for him to say in front of his kids, but I see now that there was brutality behind it. It wouldn't surprise me to learn that he called her much unkinder things when they were alone, but in the language of our family, "beatnik" was uniquely cruel.

If these were the people I was supposed to model my own relationships after, it's no wonder that I've never been particularly interested in getting married. Your father was married when I met him. I loved him, but never wanted to replace his wife.

I think I must've learned my contempt for the snitch from Agathe. I can picture her now, a few months after that makeup argument, bent at the waist, rooting around in the closet that Helene and I shared. Our bedroom was the only room on the half story of our house; the effort Agathe had put into decorating it was a daily reminder of how much she loved us. She'd spent weeks picking out white furniture from stores all over the city: our beds, the dressers, and even a small rocking chair, which held the balding teddy that had been her most cherished possession as a child. She'd given the same attention to the festive rug— Bunny was lying on it now like a log—the drapes, the other furnishings. And on top of all that, she'd made the matching floral quilts that covered our beds herself.

She'd been looking for the powder-blue suitcase my sister and I took with us when our family went on vacation to one of the black resorts in the Catskills. Having found it, she sat on Helene's bed and opened the window.

"Helene, get me a cigarette," she said, speaking in French as she generally did when Pop wasn't around. Her dress and purse were hanging over our desk chair; she'd slept in our bedroom the night before.

I watched as Agathe took a drag. She was in her Formfit Rogers Dress-Shapers, a pair of girdle panties and a pointy black bra, the kind of heavy-duty foundational garments that you could've shot her in and she wouldn't even have felt it. In that moment, hers was an indecorous beauty.

My sister curled up next to her. I thought she was our mother's favorite. They were similar, both of them independent and intensely analytical, so they understood each other.

I got out of bed and crossed to our mother. Tried to get closer to her than my sister was. She kissed us both on our temples, then said, "Marie, is your sister good to you? Does she take care of you?"

I leaned forward to look at Helene. We had the same curls, which our mother dutifully pressed for us. Her eyes were dark brown, and suggested a certain craftiness, even when she was a kid—she was always extremely vigilant, in a way that could make you feel like she was waiting for you to let your guard down.

"Before I came to New York my sister took care of me," she continued. "She was a few years older and already married."

"Is she nice?" I asked.

"Yes. I hope you'll meet her someday. You might not see it now, but you're lucky to have each other. A sister is one of the few people in this world you can really trust."

"So why did your dad make you leave Martinique?" Helene asked.

"He said it wasn't proper, me living with Sido." She stuck her arm out the window and stamped her cigarette on the brick exterior.

"Why?"

"Why? Because he was a fool. And fools like him always think they know what's best for everybody." I've met a handful of my aunts and uncles down here. Agathe's the only one who's straightforward with me about how much she resented Leon. The others treat his memory with a deference that boggles my mind.

"I would rather have stayed with my sister," she added, then fell quiet for a moment, probably thinking about the implications of what she'd just said. If she'd stayed in Martinique we would never have been born.

"What about Daddy?" Helene asked, slicing through the tension.

Agathe sounded exasperated. "A man is a reflection of the company he keeps. Look at your father's friends. They're *snitches*. All of them." *Snitches*. She'd said the word in English. Agathe looked into Helene's face then down into mine, searching it for some acknowledgment that I understood what she was telling us. I didn't understand.

"Snitches," my sister repeated, saying it dreamily.

And that was that. The conversation is tattooed on my mind because it was one of the last the three of us had before Agathe came back here to Martinique permanently, taking along with her suitcases our blue one.

For a long time I was furious with her. I thought: How could she leave her family? Pop wasn't *that* bad, as if that were a reasonable way to measure a life spent with someone.

I think the damage done to her by being forced to pass couldn't be undone, and she eventually came to feel like the only place she could truly be herself was here in Martinique. That's the narrative I've imposed on her departure anyway, to answer the questions that nagged at me.

I carried the hurt from her abandonment into my adulthood. I was angry with Agathe for years; I resented having to grow up as fast as we did without her. I spent my adolescence finding one excuse after another not to respond to her letters or speak to her during one of her rare phone calls.

I have empathy for her now that I'm an adult, but the effect her departure had on me can't be undone either. I've always promised myself that I would avoid her mistake with my own children. That I would never leave you, ever, no matter what. For a long time, the worst thing I could've imagined was the circumstances I find myself in. Now that I'm about to do exactly that.

4

I was one of only a handful of agents who deigned to live in the city, most of the others being family men who commuted from the suburbs. I had a big, bright apartment on the corner of 128th and Lenox, in a four-story brick building with a rickety fire escape draped down the front.

After work the next evening, I changed out of my suit, got a drink, and clicked on the television. Settled in on my sofa—it was a good find, a gray midcentury piece that I'd bought in an Indiana antiques shop and brought with me when I'd moved.

I watched TV for a little bit, then turned my attention to the half-dozen pin tumbler locks laid out on the coffee table. I'd learned how to pick a lock at Quantico and found it to be a surprisingly satisfying skill to practice. As I was raking one of them, the phone rang just once. Pop's code. My father always rang, hung up, and then immediately called back under the misguided assumption that knowing it was him would make me more inclined to pick up. When the phone sounded again I hesitated through a few rings before crossing to it. "Hello?"

"Your buzzer doesn't work," he said.

"You're downstairs?"

"At the pay phone on the corner."

I told him I'd be there in just a second, put on slippers, and went down to let him in.

"You look very comfortable," my father said when I opened the front door. I was wearing a pair of red gym shorts with white piping and a tank top—it was muggy out and I hadn't been expecting to see him.

He was dressed carefully, but in a manner designed to suggest casualness. He was wearing jeans and a polo shirt, a tan driving cap, and matching tan Top-Siders—what he called his Jack Kennedy shoes. I noticed the Omega watch on his wrist; he'd bought it in a Quantico gift shop when he'd come down for my FBI graduation.

He followed me up the worn stairs to the top floor and into my apartment, where I quickly pulled on a pair of jeans. I returned to the living room to find him looking around my place. I did the same, hoping to figure out what he'd comment on first—because he'd arrived unannounced, his visit felt like a surprise inspection. There was an enormous stack of newspapers on my dining table that I quickly tried to neaten. I compulsively read the news in both English and French papers. I was interested in the world outside of my own tiny corner of it.

My father pointed to a spot in the wall above one of my tall bookshelves that was split by a deep crack. "That doesn't look good."

"It's been there forever."

"I could come by one day with some compound and fix it."

"It's fine, Pop." I went to the coffee table and returned the locks to the wicker basket I kept them in.

"How's that kitchen sink of yours? Still only hot water coming out?"

"Yeah."

"I had a plumber come out to the house last week to put in a new hot water heater. We got to talking a little. I told him about you."

"What'd you tell him? That I'm a Fed?"

He shook his head and smiled. "Not the kind of thing you start with, not with a brother like him. Nice young brother though. He could really do well for himself if someone gave him a chance."

He was always trying to set me up. I never had a problem getting dates, but the pattern of my romantic life was clear: At some point I'd realize I strongly preferred my own company to the company of the man I happened to be seeing. Things tended to go sharply downhill from there.

There are only two men I never felt that way about: your father, who's widely considered to be one of the most inspiring men of his generation, and Robbie Young, who most assuredly isn't. Boys, I can't explain the gulf there, and believe me, I've thought about it a lot.

He wasn't concerned that I was lonely, he was worried that if I couldn't find a man, I couldn't give him grandchildren. I didn't share his anxiety. I always knew I'd have children eventually. I was ecstatic when you were born, the happiest I'd ever been. I'd been waiting for you my whole life.

"I could give him your phone number," he added. "Maybe he could fix that faucet of yours. Take you out for a bite afterward."

"No, Pop," I said testily, and frowned at my father. There they were in record time: those first pinpricks of irritation that always accompanied one of his visits. He was extremely proud of the fact that I was a college graduate, and was just as proud, although he'd never admit it, that military service had only temporarily interrupted his own education. While he was still a beat cop he'd gone to night school to earn his bachelor's degree. During the years he'd spent working his way up the ranks, he'd also earned a master's from Hunter. And after he'd been promoted to the office of the commissioner, he'd pursued a law degree at St. John's University.

It was annoying, the way he persisted in presenting me with men he wanted me to *drag up,* to inspire to pursue the same course of education. Never mind that spending so much energy on someone else meant having precious little left for myself.

My father was standing at the window now, looking at the ficus standing beside it. I had a number of plants in my living room, my talent for their care being something I inherited from your grandmother. "Soil looks a bit dry."

I knew it wasn't, but shrugged and went to the kitchen to fill a pitcher anyway. As I crossed back toward the plant, Pop looked up and out the window. I reminded myself that he loved me. He wasn't subjecting me to an unending drumbeat of criticism, not from his perspective. He was trying to show me he cared.

"I should go down and fix that, shouldn't I?"

I looked up from the plant and followed his gaze down to Lenox Avenue. He'd gotten a great space—his old blue Volkswagen Beetle was parked directly in front of the building, but its behind was jutting out. "It's not worth it," I said, and to distract him, added: "The Bean Can's getting up there, isn't it?"

He nodded, still looking down on the car. "Eighteen years I've had it now." He'd been talking about buying a new car for years, and although he could afford something flashier, he hesitated. He'd fit a profile in a more expensive one.

"Eighteen? It'll finally be able to vote."

He smiled weakly, and I knew his mind was still on going down there and parking it perfectly. I found my sympathy for him in the knowledge that he was harder on himself than he was on anyone else, including me.

Now he was looking at the other side of the avenue, to the party store there. A stocky man was sitting out front on a milk crate, the radio on the ground near his sneakers blasting a Chaka Khan song. The upbeat music didn't match the grim look on Pop's face.

"You all right?" I asked.

"Well, I'm just coming from the hospital."

I nodded, assuming he'd gone to visit my grandfather. A few days earlier, he'd walked the short distance from his Brooklyn brownstone to Interfaith Hospital where they'd found he had a chest infection and checked him in. I asked, "Did he tell you I was there yesterday?"

"Were you?"

"He was in a really bad mood, Pop. I think he was in a lot of pain. He wouldn't admit it though."

"He's not in all that pain anymore."

"That's good. Did they tell you when they're going to discharge him?"

He was still looking out the window. A few long moments passed before he finally spoke: "Harlem's really gone to shit."

"Pop, did you hear me? When's Grandpa getting out of the hospital?"

He turned toward me with his brows furrowed, and it occurred to me then why he'd come. What he'd meant by saying that my grandfather was no longer in pain. The news sent me reeling; I felt like I couldn't catch my breath. As the pressure of tears mounted behind my eyes, I felt myself getting angry. I hated how he always managed to blindside me. This was a problem in how we communicated that had always been there.

I went to the kitchen and returned to the living room with a bottle of wine and two glasses. I sat on the sofa. "You want a drink?"

"Yeah, I could do with a little taste on the place."

The question had been a formality. Of course he wanted one. I was my father's daughter. When I handed him his glass, he held it up to the light, and I observed him observing it, feeling the weight of his judgment on me. Pop had an oenophile streak that I considered either sophisticated or precious depending on my mood, and at that moment I didn't have the patience for it.

I sipped from my glass. I think we both understood we should've been filling the silence stretching between us with watercolor memories, but neither of us was sentimental enough. Instead we drank.

I'm sorry you'll never get to meet my grandfather, who was a quiet force of nature. He was known in the neighborhood for his motorcycle—I learned how to ride one from him—and his dog, Marmaduke, who'd died the year before. Whenever I'm over there, people still introduce me as Mr. Mitchell's granddaughter.

He'd immigrated to New York from Barbados in the thirties and worked in a grocery owned by a Jewish couple for a decade before saving up enough for a store in the south Bronx (at the time the family lived in Harlem; the move to Brooklyn was a step up that came much later). I have no idea how he accomplished all that he did. You have to understand that this was at a time when they wouldn't even have served him a meal at the Woolworth's counter, but he managed to own his own business and his home, having bought it with the help of a West Indian credit union.

"You remember Marmaduke?" I asked.

He smiled. "Of course. How'd you know he'd love that dog so much?"

"I didn't, I just thought he was lonely in the brownstone. Actually, I was worried he'd hate him. Sheryl offered to get him a dog before I even thought of it," I said, meaning one of my play cousins. "He turned her down. He told me, 'She would've bought a mutt, and I don't want no mutt in my house.' So I got him a purebred and hoped for the best."

Marmaduke had been a fox terrier, what the old folks in the neighborhood had called a Thin Man dog, because he'd looked like the one in the detective movie. And Sheryl had felt slighted, but who cared? He'd made Grandpa happy.

"He would've loved any dog you got him. He loved you."

I was embarrassed—I knew he'd loved me, but it was uncomfortable to hear my father say it. We didn't talk to each other like that. I took a drink and changed the subject to a funny story. "You remember the time Grandpa had people over to the house for a get-together and Marmaduke bit the only white guest?"

He laughed and nodded. He'd emptied his glass, so I uncorked the bottle and poured us both a little more. He took a sip and said, "He left the brownstone to you."

"What?"

"Like I said. He loved you."

I was surprised, although in retrospect I see there'd been a single, subtle indication of what he'd been planning. Out of the blue one day, he'd asked me what I would do with it, if it were mine. *Would you sell it?* he'd asked. I told him no, that I'd keep it for my kids, and he'd smiled and said, *Good. We have to own things, girl, we have to pass them down.*

"Do you want it?" I asked. My grandfather's choice probably felt like a slap in the face to my father.

"I've known for a while he was leaving it to you. I've had plenty of time to get used to the idea. And anyway, he wanted you to have it, so you should have it. You know the woman across the street?"

"Geneva?"

"That's the one."

She owned two buildings on the block, and as a teenager I used to watch her striding back and forth between them. One day, I worked up the nerve to ask her a few questions about her business, and she humored me. I still appreciate that. I had no one in my life who could really teach me about money. Pop had middle-class values: He taught me to pay my taxes in full, depend on a salary, and to avoid debt at all costs. Agathe and I never talked about money—not once—and she never worked outside the home, but the fact that she had to have squirreled some away to come back to Martinique connected money and autonomy in my mind. Robbie thought money was the root of all evil (which I took as a poor excuse for why he never had any); Helene saw money as power.

He told me how much Geneva was selling her brownstone for and added, "Yours is the same size, but in better shape. I think you could get more for it."

"I want to hang on to it."

Pop finished off the last of his wine. He nodded. "He said he knew he could depend on you to take care of it. He knew I'd just sell it." As he talked about the arrangements he'd have to make with the funeral home and crematory, I asked him how I could help out.

"I've got everything taken care of," he said.

"You sure?"

"Yeah, it's no problem. Jim's been helping. When was the last time you and him touched base, by the way?"

"It's been awhile," I admitted, thinking of Mr. Ali in his office, squinting at his word processor through reading glasses.

"I don't see why you can't give him a call. Get lunch together."

"I will, Pop."

"I mean you're right there in the same office."

"All right, Pop."

I realized I wanted him to leave. I wanted to be alone with the news he'd given me. He must've sensed it, because he asked, "Are you upset?"

I nodded. "My grandfather just died."

"I mean angry."

"I seem angry?" He nodded. "Maybe I'm tired."

"Tired?" He looked at his watch.

I tensed with irritation. Maybe I was angry, I thought, although I wasn't sure why. He searched my face for a few moments then stood. "All right. It's best I get in the wind anyway. Before some kid takes off with my hubcaps."

At the door he added, "Don't blow it off, okay? Spend a little time with Jim." I didn't know why it meant so much to him that he'd had to repeat it. I promised I would.

I went to the window and watched as Pop eased the Bean Can out of the space. I considered calling Agathe to tell her the news and went to the phone. She and my grandfather had liked each other, something she chalked up to the fact that they were both West Indian immigrants. They'd gotten to know each other while we were living with Grandpa in his brownstone, on the top floor, which he'd converted to a separate apartment. We'd moved out to Queens when I was five or six, but still went to Brooklyn regularly to visit him, Agathe always bringing him her *accras de morue*. He'd also grown up eating codfish cakes. I decided to put off calling my mother, whom I hadn't spoken to in months. There was a lot of tension between us that had been there since Helene's funeral more than a decade earlier. I was still angry about the things she'd said at the airport the day after the service.

I thought about calling Robbie, but decided not to. He would've dropped whatever he was doing to come console me, and I didn't want to impose on him that way. There was no one else in the city for me to call up, no one to speak to who would've known my grandfather. There was a specific reason for that, which I'll get into a little later if I remember. I dialed Peggy Simpson's number; she'd been my roommate at Quantico and was with the LA field office. No answer. I called Shannon, a special agent I'd befriended while I was in Indiana; her phone also rang out. I put the receiver back in the cradle.

Overwhelmed with need, with sadness, with gutting loneliness, I went to the kitchen to get a bottle of rum down from the cabinet above the refrigerator. Poured myself a large glass, then went to the living room. I turned on the television, sat on the sofa, and pulled the basket of locks toward me.

5

In spy stories, the question of what becomes of a spy's cover after it's no longer needed is rarely discussed. But we were still there. We still existed. And I can tell you exactly what we were after our mother left. We were terrified. The fall after Agathe's departure was one of the most frightening of my life. Nuclear war preoccupied my mind, my sister's mind, the minds of all of our friends. None of us expected to see adulthood. More than just being convinced we were going to die, we knew we would be annihilated (as Robbie referred to it with such relish that the word still gives me the creeps), which to me meant being somehow deader than dead.

Helene had taken over making the lunch I took to school and walking me home from the bus stop. We lived in Cambria Heights, one of the black middle-class neighborhoods in Queens. There was also Laurelton and St. Albans. Wealthy black people—doctors, lawyers, and a couple of entertainers like James Brown and Count Basie—lived over in Addisleigh Park.

In September, as Helene and I walked toward our little house, I

asked her about the speech Kennedy had given on television and what
it meant. She answered my questions as best she could, tried to be as
soothing as possible, but could tell I was still anxious. And I knew she
was too, even though she tried not to show it in front of me.

I don't know if in twenty years, when you're adults reading this,
you'll be able to understand the stranglehold that Cold War terror had
on the psychology of my generation. We were kids who wondered
what we would do if we grew up, not when.

When we got home, we called hello through the bathroom door to
Pop, who was in the shower. He'd be leaving for work soon. Helene
snuck into his room, fished around for a little bit in his desk, which was
forbidden, then came out into the hall and put Pop's dog tags around
my neck. "Hide those under your shirt."

"Why?"

"Just wear 'em," she said. After dinner, I helped Helene wash the
dishes, then went with her to the living room to watch television. When
the doorbell rang, my sister let Mr. Ali into the house. Pop came out of
his room and passed in front of the TV, headed to the closet beside the
front door. He pulled out his trench coat and slapped at the wrinkles,
then looked over at me. "Those call your name from out my drawer?"

I'd already forgotten to keep his dog tags hidden and was playing
with them around my neck.

"She has to wear them," Helene answered on my behalf.

"Put 'em back." Pop slipped on his coat. "I already told you I don't
want you two going in my room, Helene. I'm gonna start locking the
door."

"But she has to wear them. Now you'll know it's Marie even if she
gets burned up."

"Pop, am I gonna get burned up?" I pictured my body charred past
recognition, and nausea overwhelmed me. He didn't answer the question. He was distracted, looking for his wallet.

"Can we get stuff?" Helene asked.

"What do you mean? What kind of stuff?" he asked absently.

"Supplies."

"What kind?"

"Ms. Baptiste said we should get food," Helene said.

"Your teacher don't know what she's talking about," Pop said. "Canned peaches won't do nothing for nobody if those missiles hit DC."

"Pop, am I gonna get burned up?" I asked again.

"Your girls are smart; they want to be prepared," Mr. Ali said. "We could do with some nice girls like yours at work. Remember that fat old secretary they stuck me with?"

"Right before you went undercover?" Pop asked as they left.

"Ooo-wee, mean as a snake, wasn't she?" The front door closed behind them.

I turned to Helene. "Am I gonna get burned up?"

"No," she said, knowing what I needed to hear.

"You sure?"

"Yes."

"What do you think they're doing?" I asked.

"Working."

"Doing what?"

She didn't answer, but put her arm around me and kissed my temple. Then we both turned back to the television.

1965

Mr. Ali was the first person I understood to be undercover. It was only once I was older that my idea of cover became more flexible, and I realized that Agathe had also been hiding in plain sight before she left us.

I remember watching TV with Helene in our living room, staring at footage from Malcolm X's funeral. We had the news on because Pop had told us to look out for him—Betty Shabazz, who was pregnant with twins when she was widowed, had requested that the city supply black cops for crowd control at her husband's funeral, and Pop was the only one in his precinct. The camera did catch him, but only for an instant, in the background, while he was standing beside an easel spray of red and white carnations (I'm assuming; the TV set was black and white) arranged to look like the Nation of Islam flag.

Then Mr. Ali unexpectedly appeared on the screen, talking at a podium. White words appeared, superimposed over the bottom of his image, introducing him as the Nation of Islam's secretary and referring to him by a name we'd never heard before.

Helene said my name and I turned my face, resting my head on the crook of my other arm so I could see her. She was sitting cross-legged on our plastic entombed sofa, with Bunny stretched out beside her, his jowl resting on her calf. Even from where I was lying on the blue shag, I could sense the whir of her mind as she watched Mr. Ali. At first I didn't understand what had set her off. The news program had moved on to the next story before she finally spoke. "Moi aussi, je serai une espionne," she said. *I'm going to be a spy too.*

"He's a spy?"

"What else would he be on the TV for with a fake name and a fake job? You know he works for the FBI."

I thought about that for a moment, then asked her, "Where are you gonna be a spy?"

"In Cuba," she said confidently. "Or Russia."

She was twelve, a grown twelve, speaking with adult seriousness. I had just turned ten; Malcolm X was assassinated two days after my birthday. If I'd been a little older I might've challenged her, might've asked if she really expected white folks to let her do that. Go to those places. Or maybe not—when it was a question of something she had her mind set on, anything seemed possible.

A spy. The idea floored me. Helene having spoken the words made them possible, not just for her but for me. I was suddenly excited to strike out into the world too, in pursuit of adventure, provided that I could do so with my sister. I pictured walking along behind Helene on a snow-dusted street, my hands tucked into a fox fur muff. I pictured following her into a Soviet café and sitting beside her in a booth, my sister's face still red with cold, across from our handler, a balding man in a pince-nez. I still can't help but wonder at her. Where had she picked up the idea that she could do anything? *Be* anything? That the world was so much bigger than Queens?

She thought the way she did because she was naturally braver than I was. Consider the events of her thirteenth birthday, which Pop took us hunting to celebrate. We went up to the Catskills to a ranch a few miles down the road from Paradise Farm, a black resort that we used to visit in the summer. We'd ride ponies on the ranch when it was warm, but that winter we were headed to the hunting grounds.

Back then my father had a Mercury Monterey in what he called persimmon and white. We sat up front with him (this was before that Ralph Nader book), me with the aluminum foil–covered cake on my lap that our neighbor Mrs. Hawkins had made for Helene's birthday. She'd started baking for us after our mother left, and while I loved her desserts—Helene did too—it upset me when my sister would joke that they more than made up for Agathe's absence.

We drove through the city and north on the Palisades toward the Hudson Valley. At the ranch, we found a spot near a deer trail where someone had set up a makeshift ground blind out of dead branches. The three of us waited quietly, Helene and I sitting on the cold ground with our backs against a wide tree. I was nearly asleep when Pop waved my sister over to where he was and gestured toward the deer trail. A doe had appeared there and was grazing on a low shrub. He handed Helene his .30-06, and she lifted it into position. "Can she see us?" I whispered.

Pop put a finger to his lips.

"It'll kick, Helene," I whispered. "It might hurt you."

I spoke louder than necessary, trying to give the deer a chance to run. It didn't look up from the shrub. Helene took a breath and pulled the trigger. The bullet hit it in the neck; my sister was already an excellent shot, having practiced with my father at a range that bent their rules about minors shooting because he was a cop. The doe dropped to the leafy ground, legs moving like it was finally trying to run.

"Great eye, kid!" Pop clapped his hands once. "Did it kick hard?"

"If it did I couldn't even feel it," she said.

Pop told her to squat next to the doe and hold its head up. There was blood on the black nose, pooling in its open mouth, dripping down to the white fur beneath its nearly human teeth. He took pictures of her and the deer while I looked on, jealous.

As he put his camera away and got out his knife, I stood beside my sister and took her hand. I was afraid, looking in the animal's eyes, and wanted her comfort. Helene knew it and gave my hand a light squeeze. Smiling, she kissed the top of my head. "It's okay."

Pop turned the doe on its back and pressed the knife into its belly. "Your first cut is right here where the white fur starts. Then you pull up to the top of the sternum."

I can close my eyes now and still see Helene's face in profile as she watched him, her eyes alive with curiosity, the slanting winter sunshine igniting the golden down along her hairline.

As my father began to field dress the deer, I was flooded with nausea. I announced that I was going back to the car; Pop called after me to wait, but I was already on my way.

"Can I make the next cut?" I heard Helene ask behind me.

I climbed into the back of the Mercury, stretched out, closed my eyes. I saw the deer. My father cutting into its flesh, the sack of its stomach ballooning from the incision, intestines writhing like a snake's nest. There'd been so much movement. Too much, I thought, for something that was supposed to be dead. I'd looked into its eye to be sure and saw no emptiness there. The fear I'd felt then was what made me sick.

Pop and Helene arrived with the doe and strapped it to the wide trunk. We started toward Middletown and the black butcher there who was friends with Pop. As he drove, he talked animatedly with my sister about her shot. I rested with my head against the window, clutching my sister's cake, feeling jealous and excluded. I thought my sister was our father's favorite too, as well as our mother's.

The motion of the car brought my sickness back to the surface. I bolted upright and began to roll down the window as fast as I could.

I wasn't fast enough; my vomit splashed the glass. Pop pulled over. I scrambled out, doubled over, and threw up again.

"You all right?" Helene asked when I got back in the car. I said I was and wiped my mouth with a napkin from the glove box. We used the rest of the napkins to clean the window, the seat, my jeans, the foil on Helene's squashed cake. Then Pop started up the car.

"I'm sorry I ruined your birthday," I said quietly, after we'd driven a few miles in silence.

"You didn't," she said, so gently that I almost believed it, and offered me her shoulder to rest my head against.

As a child, whenever I thought of that afternoon I'd feel ashamed. I'd shown weakness where my sister had shown curiosity and courage. As I got older, I learned to hide that vulnerability and fear. I had to. It was plain evidence that my sister was my better.

6

Mr. Ali and I had agreed to meet for lunch, and he'd chosen a place in Chinatown that was close to the field office. I stepped into an alcove where an algae-green tank sat on a wide counter, the large yellow carp inside slowly orbiting each other. It was a long, narrow restaurant. Most of the tables were pushed close to the walls, and waiters in green polo shirts were working in the corridor that ran down the center.

Mr. Ali was already there. As I approached his table, he looked up from the menu in his hand and stood. His thick hair was gray at the temples now, and he was wearing a blue suit with a small American flag pin on the lapel.

He pulled me into a hug. "Marie Mitchell, pretty as all get-out. I always say it: One of these days you're gonna come to your senses and quit law enforcement."

"Maybe." I laughed listlessly. He'd been making the same joke for years.

"When you go out to Hollywood and make a million bucks, don't forget about me."

I sat. A waiter put a white teapot and two cups down as he sped toward another table.

"How are you?" he asked. "I'm sorry about your grandfather, Marie."

"Thank you."

"How's your dad? I spoke to him, but you know how it is. Hard to tell what's going on in his mind sometimes."

"I saw him a few days ago. I think he's okay."

"You having any trouble planning the funeral?"

"I wouldn't know. He said you're helping him with that."

"Did he?"

Neither of us were surprised at having caught Pop in that lie. Mr. Ali might've wanted to say something else, but the waiter returned then to ask if we were ready to order. Once he'd gone, Mr. Ali took off his reading glasses and tucked them into their soft case. "This was a good idea. It's nice to get a moment to talk away from the office." He smiled. "Say, have you heard anything from Gold about this big case coming up, the fellow they suspect of spying in the Foreign Mission office? They're putting a squad together to keep him under surveillance and you might—"

"You know I never get picked for anything high profile."

"I talked to Gold this time." He looked disappointed. "I said I wanted you on the squad, and he told me he'd see what he could do. Huh. Guess I don't have the juice I used to."

He was embarrassed. I was too. I felt bad that he'd gone out of his way to help me, and about witnessing his failure to do so. The waiter put our entrées and a large bowl of white rice between us on the table. Mr. Ali asked for a fork as he spread a paper napkin across his lap. I pulled my chopsticks apart and picked up a piece of chicken.

I watched Mr. Ali for a moment as he worked through his meal. I considered his career. He'd been one of a small handful of black special agents hired during J. Edgar Hoover's tenure at the bureau. They

were brought on to participate in the Counterintelligence Program—
COINTELPRO—and used almost exclusively to undermine civil rights
activists. Still, he was in the vanguard, and there was much to respect in
that. I could guess at how it had been for him when he'd first started at
the bureau. Hoover had his idea of the perfect agent, and Mr. Ali damn
sure wasn't it. Hoover's ideal was the white boy in a black suit, crew
cut, spit shined. The superman. He didn't even like it when his agents
drank coffee at work. Mr. Ali once told me that he'd seen someone get
written up for that.

"Your recruitment numbers are excellent though," he was saying.
"One of the highest in the division. They can't keep ignoring you forever."

"You think so?"

"Yeah. Don't you?"

"Sure," I said.

"Marie," he pressed, knowing I didn't mean it.

"I've recruited more informants than anyone else, but only because
that's all they'll let me do. I'm stuck. How can I prove I can run a counterintelligence operation if they won't even give me the chance to be in
one?"

I sighed. We only relied on recruitment numbers to quantify success
in our division because they were so easy to measure. Gold wanted me
to have as many snitches as possible because it made him look good in
front of the brass, not because doing so was an especially productive
tactic. But it was a waste of energy for the most part, and the intel was
rarely worth the money we paid for it.

"You want my advice? Keep your head down and toe the line.
That'll get you where you want to go. Hard work always pays off."

I shrugged. "I *do* work hard. I just met with an informant the other
day who I've had for almost a year now. I worked *hard* to get that
snitch."

His eyebrows went up at the word.

"The group was high on our target list, because their director was in
the Black Liberation Army and they're funded by the CPUSA. But, to

tell the truth, all they do is protest apartheid and promote Pan-Africanism. That's it. And that's perfectly legal. So how's my hard work going to pay off there? It's pointless."

"Pointless?"

"It's not going to get me a promotion."

"Why'd you become a Fed? Not for the glory, I know that. Because you have a duty. We both do. We swore an oath."

"Sure. But I also want to be a SAC, Mr. Ali."

"Because you believe in what we do," he said, responding to what he'd wanted to hear.

"I want to be a SAC. And why shouldn't I be? I'm as smart as any-one else here."

"Then take my advice. Don't rock the boat," he said, bringing the circular conversation back to its starting point.

I nodded even though I would never take his advice. His career had stalled because of his involvement in COINTELPRO, which had tar-geted Americans who weren't doing anything illegal and done so—ironically enough—through means that *were* illegal. Mr. Ali had been involved in a few black-bag jobs—unconstitutional surveillance and searches. After Hoover died, there was a sea change at the bureau, which made Mr. Ali political poison. The brass couldn't promote an agent who'd been hired to carry out illegal operations. So they'd given him a corner office and a few raises, but after thirty years he was still only an ASAC. That was how he'd been repaid for keeping his head down and following orders.

"I think I'm going to have to rock the boat a little if I want to get anywhere," I said, trying one last time to get him to understand me.

He shrugged and gave a short, patronizing shake of his head.

"Really? You never did anything that was out of bounds?" I asked. "Nothing against policy?"

"Never."

"Honestly?"

"I thought you knew me," he said, his tone suddenly defensive.

"I do."

"So why would you think something like that?"

It sounded like he had a guilty conscience, but I would never have asked why, and he would never have told me if I had. I'd asked because I was thinking of having fired Aisha. It was a tiny infraction, and yet the most questionable thing I'd done as a special agent. It had absolutely nothing to do with him.

The silence between us was tense, so I tried to backpedal by telling a version of the truth. "I have an informant I want to dismiss, but I can't get my ASAC to sign off on it. That's why I was wondering."

"Oh," he said, and once he realized that the question had been for my own sake, visibly started to relax. "I see. Well, if your ASAC won't sign off, then I wouldn't do it. Really, why bother?"

"I told you. The group isn't doing anything illegal. I want to be out helping track a spy, not wasting my time writing up reports about a sit-in at city hall."

"So you meet your informant a few times a month. Put a little money in his pocket. I don't see the harm in that. Going behind your ASAC's back, on the other hand, is trouble."

I nodded again. The truth was that I had a moral concern, and the political climate at the bureau made me feel like I could come to a sorry end if I wasn't strict with my ethics. I didn't want to participate in spying on citizens who weren't doing anything illegal. In a certain sense things were simple: I was a servant of the law. But intelligence policy sometimes descended into such murk that the dividing line between the organizations engaging in legal political dissent and the illegal—posing a military threat to the government—became impossible to see.

What the bureau had done to Mr. Ali meant, for me, that individual agents had to conduct themselves based on a choice: They could either follow bureau policy or they could uphold the law. They weren't always the same thing. I knew what I'd always pick: I'd become a special agent to uphold the law when it was consistent and fair.

I'd like to tell you I had a shatterproof moral compass—that I really was *good,* that I was nobly trying to redress past wrongs. But really, I was acting out of professional self-preservation. I didn't want to end up like Mr. Ali.

We finished our meals, and as he picked up the check, I said, "Sounds like you think I'd regret stepping out of line."

He nodded as he counted out a few bills.

"Can I ask you something? Do you feel . . . Do you have any regrets?"

"Regrets?" He looked up at me from the cash in his hand, frowning at the word. "No. No, no, no."

He paused, then spoke again: "No. But the bureau has really played dirty sometimes, hasn't it? Fred Hampton? Those Feebees in Chicago murdered that boy in his sleep."

I nodded. I thought Hampton's murder was a state-sponsored execution, and didn't feel disloyal to the FBI for thinking so. A bureau informant—a snitch—had passed a blueprint of the apartment Hampton was sharing with a few other Black Panthers to the FBI agent running him. He'd also slipped a barbiturate into the drink Hampton had with dinner the night the Chicago police raided the apartment.

Hampton's only crime had been his competence as a civil rights leader. Still, they'd fired off nearly a hundred rounds on the sleeping Panthers, killing two. Hampton had been curled in bed with his pregnant fiancée when he was murdered. He was only twenty-one years old.

I saw Mr. Ali's remorse. I believed it was sincere. But I also think that if he'd been in Chicago back then, and his ASAC had asked him to find a snitch who'd drug Hampton, he would've done it.

By the time you read this, you'll be adults. I'm telling you a lot of things, as much as I can really, and some of it you'll surely find difficult to parse. One thing I can say for sure is that I don't want you to be moral absolutists. If what I'm telling you of our story means to you that the people it involves are either saved or damned, then you'll have misunderstood me.

Mr. Ali wasn't a monster—he was a foot soldier doing what he thought was right. And if you believe he's an irredeemable villain, to be consistent, you'll also have to believe that about your grandfather—the man you love spending summer days with. I don't know what goes on when the three of you get together, only that I'll drop you off with enough clothes for the weekend, remind you about your manners, and show up again to wild men wearing exactly what you had on when I left.

I remember the two of them going out together when Mr. Ali was undercover in the Nation of Islam. I can imagine the bureau leaving a black agent dangling, without resources, without a decent partner. I can imagine Mr. Ali having to rely on someone outside of the FBI—but still in law enforcement—for help.

And I was a special agent too. So whatever you think of Mr. Ali and your grandfather, to be consistent, you'll have to think it of me too. Fred Hampton, Bunchy Carter, Anna Mae Aquash—all of them affiliated with organizations that were declared Communist enemies of the government to justify their infiltration. All of them Americans who were assassinated after a special agent like me got involved. There's a pattern there that's difficult for me to ignore, one that makes me feel culpable.

We stepped outside—it was a mild afternoon—and started back toward the field office, striding together along narrow Pell Street. On Mott, we passed a fish market, one flooded in harsh fluorescent light, where a man in rubber boots pushed a wide broom across the tile floor, and slid gray sudsy water out into the street.

We crossed by a fruit market, a gift shop with red paper lanterns hanging from the awning and shelves of merchandise crowding the sidewalk out front. Mr. Ali was quiet. I'd inadvertently rattled his cage and didn't know how to fix things.

At the Javits building, we went up in the steel elevator. Mr. Ali greeted the guard stationed in the hall as we both showed him our credentials and passed through the turnstile. We went through the set of glass doors and into a carpeted reception area where there was a secretary sitting behind a black desk. There weren't many women in the office, but she and I never treated each other with any particular sense of camaraderie.

Mr. Ali walked me to my desk, where I saw that a pile of investigative requests had accumulated beside the word processor. Without having to flip through them, I knew they were rookie leads that had quietly circulated the division office and wound up with me because no one else wanted to handle them. Forward criminal so-and-so's birth certificate to agent so-and-so in Salt Lake; forward criminal so-and-so's identity history summary—their criminal record—to agent so-and-so in Atlanta.

There was also a memo from Gold, which I picked up. Coincidentally enough it read: *Want to meet with you re: PLC.* I let out a nervous laugh.

"Everything all right?"

I looked up at him. "It's a memo from my ASAC. Guess what it's about."

"What?"

"He wants to talk to me about that organization I mentioned at lunch. The Patrice Lumumba Coalition."

"The one with the informant you want to cut?" he said with a lowered voice. "Good thing you didn't. Told you. Not the hill you want to die on, girl."

I stretched my mouth into a smile.

"That was fun. Let's do it again soon." He surprised me with a kiss on the cheek that made my face flush with embarrassment. I saw my training agent notice—his desk was near mine and he was a gossip. Mr. Ali should've known better than to do things like that when we were around colleagues.

I'd been at the New York field office for two years, but could still sense the assumption that he'd gotten me my job lurking around the carpeted halls. And I wouldn't have been surprised to learn that the more bad-minded among them believed I'd slept with him so he'd do so. These were men for whom it somehow made more sense that a politically castrated old man had ushered me through a back door and into a highly specialized career with a rigorous screening process. The notion that I worked as hard as they did (or a whole lot harder in some cases) never crossed their minds.

Mr. Ali said he'd see me Sunday at the funeral, and started toward that enviable office of his, which was large, nicely furnished, and had wide windows that looked out onto downtown's farrago of skyscrapers. It was a beautiful office that he was boxed into: unable to advance, unwilling to retire.

7

I want you to understand my sister, because what happened at our house in Connecticut started with Helene.

When she was thirteen she was obsessed with spies, and read as much as she could about them. For an outsider, it might've seemed like her preoccupation was unusual, that it was surprising for a black girl from Queens to know so much and have such strong feelings about Ethel and Julius Rosenberg. For me, that was simply who she was.

She'd started grilling Mr. Ali about his work, and to his credit he took her seriously. He answered her questions thoughtfully, treating her like a potential agent instead of dismissing her as a girl child. It was through their conversations that she decided she didn't want to be a spy anymore because she didn't want to be anyone's lackey. She wanted to *run* them.

Every summer, the three of us (me, my sister, and Bunny) would stay at our grandfather's in Brooklyn for a few weeks. When *Goldfinger* came out we went to see it at the Sumner Theatre, which was in walking distance of his brownstone. While I'd thought it was sexy and cool and a little scary, she'd thought it was ridiculous. She said Ian Fleming was no match for John Le Carré, whose spy novels were advertised as the real thing. He was in MI6, she'd said, eyes shining.

I've since read the Le Carré biography that argues he was interested in spies and secret lives because his father was a confidence man and a professional liar. I think that conclusion was drawn too neatly—people are too complex for such simple arithmetic—but I understand the purpose it serves.

Our mother could pass; she could hide in plain sight. And then one day she suddenly left us. That is all a spy does—they hide in plain sight, and once they've exploited all they can from their relationships, they leave. I know what would've been written in Helene's biography.

Our grandfather would send us to a black day camp run by St. John's Rec Center in Prospect Heights where we were given yellow T-shirts and green plastic totes in which to keep our lunch and bathing suits and whatever money we had.

At thirteen, Helene felt she was too grown up for camp, but went because she was popular there and because I liked it so much. They would take us on field trips; my favorites were the ones to McCarren pool, in Williamsburg, on the other side of Brooklyn.

Both Helene and I could swim; that we should know how to was one of the few things our parents agreed on, Agathe because she was from an island, and Pop because he'd learned at the Harlem Y. Growing up near a pool that black folks could use was one of the privileges he'd had that made him think of his childhood as a lucky one.

As I was sitting at the edge of the pool, tucking my pressed hair up under my bathing cap, running footsteps drummed behind me. I turned to see two boys my age jump in; while one of them bobbed up immediately, the other took so long to ascend that it scared me. Inwardly I chided myself: *He's fine. Don't be so afraid.* Still, when the boy broke the surface coughing and laughing, gems of water slipping out of his black hair, I was relieved.

I climbed down the ladder, tread water for a bit, then tentatively dog-paddled along the edge of the pool toward the deep end, avoiding the groups of kids who were shrieking and laughing as they played. I was almost to the far wall when I felt a pair of hands on my shoulders. They dunked me under. I flailed, sending off plumes of bubbles as I tried to fight the hands off. Through the hazy water I recognized Rhonda's worn-out green bathing suit.

Rhonda was probably twelve that summer. The hardness of her features, her sinewy neck, and the scars on her legs made her look rough, but she also always wore bows in her hair and floral dresses under her yellow camp T-shirt. Her appearance is seared into my memory because she picked on me. Little things mostly: a shove in the back, a yank on one of the braids Helene had done for me. Her behavior wasn't exactly vicious; it was more like she wanted attention and had run out of good ideas.

I surfaced, coughing, heard a whistle tweet as Rhonda dunked me under again. I scratched her and she recoiled. I got free for a moment and broke the surface of the water. "Rhonda! Stop!"

She laughed and shoved me under a third time. I tried to push her hands off me, but she was much stronger than I was. I fought her until the strength started to course out of me. She was still laughing. I could hear it, muffled and coming from far above.

Helene's skinny legs sliced into the water, causing a surge of bubbles. She tackled Rhonda, and I floated up to the surface of the pool, limply paddled to the closest ladder, and pulled myself out of the water, panting.

Helene pushed Rhonda's head underwater and kept it there until the lifeguard blew his whistle. She let go and Rhonda bobbed up. As she was climbing out of the pool, my sister, who was just behind her on the ladder, yanked on Rhonda's ankle, and she tumbled to the concrete pool deck. Helene pulled herself out of the pool and stood over her. A counselor flew to Rhonda's rescue before Helene could land a punch.

"Calm down!" the counselor shouted at Helene, which never failed to further agitate her.

"You could've drowned her!" Helene shrieked.

"I was just playing," Rhonda said.

"What's the matter with you? Who plays like that?"

She turned away and came over to where I was sitting. "You okay?"

Still coughing, I nodded.

"You don't look it."

"I'm fine," I said as Rhonda and the counselor approached.

"Listen," he said to her in front of us. "You can act like that around where you live, but you can't do that here. Apologize."

Rhonda muttered that she was sorry. Helene screwed her face up, and I braced myself for an explosion—my sister had an unusual capacity for rage. I didn't understand all of the reasons for it and never will, but I do know it wasn't a coincidence she got into her first fight only a couple of months after Agathe left.

Something unexpected happened though. Her face suddenly relaxed. She took a breath, smiled. She said: "It's okay. Marie's all right. Aren't you?"

I glanced at her, at that point more concerned by the strangeness of her reaction than having nearly drowned. "Yeah."

As they walked away she touched her head. "Made me get my hair wet," she muttered, appalled.

A year later, the summer I was twelve began quietly enough. My favorite thing to do when school was out was read. I liked to keep to myself, which isn't to say I was a disagreeable kid. In general, when people first met me they liked me, and that's still the case. I close up though when they start getting familiar; I can't run the risk of caring too deeply about too many people. The result is that I've never had very many close friends, but have always excelled at being an acquaintance.

Helene, on the other hand, always had a lot of friends, and she'd started counting Rhonda among them. When we stayed overnight at our grandfather's house, they'd wander the neighborhood together, and occasionally Rhonda would come all the way out to Queens too, which was so far to travel that she'd usually sleep over. She adored Helene, and had attached herself to my sister with incredible speed and loyalty. If I wondered about what Helene got out of the friendship, I probably settled on it being some exercise in the power of kindness. Whatever she was doing had worked: Rhonda was as sweet as pie to me.

Helene's best friend was Robbie Young's sister, Pam. They lived with their uncle Chickie, who worked as a porter somewhere in the city, and his wife, a God-fearing Seventh-day Adventist who saw herself as persecuted for righteousness' sake because none of the badass kids living up underneath her roof were hers.

Sometimes Helene forced me to go outside, and we'd ride bikes around the neighborhood, or I'd look on as she and some of the other girls jumped double Dutch, too afraid to jump in myself. Pop still worked a lot, and often at odd hours, so it fell to my sister to give me chores, send me on errands, and help me with my homework. My grades were more important to her than her own. She said that was because I was smarter than her, that if I used my brains and got A's I could make a million bucks.

But Helene was plenty smart. Actually, I think her intelligence was the reason she was barely passing her classes—because so much came naturally to her she couldn't stand having to apply herself. If she couldn't understand a concept within twenty seconds, she considered it a waste of time and dismissed it. Being her sister often felt like trying to catch up to someone who was beating you so effortlessly that they weren't even aware you were trying to compete.

Pop had put up a wall to split the room we shared in two, which meant Helene had to pass through mine to get downstairs. One afternoon, as I was sitting at my desk, she came out of her room and asked in French, "What's that you're reading? One of the books on the list from your teacher?"

I nodded. I was being skipped ahead to eighth grade, so the school had given me a summer reading list to make sure I didn't miss any of the hits on the seventh-grade curriculum.

"I'm going over to Chickie's with Rhonda. Take a break and come outside. You need some fresh air. And I want you to go pick up a few groceries."

I grudgingly agreed and followed her downstairs where Rhonda was waiting. She'd slept over; the blanket and backpack she'd brought were sitting neatly on the sofa. The three of us left the house, Helene closing the door behind us in Bunny's disappointed face. Chickie's house was a few blocks from our own, directly across the street from the neighborhood convenience store that belonged to Mrs. Menoni.

Our neighborhood was full of kids; on the way we passed some of the boys from Helene's grade, who were shooting craps between two parked cars, the game obscured from the view of any parent that might look out their window.

At Chickie's house, his two youngest nieces were playing jacks on the front walk while Pam and another girl lounged on the front steps. Helene and Rhonda passed through Chickie's gate and I continued to the store.

Mrs. Menoni farmed a small plot in the yard at the front of her property, which may sound odd considering I grew up in Queens, but she'd lived in the neighborhood for so long that I'm sure she could remember when it was all farmland. And when it had all been Italian too; by the time I was growing up, the only ones left were too old or too broke to have joined in on the white flight. Helene's friend Matt Testaverde's family fell in the latter category; his father beat him with a belt every time he caught Matt hanging out with the rest of us, but that didn't stop him.

Inside Mrs. Menoni's dim, old-fashioned shop, she was sitting on a tall stool behind the counter, swaying gently to the classical music pouring out of the radio on the shelf behind her. She was in her eighties and, as always, was wearing a black dress and shawl. I liked her even though Matt Testaverde said she was a witch. He'd once told me that she could look at any pregnant belly and know the baby's sex, and that she could put the evil eye on people too.

She smiled when she saw me. "Maria. Come va?"

"Non c'è male. E Lei?" I replied. *Not bad. And you?*

She laughed as she always did when I spoke in the minimal Italian she'd taught me, and answered, "I'm good."

I picked out a loaf of bread, a carton of eggs, and onions, and put them on the counter beside a box of wrapped penny candies and a jarful of the Spaldeens we used to play stoopball with. After I'd paid, she pressed a piece of candy into my palm.

"Grazie," I said, pronouncing all the letters as she'd taught me— *graht-ʒee-a*—then walked out of the store, the bread and onions in a paper bag. I heard a bloodthirsty chorus of kids' voices shouting and jeering, and ran across the street to join the group clumped in Chickie's front yard.

Helene had Rhonda pinned down on the patchy lawn and was punching her. I called for her to stop, but it was like she was in a fugue state, unaware of anything but the mechanical beating she was giving her friend. No one intervened. Then Helene landed one last punch and stood abruptly, like some kind of internal timer had dinged. By then all of the spectators had fallen quiet. I'd witnessed a lot of fights growing up, even a few where someone was hurt worse than Rhonda, but none had ever struck me as being so strange, or quite so brutal.

"Damn, Helene," Matt Testaverde said.

She came over to me. She asked, "Did you remember to check the eggs?"

I held out the carton. She opened it, moved each of the eggs around to make sure none were cracked, then gave it back. Her expression was as calm as still water, her face was streaked with dirt and blue chalk dust from the skelly board one of Chickie's charges had drawn on their front walk.

Rhonda was still curled on the lawn, crying. As we started back toward our house, it was only once we were almost out of earshot that Rhonda got to her feet and weakly threatened to have my sister jumped.

"Your nose is bleeding," I said to Helene in French. Her lip was split too. She touched the tip of it lightly and sniffed hard at the blood creeping out.

"Are you okay?" I asked.

"I'm fine."

"What happened? What did she do?"

She shrugged. "Nothing."

"What?"

"Nothing recently. She tried to drown you though."

I started to ask what she was talking about before I remembered. "But I thought you all were *friends*."

She was amused. "Really?"

Confounded, I turned to her. She put her arm around me as we crossed the street toward our house.

"No, I was practicing something. Spies have to be able to get close to people, then turn on them. Just 'cause I'm not gonna be a spy myself doesn't mean I shouldn't know how to do it. You should never ask someone to do something you can't."

Helene opened our side door—it led into the kitchen, which was avocado green and had a large, generically African mask hanging on the wood-paneled wall. I followed her through the house, going first to the living room, where she grabbed Rhonda's bag and blanket and tossed them out onto the front steps, then to the bathroom where she washed her face. I followed her to the kitchen where she announced she was going to start dinner. I couldn't get over how calm she was. Holding up one of the onions I'd bought, she said in French, "Cut this for me, please? And set the table. After that go get your book. You can read it down here."

Helene was at the range when our father came home. He was wearing his uniform. "Smells great!" he said cheerfully.

His good mood deflated the second he noticed her split lip. He lifted her chin and held it firmly in place. "What happened here?"

"Nothing," she said as she tried to push his hand away.

"I told you already I'm tired of this." He let her go and she turned back to the stove.

"You don't have nothing to say for yourself?" He watched her back as she silently spooned rice onto a plate.

His voice was full of malice when he said, "No, of course you don't. Just like your damn mother."

He turned to me. "Marie take your food upstairs. I need to talk to your sister."

I left the kitchen and hid on the staircase to eavesdrop on him shouting at her. Pop was furious. Her behavior reflected badly on him, he said, and he was going to do something about it. She didn't say a word, but at one point in his tirade I heard her shriek—it sounded involuntary and made me think he'd hit her. Scared, I ran up to my room and read at my desk until I heard Helene on the stairs.

I looked up from the book. Her eyes were red and her face was puffy. I asked, "What happened?"

"He said if I'm gonna act so much like Maman I might as well go live with her." She went to her door. "He's sending me to Martinique."

Before I could respond, her door closed and locked. I couldn't believe it. How could Pop separate us so abruptly? I went over and knocked on her door, but she didn't respond.

"When are you going?" I called.

She put on some music. Turned it up loud. The wall was thin—she did that sometimes when she didn't want me to hear her cry.

I missed Helene more than I ever had Agathe. Or maybe the way I missed my sister was simply less bearable—the difference between the sharp pain that takes you to the hospital and the dull ache you can ignore because you've always had it. I'd felt like I needed to be insulated against my mother—in the five years since she'd left, I'd spoken to her only occasionally, far less than my sister did.

But I wrote Helene once a week and spoke to her as much as I could, even though an overseas call was an expensive rigmarole back then (you had to book it through the operator and get rung back when the call was ready). That was when I first learned that Agathe owned a cattle farm with one of our uncles—a *farm*! I couldn't picture it.

I felt guilty about Helene's banishment—she'd gotten in that fight with Rhonda because of me. And I was lonely without her; she was without question my best friend. But I resented her too. She'd been rewarded for her bad behavior with an extended Caribbean vacation, and I thought Helene was the only one of us who was welcome at our mother's, which triggered that old jealousy.

When Pop picked her up from the airport and returned her to our house in Queens six months later, she had a golden suntan and was ostensibly reformed. She walked through the door and said, "Jesus, neither of you know how to use a broom?"

It was true that the household had fallen into shambles while she was gone. I hugged her hard as Pop came through the door behind her. She handed us both small parcels wrapped in newspaper—always a practical gift giver, instead of souvenir tchotchkes, she'd brought Pop back a Swiss Army knife that he still has, and gave me a little red address book that I kept for years.

And later that night, when I was in bed, I asked her in French how it had been down there. We could hear each other through the wall, and sometimes it was easier to be honest when we couldn't see each other.

"It was fine. Good."

"That's it?"

"What else do you want me to say?"

"What was it like being with her?"

"Nice. She took care of me. Made pancakes sometimes. And she took me to the beach. Not all the time though, don't be jealous. There's a lot of work to do on a farm."

"A farm. With animals and everything?"

"Of course. Cows and chickens."

"I can't picture it. I can only see her here, you know? In the city. In the kitchen. Or in Ohrbach's that time when she bought me that nice coat with the toggles. Or the three of us in the button store on Delancey."

She started to laugh, and I knew why. I said, "You thinking about that thing I did with the sample button?"

"Uh-huh."

Every wall in that button store had been lined with shelves, and stacked on each were thousands of two-inch-tall cardboard boxes. Glued to each box was a sample of the button inside. They were organized by color; the effect was surreally beautiful. The samples were as appealing to me as candy, so once when no one was looking I'd ripped a round button off a box, and not knowing what to do with it once I had it, shoved it up my nose. I was six. It had seemed reasonable.

I remember a young clerk in a yarmulke holding my face and trying to claw it out of my nose, while a second one, fat, suspendered, his face red, had shouted, *No! Get her to blow. Put a finger over her nostril and get her to blow it out!* My sister hysterical with laughter, my mother frozen with mortification.

"You never did stuff like that," she said, still giggling. "Maman got so mad at me for laughing, but I couldn't help it."

"Helly, are you glad to be back in Queens?"

It took her a few long moments to answer. "Yeah. I'm glad I'm here."

It seemed obvious she was lying, which upset me. If she'd wanted to stay in Martinique, then she should've stayed. Sometimes I still worry that she came back out of obligation to me—out of guilt—and feel awful for taking her away from a place that made her happy.

Staying in Queens was contingent on her behavior, so Helene committed to being *good*. At least that's how it looked to everyone else. She did better in school, just well enough to stay out of trouble. She joined the cheerleading squad and started dating a basketball player my father strongly approved of. She never got into another fight that I heard about. But I suspected she wasn't really reformed. I could sense that her new personality was manufactured, and who she'd always been was still present just beneath it. I couldn't prove it though—how do you expose a dormant sleeper?

1971

In our tiny corner of Queens, the shift in culture had been abrupt— suddenly everyone was wearing shades in school, military apparel, Afros. Bullets around their necks and lions' teeth; red, black, and green flag buttons on their jackets. But I continued to look *good*. I kept pressing my hair, and when I applied makeup, it was with a light touch. I kept wearing the cream-colored blouses and wool pencil skirts that pleased my father. My mother had been gone for years, but I still had good home training. I spoke and dressed well, did well in school, accepted that I had to be twice as upright for white folks to think I was half as virtuous.

Robbie Young, according to my father, was the single corrupting element in my life. Pop hated Robbie; having known him for as long as my family had lived in Queens and being able to remember him as a goofy, happy little boy did nothing to strengthen my father's affection for him.

Still, when Robbie was sent to jail at sixteen—to Spofford, a notoriously violent juvenile facility in the Bronx—my father pulled some strings to get him transferred to a reform school upstate. Pop was the type who would never hesitate to put his personal feelings aside in order to do right by a young black man.

While Robbie was at Warwick he'd mailed a package to our house. In it were two items. The first was for me—it was a picture of him posing solemnly in a flannel shirt, pointing at the camera with a hatchet. The second was for my father: Robbie had lopped the paw off a badger, preserved it, and wrapped it up in a bit of newspaper as a gift.

I think his intention was to make a lucky trinket, like a rabbit's foot. Now I'm not going to pretend it wasn't ghoulish, but Pop's reaction surprised me: He took it as a threat. He must've believed that Robbie was rotten right down to his center, and everything he did was an expression of that rot. He told me that when Robbie got back I was forbidden to see him. I didn't argue, but when Robbie was released, I gleefully ignored the ban. People thought I was the good sister, but really I was only good at being sneaky.

I saw him every day for a few weeks until one evening when Helene, with feigned casualness, broke the news that Robbie was back in the city. She'd picked her moment: Mr. Ali was also in the kitchen, having just dropped Pop off after work. He shared my father's opinion on my boyfriend, which I knew because he'd lecture me on it. Even though, strictly speaking, it was none of his damn business.

"I hope you're not planning to see him," Pop said.

"Why would I? You already told me I couldn't."

"Hm."

Mr. Ali put his nose in the air and took a deep sniff. "That boy. You can smell the recidivism coming off him from here."

I smiled to hide my annoyance. He'd been right, of course. I knew Robbie well enough to know he thought he was smarter than everyone else, and by extension, that the rules shouldn't apply to him. But what teenager wanted to hear their boyfriend condemned by a man who wasn't even their father?

After Helene ratted me out, I didn't see Robbie again for about a month. In that time he moved out of Chickie's house and started sleeping on the futon in a foul little East Village one-bedroom, he and his roommate paying something like ninety dollars a month and "liberating" their electricity by patching into the building next door. This was the summer before I started college. I was sixteen; I'd been advanced in school a second time, so I was in the same graduating class as Helene. I took an inconsequential job because it was near Robbie's apartment, and felt free to see him whenever I wanted because my father's house was so far away.

One afternoon, the phone rang while I was at his place. He picked it up, then held out the receiver and told me it was Helene. She said she was at a pay phone nearby and that she needed to tell me something in person. She asked if I'd meet her in Tompkins Square Park.

Robbie insisted on coming with me. On the way there, we stopped at a pizza place and ate quickly at one of the Formica counters. We were having a good time until, as I was throwing out our paper plates, I looked over and saw him glance at the cashier, whose back was turned. Then he reached over the glass counter, opened the register, removed the stack of twenties, and reclosed it so smoothly it didn't even ring.

"You dummy," I said when we were out on the sidewalk. The insult was a part of our patter, but I was also annoyed. He tried to put his arm around me, but I shrugged him off. "I don't care what you do when you're alone, but don't get *me* in trouble. If he'd called the cops they would've arrested us both."

"You got to read *Steal This Book*. Then you'd understand."

"Don't give me that."

"It's true."

I sighed, resigned. "I'm already reading *Soul on Ice* like you told me."

"Read it next," he said, and added with a sarcastic smile: "Off the pigs. And welcome to the revolution, baby."

I loved Robbie, which meant he could truly make me furious. In too much of what he said, I heard overconfidence about his limited life experience and in his aggressively average intelligence. He was the type of guy that, had he been born white, especially if he'd grown up with a little money, would probably have wound up at an excellent business school.

We walked into the park. Helene wasn't there yet, so we took a free bench beside the monument where she'd told me to meet her. Tompkins Square was teeming with people: other teenagers, men playing chess, the homeless. Lively salsa music floated down from a nearby apartment building and mingled with the guitar that a cross-legged hippie in overalls played under a nearby tree.

Helene appeared with a backpack on. She'd gotten really beautiful. We both looked like Agathe, but Helene was also built like our mother's family: tall and with an athletic body. I was much curvier, like the women on Pop's side.

"Hey, Helene," Robbie said as I hugged her.

She ignored him. "I thought we'd be able to talk alone, Marie."

"What's going on?"

"Well. I enlisted."

Anger at the news flashed up in me, but I hid it as best I could. Robbie on the other hand couldn't contain himself. "What's the matter with you? They still fighting! You want them to send you to Vietnam?"

She gave him a withering look. He was wearing green fatigues, dark glasses, and a goatee, having started styling himself after the Panthers. "I don't want to go over to Vietnam. I want to be in the army."

"What's the difference?"

"I enlisted to become an intelligence officer."

"That's crazy." He laughed. "If I get called up when I'm eighteen I'm going to Canada."

"Yeah, well, you always been a coward, Robbie."

"I'm not no coward just 'cause I don't want to go over and kill a bunch of people who never hurt me. What you want to do that for, Helene? What Vietcong ever called you nigger?"

"I told you. I don't want to kill people. I'm going into the army so I can get into intelligence."

"And what's that going to get you?"

She sighed as if he was the stupidest man on Earth. "A job with the CIA."

He laughed again. "The CIA. Out your damn mind."

"Robbie . . ." I started, but Helene waved her hand, to signal that he wasn't worth it. She'd become immune to hearing no from everyone—even people who were supposed to be allies—and was still confident that she would succeed. Defiant about it.

"Marie, she needs to hear this." He looked to her. "You really think the CIA's going to make a black girl from Queens one of their agents?"

"Officer," she corrected. "They're going to hire me as an officer. Agents are spies."

"Yeah right. Good luck," he said, and although he was being sarcastic and mean, he was also saying a lot of what I longed to. As the reality of her news settled over me I got angrier. She was putting her life on the line and for what? Some stupid, unrealistic dream she'd had as a kid?

"What do you know?" she said coolly. "And where do you get off acting so high and mighty? You never been about shit."

"Hey," he said, suddenly serious. "Don't talk to me like that."

"I'll talk to you however I wanna talk to you."

He looked to me. "Tell your sister to be cool."

Helene and I exchanged a glance—he didn't know me well if he believed I'd ever say something like that to her because he'd told me to. She said my name, but I was still too stunned to say anything coherent.

"I should go." She turned in the direction she'd come from.

I told Robbie I'd be right back and followed my sister.

"When do you have to show up and . . ." I trailed off not knowing enough about the army to finish the sentence.

"When do I start basic training? Next week."

"You kidding?" I said, shocked at the speed, then composed myself. "You're not gonna walk at graduation?"

"No. I don't care about school like that."

"I'm walking. You're not gonna be there to see it?"

She turned to me. "Can't you be happy for me?"

"I *am* happy for you," I assured her. "I'm just worried. And I'm disappointed you won't be at graduation. Does Pop know? He's gonna be pissed."

"He already kicked me out. What else can he do?"

She said it casually, but the fight they'd had must've been intense. I'd never seen him as angry as he was after Helene enlisted—for months I couldn't even mention her name. His reaction was as strong as it was because he was scared, and also because she'd blindsided him. He hated being sucker punched as much as I did, and had been unable to anticipate that one of his children, one of his girls, would choose military service over education.

"Where are you going?"

"Uptown. I'm going to stay by some friends of mine for a few days."

"Will I see you before you leave?"

"Of course." We'd exited the park. She stopped on the street corner and turned to me. Her eyes were glassy with tears.

"Helene . . ."

"I *really* need to go now. Okay?"

I nodded and hugged her. Watched as she jaywalked across the avenue then turned back toward the park. Robbie was still waiting where I'd left him.

"She's going to basic training in a few days," I told him.

"I don't understand that girl sometimes," he said, and when I didn't respond he went on. "But don't nobody really *know* Helene, do they?"

"Pop kicked her out."

"Where she staying till she goes?"

"She didn't say. Uptown."

"Must be with some white friend of hers that goes to school up there. Who else would let her stay by them now?"

"Maybe she could crash with you for a few days so I can see her."

"Roy's not gonna want no sellout at our place."

"That's my sister," I said.

"I know."

"Anyway, Roy's white."

"Yeah, but Roy's down. He's a hippie."

"Abbie Hoffman's white."

"You trying to misunderstand me on purpose?"

"I'm just saying you don't even stick to your own rules about who's down and who's not. I admire Helene. She's ambitious."

"Yeah, you *would*. You and your cop daddy, all y'all are just alike." He clipped a section of my hair between two of his fingers. "That why you still straighten this?"

I pushed his hand away. "I'm not down 'cause I press my hair?"

"Well, if I'm being real . . . it embarrasses me. You're my woman. Reflect me, you know?"

"It's my head, Robbie." I screwed up my face as I stood. "Listen, you not better than nobody. And you not part of no revolution. You just a thief, and you been one since long before you ever heard of Abbie Hoffman."

As I started toward the exit, he called after me but I ignored him. He said he was a radical, and counterculture, but so was everyone we knew. In that context, how was he any less conformist than the people he dismissed as mainstream? Helene was the only genuine nonconformist I knew, and through example she taught me to look for that in the people I chose to love and respect. Because I took the lesson seriously, after that argument, Robbie was permanently diminished in my eyes. It wasn't until the day I met your father that I understood why I'd felt so disdainful: I loved Robbie and wanted him to be the revolutionary he thought he was. The fact that he wasn't disappointed me.

I saw Helene only once more before, as promised, she left for basic training at the Women's Army Corps Center at Fort McClellan in Alabama. Meanwhile, I started at City College. My favorite course was a literature seminar that took place in a young professor's apartment on the Upper West Side—I'd never really had any business visiting the neighborhood before then, and the first time I did was like an expedition into a new world. So *this* is how wealthy white people really live, I'd mused with an anthropologist's zeal as I observed the scenes around me. I'd thought it was exotic stuff.

The class itself was pleasant and easy: We'd sit on pillows in a ragged circle on the floor and talk about how certain books made us feel. But I made a male acquaintance there that Robbie became unreasonably jealous of. That, combined with the frustrations that our fight in Tompkins Square had highlighted, precipitated the first off-again phase of our relationship.

After basic training, Helene was stationed at Fort Bragg. She came up to the city sometimes, when she could get space on a military hop, and would stay at a friend's house where I'd go visit her. Things were still hostile between her and Pop. Thanks to my intervention, the tension had eased to the point where she came to the house once for dinner, but she still wouldn't spend the night.

I went down to North Carolina as much as I could despite the unspoken friction between us. On my side, I was still resentful that she hadn't been at my graduation and that she'd given me no indication she was planning to enlist before she did it. I don't know why she was upset with me, and she wasn't the kind of person to lay her grievances out on the line. While her gift for secrecy put distance between us, it also taught me the value of intelligence: I learned that a secret is power, that power in application is force, that force is strength, and strength advantage.

Helene lived off base in one of the small aluminum-sided homes that featured so prominently in the anonymous suburban sprawl squeezed between Fort Bragg and downtown Fayetteville. We pretended things between us were as they'd always been by doing all sorts of things— had it really been as it always was we would have hung around and done nothing. She snuck me into a disco (I wasn't yet eighteen) where we partied with her WAC friends. We raced in Chocolate Chip, the tiny used Honda Civic she'd bought, and I never let on about how much it scared me. She taught me to box; she'd joined a WAC team and said I might like the sport because—as she put it—I had some aggression I needed to work out. I'd laughed at the comment even though the assessment made me angry. We went to all sorts of parties—she knew a lot of people. It was all out of character for me; I'm not a traditionally fun person, but Helene was in her element.

One weekend she said she was taking me to a bar, so I put on flares and a striped shirt. She was more dressed up—wearing a white mini-dress with puff sleeves. She looked beautiful and I told her so.

When we arrived, she waved to a group of men sitting at a table along the wall; one of them saw and waved back.

"Who are those guys?"

"Eighty-second Airborne."

"Oh yeah? Any of them radio operators like Pop?" I asked, teasing her.

"Shut up," she said with a smile as we walked toward the group. One of them, the only white guy at the table, stood to shake my hand and insisted that I sit beside him. I looked at him. Pressed to guess, I would've said he was twenty-five or so. He had piercing dark blue eyes, a hawk nose, chestnut hair. I naturally had a good ear for accents, which I would later hone, and could tell he'd grown up in Texas.

After he'd been talking to me for a while, it occurred to me that Helene must've asked him to, presumably because before I'd come down for the visit, I'd mentioned wanting to get back together with Robbie. But I found her friend off-putting: His eye contact was too intense, he laughed too hard at his own jokes, and said my name an unnatural amount.

Toward the end of the evening, Helene pulled me toward a photo booth and we tumbled into it. Took a series of silly pictures.

"You still think you want to go to med school?" she asked, as we waited for our photos to develop.

"I don't know." I was already ambivalent about the plan even though it was a new one. I'd started telling people I wanted to be a doctor because it felt crude to say what I actually wanted, which was to be wealthy and respected.

"Have you ever thought about working for an intelligence agency?"

I shook my head. "I don't want to join the army."

"You wouldn't have to. You're going to have a degree in a couple of years." She sighed and tipsily let her head fall back against the booth. "Marie, I'm not stupid. I know the CIA's a long shot for me. But if it doesn't happen, I'll find something else. The intelligence community is big. What Mr. Ali does, that's intelligence. And if he can do it, I know I'll be able to find my way in at some point."

"I believe it."

"Once I make officer, that's when I'll start pushing. If I learned anything from Pop, it's that they may not want us, but we're Mitchells. They'll get us anyway."

I made a quiet, dissenting noise.

"What?"

"If they don't want you, then don't fight their wars."

"It's that easy, huh?"

"It is," I said.

"Not for me," she said. "If no one will hire me, I'll start my own firm." I nodded. Spite was often a motivator for both me and Helene— it was never wise to tell either of us that we couldn't do something.

"Is that something you'd want to do?" she asked.

"What?"

"Work in intelligence."

"Me?"

"Promise me you'll give it some thought. You'd be good at it. I know it."

"If it was our firm, maybe. If I was working with you. I used to think about that sometimes when we were kids. Sister spies."

"Yes!" she said, drunkenly excitable. "Promise you'll look into it."

"All right," I said.

"Say you promise."

"I promise."

She smiled. "I love you, Marie."

Before I could respond she added, "I bet the pictures are done."

She woozily stepped out of the booth and took the strip from the dispenser. We looked them over together then she tucked them into her purse.

She woke me up punishingly early the next morning—I still had a hangover, but she seemed to be in high spirits. Over breakfast she said she wanted to box, so after we ate, we got into Chocolate Chip and started toward the base.

"Did you have a good time last night?" she asked in French as she drove

I nodded. "It was fun."

"Those guys I introduced you to, my friends, you thought they were all nice. Right?"

"Yeah."

"How's Robbie?" she said, her voice dripping with disdain.

"How come you don't like him?"

"What's to like?"

"I'm serious. Is it because you think he's a bad influence on me?"

"Bad influence? No, I don't respect Robbie because he keeps getting caught. He's not good enough for you."

"I like him more than that guy you tried to set me up with."

"Which one?"

"The guy I was sitting next to. Wasn't that a setup? Not my type at all. He's kind of creepy."

"I could tell he was really trying to be nice," she said, sounding wounded.

"What's his name again?"

"Daniel Slater. He's a sweet guy." She looked around and spoke with a lowered voice: "The CIA approached him. They want to recruit him once his contract with the army is up."

"Did he tell you that? They made a bad choice if he goes around telling people that."

She didn't laugh. "I can hear it in the way he talks. I've met a few guys down here that I think are recruits. They all act like they're tactical geniuses."

"Does it bother you that they're recruiting your friend?"

"Why would it?"

"Because of what you said last night."

"What'd I say? I don't remember. I was drinking shots."

"Forget it."

"I've been seeing him for a few months," she said.

"Really?" It should've occurred to me earlier that he'd been her boyfriend, but I hadn't guessed that my sister would have picked him. It wasn't that he was bad looking, and in fact I could see how Helene might have found his face charming, but he didn't seem like her type. He was nothing like Freddy, her high school boyfriend.

"It's not too serious. But, I like him."

"Pop's not gonna be happy about you dating a white guy."

"That's all you have to say?" She flashed me an angry look and we drove the rest of the way in silence.

On the base, she parked in a lot near the fitness center. It was large, brightly lit, and empty except for an older, muscular officer who was jumping rope. As I put on sparring gear, I asked her to go over some of the basics again.

"Let's practice some footwork first," she said, and I copied her re-flection in the mirror. Maybe all sisters say this, but Helene was the prettier one. She had box braids then, high cheekbones, a full, pretty mouth. Her face was still changing—she was only twenty—and in the last few months her features had gotten sharper, giving her a regal look.

After she'd shown me the basic stance, then the four punches, we faced off and began to gently spar, my sister giving me advice about how to throw my punches with a bit more strength.

I sent her a shot to the chest that she wasn't expecting, one that knocked her back against the mirror. I kept her pinned there, hitting her with shots that weren't particularly hard but were brutal in their consistency. It felt like I was exorcising whatever anger I still had. She protected herself, and when she didn't try to hit me, I thought it was because she couldn't. Her watch beeped to signal the end of a round. We broke apart and sat with our backs against the mirror.

"You're good," she said.

"I *feel* good."

She sipped from her bottle of water and gave me a smile that was hard to read.

"Ready?" she said as she got to her feet. "I'm gonna go a little harder on you now."

I nodded as I put my gloves back on. We started to spar. Her glove immediately slammed into my temple, so hard that I saw a starburst. She hit me in the chest and ribs, absolutely clobbering me until, disoriented, I lost my balance and fell to my knees. The briny taste of blood jumped in my mouth.

"Come on!" she shouted. "Get up! Hit me!"

I looked up into her face, and for just an instant I saw that wild, girlhood fury of hers before she regained control of herself and backed away. She pulled off her gloves and her headgear.

"We're done," she said as she started toward the locker room.

8

As it turned out, it wasn't only Gold who wanted to speak to me about the Patrice Lumumba Coalition. I was told an officer from the CIA would be coming to the field office to meet with me too—apparently he wanted to talk to me because one of their targets had a connection to the PLC.

I was nervous about the meeting because I'd forged Gold's approval signature on Aisha's termination paperwork and submitted it to bureau HQ. It would be especially embarrassing if that came up in front of an officer from another agency.

I was also excited about what the CIA might ask me to do. Through executive order, Ronald Reagan had changed the nature of our foreign surveillance operations. For the first time ever, the agency was allowed to investigate a foreign target anywhere in the world, including our own soil. Which meant that I could be working with them to spy on virtually *anyone*. I'd convinced myself the target was high profile.

A few days after I'd received Gold's memo, I went down to squad bay B and sat beside him at an expansive white table, our backs to windows that looked over the city. We waited quietly, Gold working a toothpick between his teeth. I remember the wall clock being exceptionally loud, although that memory might just be an expression of my anxiety at the time.

An officer approached the squad bay—I could tell from the way Gold straightened his back and nervously smoothed his blazer that he was CIA. As he came into the room, both Gold and I stood to shake the officer's hand.

The first few moments after you meet someone are precious, because the data on them is plentiful and your own subjectivity has yet to interfere. I've always been good at making guesses about who people are, and often used the skill when I was recruiting informants. I generally kept what I knew to myself though; my talent for observation put most people on guard, and my memory could cause the same problem. When it's a question of how much you remember about an acquaintance, a colleague, or a snitch, there's a fine line between what's flattering and what gives them the creeps.

The officer gave me some deliberately direct eye contact, his face wide open, his eyebrows up as he smiled slightly. When I first approached a target, I did so with this very same look on my face. It was a basic step, one of many I used to suggest to my targets that I was trustworthy. I imitated his expression; right from the start we were working each other.

He introduced himself as Ed Ross. He was in his early forties and handsome in a corn-fed kind of way. The strong light pouring in on us from the window had a clarifying effect on his features that worked in his favor, illuminating a dusting of light freckles that made him look boyish and the laugh lines etched around his eyes that made him seem warm.

"Good to see you again," Ross said as he vigorously shook Gold's hand.

"You too, Ed, you too." Gold smiled. "Season's coming up fast. You betting on Duke this year?"

"Do what now?" Ross asked.

A few years earlier, a sociolinguist I admired had published an excellent book on a university press, an enormous work that I'd liked so much I'd gone to the one sparsely attended book event that was held for it in the city. In the book were a series of overlays on maps of the United States representing the influence of race, class, gender, education, socioeconomic status, and a handful of other factors on American regional dialect trends. The book had also come with hundreds of dialect samples on tape, which I listened to all the time: in my car, or while cooking, or sometimes when I was jogging back home from the gym. I found them oddly soothing. I listened to them so much that I'd wound up committing most of the notable linguistic characteristics to memory, augmenting my natural talent for accents.

I knew from Ross's accent and from the turn of phrase he'd used (*do what now?*) that he was from what the linguist had categorized as the inland South, which included small swatches of Tennessee, Georgia, and western North Carolina. His strong aversion to the idea that Duke might win suggested an allegiance to the Tar Heels. My guess was that he was from North Carolina.

A thicker version of his accent didn't seem far out of reach. I supposed that one of the first things he'd found out about himself was that how he spoke led people to presume a lot about him. As a younger man he'd learned to shift his voice, his speech, to make them different things for different people, and he could now do it without much thought. I hope you can see me well enough in these journals to understand why I instinctively recognized this ability in him.

I saw other things about Ross. His suit had been cut from very high quality wool and fit him well. Truth be told, it looked so expensive that it raised practical questions about how he could afford it on a federal salary. As Ross and Gold continued to talk, I glanced at Gold's suit. His was what I'd become used to seeing in a government office: ill-fitting polyester, plastic buttons. It was a suit that belonged to a man who had children and a mortgage. Who couldn't afford to have taste. The three of us sat, Gold and me on one side of the table, Ross on the other.

"You two know anything about Thomas Sankara?" Ross asked.

"Only a little," I said, when in fact I knew a lot. I've accused Helene of being secretive, but I'm not in the habit of tipping my hand either. General knowledge wasn't a trait that was rewarded at the bureau; it wasn't a game show. Hard work and ambition and the benefits of favoritism were how you got ahead. In fact, I preferred for my colleagues to believe I was ignorant. That way they didn't see me as a threat.

"Yeah. He's the president of, uh, Upper Volta," Gold said.

I glanced at him. Thomas Sankara was the president of what was *formerly* Upper Volta, and the story of how he'd seized power in the country was a fascinating one. I'd followed it closely.

Ross gave us fact sheets that outlined Thomas Sankara's biographical information, which we both only skimmed for different reasons: me because I knew much of it, and Gold because he wasn't interested. Obviously, I can't remember everything on the sheet, but I should tell you what I remember of the history.

It's important to understand that he came to power backed by a popular movement. In the early 1980s, there'd been a quick succession of military governments in the country, each of them toppled by coups. In May 1983, Sankara was prime minister. Clashes he'd had with the president, Jean-Baptiste Ouédraogo, led to Sankara's removal from his post and his arrest, triggering widespread student-led protests in Ouagadougou, the capital city.

Sankara's closest friend, Blaise Compaoré, was the head of a military training center in Pô, a city in the south of the country. He organized a rebellion there, which put political pressure on Ouédraogo that led to Sankara's release. The second he was free, he began to organize his coup. He was in Ouaga, the beating heart at the center of a network of dissenters.

On August 4, Compaoré began leading his troops from Pô toward Ouaga in trucks seized from a Canadian construction site. It was night when they arrived. As Sankara had instructed, civilian members of his revolutionary network cut the power lines in the south of the city, disorienting the president's armed guards who were stationed there.

Meanwhile, other members of Sankara's network helped guide Compaoré's troops through the darkness toward the presidential palace.

Employees of the national telecommunications company, led by Mousbila Sankara, Thomas Sankara's uncle, cut the phone lines near the palace, effectively isolating Ouédraogo from his guards at different outposts throughout the city. Suspecting something was up, Ouédraogo fled from the palace to his home. When Compaoré's troops arrived at the palace, the presidential guards there, realizing that their leader had deserted them, immediately surrendered.

At 10 P.M. on August 4, 1983, Thomas Sankara went on the radio to declare himself president of the National Council of the Revolution, the CNR, and appointed his friend Compaoré minister of state, effectively making him the second most powerful man in the government. Right from the beginning, they functioned as a pair—Thomas Sankara being the strategist and Blaise Compaoré being the force.

Thomas Sankara renamed the country Burkina Faso—the Land of Incorruptible People—and wrote the national anthem. He'd been young when he'd come to power—just thirty-three years old. He was charismatic, an excellent public speaker who played guitar in a jazz band, and sped around Ouaga on a motorcycle. And troublingly, he considered himself a Marxist revolutionary.

When I looked up from the pages in front of me Ross said, "He's coming to New York next month to speak to the UN General Assembly. And the next day he'll be speaking at a rally the Patrice Lumumba Coalition is organizing. Mitchell, we want you to help us keep him under surveillance when he's talking to the PLC."

"Is there specific intel that you're hoping my asset can get you?" I asked, wondering if I could pay Aisha for a one-off job.

"Yes. We want to know how much Sankara knows about our involvement in the ULCR, a political party that we've formed within his government."

"What's his government called?" Gold asked.

"It's in the fact sheet. That's why I gave it to you," Ross said, a little testily. "The CNR."

"You have operatives in the CNR?" I said.

"Yes. Our problem is that while Sankara's government presents it-self as a coalition of several political parties who all get a say in decision making, in fact only a small handful of his closest allies truly do. We don't yet have access to anyone with any real power."

"Sounds like he's a dictator," Gold put in.

"Unfortunately, you're right about that," Ross said. "But we're completely in control of the ULCR, and through the party we're agitating for electoral reform. Over the last year, we've been putting increasing pressure on Sankara's government to create a multiparty system."

"Why's the CIA precipitating that push?" I asked.

"Because a multiparty system is a basic element of democracy," he said, chiding me.

"It's an odd agenda for the CIA to have when *our* government isn't a multiparty system." My tone was just a shade away from flat-out sarcasm. I didn't like being spoken to as if I were a child. And it wasn't unreasonable for me to assume that the CIA was meddling in a foreign government out of more than just the goodness of the agency's heart.

"Well, this is a former French colony," Ross said. "An electoral system similar to what the French have is one that will be a better fit. The people are more familiar with that."

"So you're trying to establish a French-style electoral system. A two-round system."

He shook his head. "We only want to embrace the French way up to a point. But this is all too big picture. Let me lay out what we want from you—"

"Why's it so important to know if he knows that the CIA is in control of the ULCR?"

"Mitchell, come on." Gold, tired of my questions, shot me an angry look.

"There are a couple of ways to answer that question. For now let me just leave it at contempt."

"Contempt," I repeated with some contempt of my own for his having given me such a vague answer to a direct question.

"Sankara has contempt for the politicians in his country that he considers corrupt, and it makes him underestimate his rivals. We want to know just how much that contempt blinds him. If we can understand that, we can better understand how to give his more prodemocratic rivals an advantage come election time."

"Hm," I said, because I didn't believe him. I said slowly, "Let me be sure I understand you. The CIA wants to establish a French-style electoral system in Burkina Faso."

"Yes."

"That's not a two-round system and therefore not actually French—"

"We don't think it needs to be."

"Because you hope to create a free and open election—"

"Yes."

"Of the candidate that the CIA plans to back. You already have your pro-American candidate picked out, don't you?"

"Prodemocratic," Ross corrected. "He's a *prodemocratic* candidate."

"I don't think their long-term goals in the country are any of your business," Gold said. He seemed embarrassed. "Or at least not anything you should be interrogating him on."

"I just want to understand the nuts and bolts. Don't you? Obviously, it's an elaborate sham, which is interesting." I smiled despite my clear hostility. I was annoyed. This man had approached me to participate in an operation, but didn't have enough respect for me to be honest about what he was up to.

Ross seemed amused by my reaction. Speaking to Gold, he said, "I didn't think she'd be able to connect all those dots. It was a mistake to underestimate her." He turned back to me and looked me deep in the eye. "One I won't make again."

"Look, it's win-win," he continued. "We're giving a fledgling government a recipe for democracy. Admittedly, it's a poor country, but their loyalty to our ideology matters. Sankara has visited the Soviet Union several times, and they're supporting his government financially. They're supporting his dictatorship. We need to win back hearts and minds from them."

"That I can understand," Gold said. "If they're funding his government, that's just a way for them to expand the scope of their power."

"I agree," Ross said. "Which is why we have to counter their threat everywhere it crops up in the world."

I thought about this as I observed Ross. The subtext, of course, was that we would be countering Soviet expansion with our own—the plan was that they'd remove a wildly popular president from power in favor of a rigged electoral process that would install a pro-American candidate.

But that didn't bother me, despite the irony. What bothered me was my nagging awareness that Ross was leaving something out. I could tell from his expression and my intuition.

"What's your asset in the PLC like?" Gold asked me. "Could you get your guy to wear a wire and take Sankara and his delegation out to a strip club? They might talk politics in front of him."

"That approach isn't going to work on Sankara. He's not that type," Ross said.

"They're all that type," Gold said. "They come to New York, and they want to have a little fun."

"Does your asset even speak French?" Ross turned back to me, politely ignoring Gold.

"No," I said.

"Well, that's a shame. Because we really want someone who can speak the language. That way they could spend a little time with Sankara after the rally, and try to find out what he knows about the ULCR. Maybe also learn what his next steps will be."

I stared across the table at Ed Ross. It didn't seem at all like a coincidence that I spoke French and that he wanted to use an operative who spoke it. I realized then that from the start, his agenda had been to involve me in his operation. And it was unsettling—why all the subterfuge?

"Yeah," I said. "That really is too bad."

"Wait a second, Mitchell," Gold jumped in. "Don't you speak it? Isn't your mother French or something?"

"I speak a little," I conceded, surprised—and annoyed—that one of my biographical details had managed to stick in Gold's mind.

Ross lifted his eyebrows. He said, as if it were the first time it had occurred to him, "Well, we could post *you* at the UN. If you wanted to go undercover. I know someone in the chief of protocol's office."

"Oh, is that right?" I said, my tone equally as performative as his. I noticed him catch it.

"You might be a better fit than your informant," he said. "Sankara likes women. Respects them."

"And what a thing to use against him." It was out of my mouth before I realized it. His condescension had gotten to me. In my rush to prove that he was underestimating me, I'd let slip things about myself that were too revealing.

"I think we could get you closer to him than we could get a man," Ross pressed.

On the surface it looked like exactly the operation I'd been waiting so long for, the one that would give my career a boost. The target was a president, so it would be a high-profile case. But while Ross had told me that I'd just be gathering information, and there was nothing illegal about that, I'd seen the way his eyes lit up as he'd taken in my appearance. He wanted to use me because I was a woman, because I was black, because they expected Thomas to find me attractive.

So I had to turn it down. There was just too good a chance that accepting his offer would backfire on me. I looked to Gold. "Perkins speaks French too, doesn't he, sir? Maybe he could help them instead."

"So you're not interested," Ross said.

"No. But I'm sure there's someone else here who could help you get the intel you need."

"Mitchell." Gold was glaring at me. "There aren't too many people here with your, uh, *profile*. I can't think of anyone else who—"

"I'm sorry." I was speaking to Ross. "I'll give you information about the PLC—maybe you can find someone on their roster who can help you. But I'm not interested in going undercover."

"Not a problem," he answered. The expression on his face was difficult to read. "We'll just have to figure something else out."

He smiled—it almost looked sincere—and asked to see the reports I'd mentioned.

I left the squad bay for my desk. As I was looking through the file organizer, I saw Gold approaching and braced myself. "What the hell was that?" he hissed. "They want to run a joint operation with us. It's always good to make nice with those guys. Build bridges."

"I'm being helpful, sir. They'll find someone else." I held up the folder I'd been looking for.

He snatched it from my hand. "You're not a team player. That's your whole problem. Fix that or you won't get very far here. I'll field the rest of the meeting. You stay."

I watched him walk back to the squad bay. I couldn't let Ross use me. When Mr. Ali had let the bureau use *him*, it had trapped him professionally. It's only a fool who doesn't learn from the experience of others. Fuming, I left the office as soon as Gold was out of sight.

There wasn't too much to my neighborhood boxing gym: a ring, of course, two heavy bags dangling over the thin strip of linoleum floor, and walls that were covered in peeling white paint.

"Shoulders down. Keep 'em down!" the trainer said as I hit the focus mitt on his hand. "One-two-three-two. Come on! Forty-five more seconds!"

I hit the mitt as hard and fast as I could, using up my last bit of energy. Boxing always reminded me of Helene in the fitness center at Fort Bragg, the angry look on her flushed face before she decked me. And yet I did it once or twice a week. The trainer started to count down from ten. Then: "That's it! You're done. Good work."

I thanked him, my muscles still screaming, my heart racing, then stood there panting for several seconds with my gloved hands on my hips. Once I'd caught my breath, I slipped through the ropes and down to the linoleum. A heavyset boy in a striped shirt and shorts, like a black Pugsley Addams, was leaning against the wall watching us. Most of the people I crossed paths with there were boys and young men. It was the kind of gym that the trainer, who also owned the place, had founded in hopes of providing kids with something constructive to do so they'd stay out of trouble.

"Your turn," the trainer called to Pugsley. The boy looked panicked as he approached the ring.

I wiped my face and drank from the water fountain. Took my gear off, changed into my sneakers, and pulled my Walkman from my backpack. As I was leaving, I called goodbye to the trainer.

"Take care, sis," he shouted back. "See you Wednesday."

I went out to the concrete stairwell, where maybe a dozen Iz the Wiz throwies lined both walls, each one a different, vibrant color. Every time I saw them I was uplifted, and wondered what kind of Fed I was if I could find graffiti beautiful. I jogged down the steps, through the metal door propped open with a cinder block, and out into the bright, open city.

"The six-million-dollar woman! All right!" That was from the incense vendor on the corner of 125th Street and Adam Clayton Powell. I pretended I couldn't hear him; I'd long since stopped feeling obligated to respond to every strange man who spoke to me.

I went north up the boulevard. Weaved around two women carrying Conway shopping bags in that trademark pink, then crossed east at 128th Street in the direction of Lenox. On that corner another man called after me. I pretended I hadn't heard him either.

I jogged past the building halfway down my block that had black smoke stains on the exterior and plywood in the windows. Past the detritus-peppered lot beside it, the gap of the building that had burned down there was like a missing front tooth.

The street was deserted, but up ahead on Lenox I could see pedestrians waiting for the light to change. They were close enough to hear me scream, I found myself thinking, nervous because of the black car that had been creeping along behind me since I'd turned onto 128th. It suddenly sped up until it was in my peripheral vision. Ed Ross was peering at me from the passenger side, his face framed by the black car and gloomy interior.

I pulled off my headphones. "You scared the hell out of me."

"Sorry. I called after you on the corner, but you didn't hear. What are you listening to?"

"It's a book on tape," I said, embarrassed to admit it. At least it wasn't one of those dialect tapes, which would've been even dorkier.

He smiled. "I have a very good friend who likes those too. Which one?"

"*Against All Hope*, by Armando Valladares." I stepped off the sidewalk and went toward the car.

"You know the Cubans think he's CIA."

"Is he?"

He smiled again and shook his head. "Not as far as I know."

"What do you want, Ross? I made myself clear in our meeting. Which I caught hell for from my ASAC, by the way."

"I came up here to invite you to dinner. I'll be in town for a few more days. There's an excellent restaurant in the lobby of my hotel. Give me one more shot to convince you to come work for me."

"I'm not going to change my mind."

Despite what I'd said, he extended a business card to me. After a moment's hesitation, I took it.

"Listen, I have to try. That's my job. But there are no strings. All I'm asking is for you to come listen to my pitch. Enjoy a free meal, some nice wine. You say no and I'll never darken your doorway again."

He sounded like he was trying to sell me a timeshare, but it was working. I didn't feel as hostile to him as I had in the meeting, because he didn't seem as keen as he'd been before to lie to me. Willing to start fresh, I said, "I'm not stupid, Ross. You weren't telling the truth. I can't work for you if you're not straight with me."

Clearly amused by what I'd said, he answered, "I couldn't tell you everything in front of your ASAC. But I will if you come to dinner. Hear me out. Make your decision then."

I considered his invitation. "Just to be clear: This is only about work, right? Nothing else?"

Once more he seemed genuinely amused in a way that left me feeling like there was some joke that I wasn't in on. "No funny business, I promise. You free tomorrow?"

I decided I was and he gave me the hotel's address. He told me if anything came up that I should give him a call. I looked down at the card he'd handed me. It gave his title as *consultant* in a firm called Primary Consulting, a phone number but no address.

It was my turn to be amused, by the work of constructed meaninglessness I was holding.

"I'll see you, Marie," he said, and I looked up at him again.

In his words I'd heard more than a simple salutation—I heard his confidence. I knew that if an informant was willing to meet with me on their own, I'd already persuaded them to work for me. We both knew that.

I watched as the car Ross was in continued on to the corner, turned on Lenox, and disappeared from view. As I went toward my building, I thought about his approach, which was much less subtle than my own. It was my style to gently, slowly insinuate myself into a target's life. I got Aisha used to me first by appearing every day at the park near the St. Nick projects where she took Marlon. I acknowledged her with a nod but never spoke to her, those initial interactions never lasting more than a few seconds. I'd let a couple of weeks pass that way, because I'd wanted her to know I wasn't a threat and also to make her as curious as possible about what I wanted. It had worked. When I finally spoke to her, she'd already bypassed the guess that I wanted to sleep with her and moved on to the suspicion that I was a Fed.

As I climbed up my building's peeling stone stoop, two boys came outside—the one I recognized as a neighbor's son held the door for me with a bright smile. The interior of my building was gloomy, and the scent of fried meals hung in the air. I ran up to my apartment where I did push-ups and sit-ups, took a shower, dressed. In my bedroom, I glanced at Ross's card on my dresser. It was surreal to find myself being recruited, having spent so much time recruiting people myself.

The room looked out onto 128th Street, which was much quieter than Lenox. In the window across from my own, a girl was reading a pocket-sized book, a Bible probably, her legs outstretched and crossed at the ankles, her hair wrapped in a doobie. I could hear the *thock* of a Spaldeen against the building—the boys I'd seen earlier must've been playing stoopball, which according to the sociolinguist's book, they called pinners in Chicago.

9

I called a car service, and on the ride downtown, tried to guess at how Ross would make his pitch. I walked into a small, elegant restaurant and found that he was already there—I was surprised to see him sitting with a blond man. Both of them stood as I approached.

"Marie, this is Phillip," Ross said, and gave no further introductory description, referring to him as neither a colleague or a friend. All three of us were aware of the omission.

"Nice to meet you." I shook Phillip's hand.

"Marie," Ross said. "I didn't know you had so much hair. It's beautiful."

I thanked him, even though it wasn't just a compliment. He was appraising me. I knew I did look good though, in my favorite black cocktail dress and with my hair down. Although I always wore it pulled back at work, I felt more myself with my curls free.

The three of us sat, and a few uncomfortable moments passed in which I could think of absolutely nothing to say. Luckily the waiter came to our table and broke the silence. Phillip ordered a bottle of wine.

"I thought you two should meet," Ross said. "You're the only two people on the planet who listen to books on tape."

Phillip laughed. "So you're the other one."

"Guilty." I smiled. "What are you listening to these days?"

"Not too much right now. I'm too busy to read for fun during the semester."

"Phillip's a lit professor down near us in DC," Ross said.

With some prodding, Phillip listed a few of the books on his syllabus that semester, including *Passing*.

"That's one of my favorites," I told him.

"What attracted you to it?" he asked. "I'm always interested in what makes someone pick up a book."

"That's hard to say, I read it so long ago. I was a teenager." I must've initially been attracted to it because I thought it might teach me something about your grandmother—the premise of the book is that the main characters are both black women who can pass for white. But I was aware that Ross was listening, and not wanting to reveal too much about my background, settled on telling Phillip, "I like melodrama. That's probably what appealed to me. How about you?"

"I'd heard it was way ahead of its time. Clare and Irene are clearly romantically obsessed with each other, so the title also refers to sexuality. They can both pass for white *and* for straight. And that book came out, what? Almost sixty years ago? It's revolutionary."

I thought about his answer for a moment and nodded in agreement. I'd never considered that before, but he was right. Most of the conversations I had were with colleagues—I couldn't remember the last time one of them had said something as intellectually stimulating. It was refreshing.

He glanced at Ross. "We're boring Ed."

"Not at all," Ross said.

"You should read it," Phillip told him.

"I have. It's not bad."

"You did? When?"

"Hm, maybe a month ago? You left a copy on the coffee table. I was bored and read it in a few hours. It's short."

"Why didn't you tell me?"

"You know why." He looked over at me. "I'm not afraid to admit it: I don't like talking about books with him."

"You see how he is?" Phillip asked me.

"You see how *he* is? I don't like it because he asks impossible questions."

"I ask your opinion!" Phillip was still grinning. "There's never any right answer."

"Yeah. You just want to know how I feel about the things you ask me to read."

"Exactly."

"But they don't make me feel anything. And you refuse to accept that."

"Because everyone has feelings!" Phillip ran a hand through his hair, causing it to stand on end.

"See?" Ross laughed. He reached out and patted Phillip's hair back down. "Impossible to give the right answer."

So this was how he was making his pitch, I realized. He was hoping to foster my trust by suggesting I had his. Once I understood what he was up to, I started to let my guard down. Although he had an agenda for giving me a glimpse into his personal life, and although I believed he was performing his part of their intimacy for me, I could still let myself have fun. By the time our meals came, the discussion had subtly shifted to politics. I was happy. It was the first time in a long time that I'd really enjoyed a conversation. That is until Phillip leaned in and whispered: "I *know*."

"Know what?"

He pumped his eyebrows.

"I told him you're FBI," Ross said.

I nodded. "It's not a secret."

"I haven't met any of Ed's colleagues for obvious reasons"—he glowered at Ross—"but I assume none of them are like you or like me."

"I don't fit in at the field office," I said agreeably, skating over his presumption that we were alike.

"Then I have to ask—"

"Phil, don't be nosy."

"Why'd you join the FBI?"

"When you could've been a CIA officer instead," Ross put in. "That's what he means."

"That boys' club?" Phillip scoffed. "You really think those white-shoe assholes you work for would've hired her?"

Ross moved Phillip's wineglass out of his reach—it was a jokey gesture. Phillip grabbed it back and took a long sip. "Ed's a legacy: His dad's CIA, and his brother too. And one of his uncles. He was pretty much guaranteed a job. Because it was so easy for him, he doesn't *really* understand that's not the case for everyone."

"Listen, I admit there might be biases," Ross said. "But I think they'd hire a really strong candidate even if she was a woman."

Phillip looked at me and rolled his eyes. "See?"

"It's not just that I'm a woman," I said. "I'm a black woman. Two strikes against me."

"Why feel obligated to people that you can't even really be yourself around, that's what I want to know."

It was obvious they'd had this argument a thousand times before, and that there was no resolution to be had. What I thought was interesting was how confident Phillip seemed that he knew who Ross really was. Even if they'd known each other for twenty or thirty years, even if they'd known each other from before Ross joined the CIA, now, his stock and trade was subterfuge.

"He should've been a painter. Or a psychoanalyst," Phillip said. "I would've been much happier."

"I was never a very good artist." Ross laughed. "And anyway, I think Marie can understand the obligation I felt to my family."

I glanced at him, curious about what he'd meant by that. His face revealed nothing.

My mind was on what he'd meant about my ability to understand familial obligation. I wanted to know more about Ross's past. If there was a connection between us. "So, Ross, you spent some time in the field?"

"Yes."

"Where were you?"

He hesitated for a moment as if he was weighing whether or not to tell me the truth, and it struck me as a strange thing to be cagey about. "I was station chief in Ghana. I came back here last year. For Phillip."

"It was a real strain on us, his being out of the country most of the time." He added, "I have to remind myself that he's a legacy all the time. It's the only way I can make any sense of what he's chosen to do for a living. Although I can't figure out why he even bothers trying to please that old bigot."

"As I'm sure you've guessed by now, Phillip's a radical," Ross said.

"No I'm not. It's not like I ever blew anything up."

"And that's your measure? Whether or not you've blown up something?"

Phillip laughed.

"You've been arrested," Ross said.

"Just for protesting."

"That's a crime."

"No, it isn't, Ed."

The conversation had shifted permanently from the one I'd been trying to have about Ross's past. He turned to me. "He's been arrested a half-dozen times."

"Are you trying to embarrass me? It won't work." I could tell it really wouldn't. He looked pleased; they both did in fact. "What should be embarrassing for you is that you ran a background check on me."

"I had to. It's policy."

"That's right. You don't make the policy, you just follow it." Phillip's eyes were swimming from the wine. "I'm over it now, but I was ticked at him. Can you imagine? 'I love you and I trust you, but can you tell me about this time you went to jail?' We took a little break after that. I couldn't talk to him for months."

"But now he's back to his old ways. He was arrested, what, two months ago? Up here, actually."

"Yeah well, Burroughs Wellcome ought to be ashamed. They think they can charge whatever they want. They're gouging sick people. People in our community who are dying. It's immoral."

"See. A radical."

"If I'm a radical, then Ed is . . ." Phillip trailed off and picked up his glass of wine. He didn't need to finish the sentence; I knew what he was implying. A sellout. Helene had heard it plenty when she'd wanted to enlist, and I thought it sometimes too, about myself, sitting at my chocolate-colored desk surrounded by all those white lawmen in suits and ties.

Ross cleared his throat. They'd been play-sparring all night; this was the first real moment of tension between them.

"I used to really like that TV show *The FBI*," I said suddenly, to ease the strain. They both looked over at me.

"That's why I became a Fed. I used to watch it all the time with my dad."

"Oh," Ross said. "I remember that."

Phillip was incredulous. "Because of a TV show?"

"I've heard crazier reasons," Ross said with a smile.

I was lying. While I actually did watch the show (with Helene, not Pop, but I didn't like mentioning her and opening myself up to questions), I'd stolen the answer from one of the trainees in my graduating class at Quantico. He'd said it during orientation.

After I graduated from City College, Pop suggested I meet with Mr. Ali—he said it as an offhanded bit of advice—so I went into the city, we had lunch in Chinatown, and he told me about his job. And that, to get it, I'd have to sit a written exam; nearly nine thousand candidates had already taken it that fiscal year, and the bureau was planning to hire only about a tenth of the total applicant pool. I applied because that all appealed to my competitive nature, but I stuck with being a Fed because of my sister. I wanted to be the version of myself that she'd believed in.

"But, Marie, seriously. How can you work for an organization like that?"

"You mean, as a black woman?" I said, wanting to be clear about how precisely he was dictating what my experience should be.

"Let it go," Ross said, having heard the sharpness of my tone. "Maybe she feels like I do, like I have to make a place for myself. Even if the agency doesn't want me."

I glanced at him. It was the second time in the conversation that he'd said something that reminded me of Helene.

"Let it go?" Phillip asked. "You let too much go. That's the difference between us."

"I don't know how you can be so sanctimonious," I said. "If I'm culpable, you are too. You'd never catch me pretending to be a radical if I were in your shoes. Ross is in the CIA. If you're a radical, you're supposed to hate everything he stands for. But you don't. And you benefit from what he does for a living, every day."

I finished what was in my wineglass. Ross let out a loud, forced laugh. He said, "Phil, do you mind if I meet you upstairs in a little bit? I need to talk to Marie alone for a few minutes."

Phillip stood. He took my hand and said disingenuously, "Listen, it was really great to meet you."

"You too."

"If you're ever down in DC, you should drop by. I mean it." He didn't. We both knew that.

"Good night, Phillip," I said as I leaned forward and kissed his cheek.

Once he was gone, Ross and I glanced at each other. He put a finger up to order one last round of wine.

His choice to invite me into his life was a customized recruitment technique. I'd said what I had to Phillip to short-circuit the tactic. I could imagine them upstairs, before they came down to the restaurant, Ross telling his lover to play up his politics. It wasn't dissimilar to the toys I used to bring Aisha for Marlon. There are elements of recruit-ment that aren't unlike seduction, and although what he was doing was transparent to me, I'd been so starved for pleasurable conversation, and for anything that looked even remotely like friendship, that at first I'd been willing to pretend I didn't understand precisely what was happen-ing. I'd come to my senses.

And now I had the advantage. Now I could decide what dangling Phillip's friendship like that meant Ross had divined about me. He knew I was lonely, and that I wasn't really politically neutral. I'd learned things from the move as well—that he was smarter than the people I was used to. And more manipulative.

He cleared his throat. "So how's it going over at your office?"

I told him things were great, but the truth was that the high-profile case Mr. Ali and I had discussed, the one involving a spy at the Foreign Mission, had thrown the division into turmoil.

"I hear you're a talented agent. Hopefully they're not wasting you over there."

"They're not," I said, lying again. I'd been hopeful that Gold would ask me to participate in the suspect's interrogation. Instead he'd as-signed me to the evidence seized from his apartment. I'd spent a day sifting through and logging the items a squad had found in his safe: his tax and bank records, his diplomatic passport. A black address book with two tickets stubs for a Saturday matinee of Verdi's *Macbeth* inside.

He must've known I wasn't telling the truth, because he said, "These organizations aren't savvy. If the agency knew I was . . . the way I am, they would assume I was a liability. Out in the field, I had to hide everything about who I was because it made me vulnerable as an officer. And at Langley now, I still have to hide. That's a choice I made. A personal sacrifice. It was worth it, because I swore an oath of service to all Americans. That includes kids like me. They should have some-one to look up to. And I bet there are little girls like you—"

"Black girls."

"Who want to grow up and become special agents. Don't you want to blaze the trail for them too?"

"Yes," I said, although to tell the truth, what he was describing sounded absolutely exhausting. Why should I subject myself to professional torture for the sake of some hypothetical black girl who might want to be a Fed? I was too tired. I wouldn't realize how tiring the last few years had been for me until I was forced to take a break from them. Which isn't to say it wasn't tempting, the way that Ross wanted me as an ally. To join him in his own secret war—pushing back the goalposts at our respective agencies. I just wondered if it occurred to him that the posts might need to come down altogether.

"Listen, Officer Ross—"

"You can call me Ed."

"I'm ready for your pitch. I should warn you though, I've read a little bit about Burkina Faso since our meeting. I know it's never done as well as it's doing right now."

"What exactly impresses you?"

"The CNR has improved the lives of millions of Burkinabè in just a few years."

"That's true. There was the vaccine campaign," he said, and counted it on a finger. In 1984, Thomas Sankara had made it his goal to vaccinate as many Burkinabè children as possible in two weeks against three diseases that they routinely died from: yellow fever, measles, and meningitis. Despite UNICEF's misgivings about the project's feasibility, they supported it, and two million were vaccinated. And in that way, Sankara had helped save the lives of thousands of children.

"And Alpha Commando," he added, and put up a second finger, counting the CNR's accomplishments in as dismissive a way as possible. That was a similar campaign designed to combat illiteracy in the most rural parts of the nation. It had increased both the literacy rate and school attendance. Before he'd taken office, less than 10 percent of the population had been literate; in two years, the CNR increased that number to 25 percent.

Sankara argued that a society that oppressed women couldn't be a successful one, and committed himself to women's rights: banning forced marriage, polygamy, and female genital mutilation. He argued that the poorest on the globe were the most vulnerable to climate change and started a tree-planting initiative to stop the encroaching desert.

"It's rare for one man to have done so much good for so many in such a short time. I can't think of anyone else who's done it. It's impressive."

"Fair enough." He inclined his head. "But you'll have to forgive me if I don't understand the point you're trying to make. Is it a bad idea for us to gather intel on a hostile government because of its social initiatives?"

"Is it hostile?"

"By definition, all Communist governments are hostile. All dictatorships are hostile." The lightness that had been the companion to his attitude all evening had suddenly dissolved. "I won't tell you that Sankara's not doing a lot of good. I can see it. But I don't think there's much value in looking only at short-term social improvements, while ignoring the potential for long-term economic gains. It's a fact that Communist governments inhibit the economic growth of a country. End of story. And when Sankara runs out of what little money his government has, what do you think'll happen to all those programs?"

"Good point," I said. "Now let me ask you something else."

He leaned forward and clasped his hands. "Shoot."

"What do you really want from me?"

He smiled. Once more, he seemed entertained by my ignorance of something. It was becoming condescending.

"Here's the truth. Getting you *close* to Sankara is at the heart of SQLR," he said, using the operation's code name for the first time. I assumed it was a meaningless acronym, probably one that followed CIA conventions on such matters. After all, it wouldn't be a very good code if it hinted at what the operation was about.

"Have a good night." I started to gather my things, having finally understood what he was leaving out. They expected me to sleep with him. For intel. Although I was angry and insulted, I was unsurprised to learn that this was the best way they could think of to use my talents.

"You're going? You haven't even asked about the money."

He told me how much the assignment would pay. It was a lot, an obscene amount in fact, so much that it shocked me. And further convinced me that they wanted me to have sex with him. For *intel*.

Off my expression he said, "I think a lot more things are about money than people care to admit."

I'd made it only a few paces toward the exit when he played an unexpected card. "Do you know Daniel Slater?"

My mind raced back to the night I'd spent sitting beside him at that bar in North Carolina. I turned back to Ross. "He knew my sister."

"He recommended you for this assignment."

"Why?" I said, unable to hide my surprise.

"He thinks you'll be successful."

"It's his idea for me to get *close* to Sankara?"

Ross shook his head. "The assignment is getting the intel. I'm being honest with you about what you'll need to do for it."

I sat down again across from Ross. "Where is he? Slater."

"I can't tell you that."

"Please," I said. I heard the strained, begging note in my voice, but wanted too much from him then to bother with being embarrassed by it. He shook his head. I said, "Did you know Helene too?"

"No. I've heard about her though. From him."

"How can he vouch for me? Is he in DC?"

"He's in the field. That's really all I can say."

"What did he tell you about her?"

"I know he loved her."

I thought for a few moments before I spoke. "So, you just want me to find out how much Thomas Sankara knows about CIA involvement in his government."

"Yes. But to do that you'll have to get close to him."

"What do you mean?" I asked, trying to pin him down.

"You're smart. What do you think I mean?"

"I think you want a particular bit of intel and it's up to me to figure out how I get it."

"All right."

I thought he was radically underestimating me. I knew I wouldn't have to sleep with Thomas Sankara just to extract a little bit of intel. That was crazy. And if all he was willing to admit to was that he wanted this bit of information, then I had no problem participating in SQLR. Because I could do it on my own terms. I could outfox him—a thought that was pure Helene. She often believed that. I said, "Okay. I'll get the intel. But I want something in exchange."

"Something other than the cash?"

"I want to talk to Daniel Slater." I had questions about Helene that only he could answer. The chance to ask them was worth far more than the money to me.

"I can't make any promises," he said. "But let's say SQLR was successful. I could see him surfacing to congratulate you. And to take credit for recommending you."

"And I could ask him my questions."

He nodded.

"Then I'll do it."

I reached out my hand to shake his. As he took it in his, he seemed very pleased. I thought that once he realized his vagueness had given me a loophole I was planning to slip through, he would no longer be so self-satisfied. He said, "Let's meet again tomorrow. I'll brief you on everything you'll need to know."

"We can do that now."

He gestured for the check as he shook his head. "It's getting late. Go home, get some rest. We'll talk in the morning."

After he'd paid the bill he said, "Come on. I'll hail you a cab."

"A yellow one?" I asked tentatively.

"Yeah. What's the problem?"

"He's going to hate having to take me to Harlem."

"We all have to make concessions to serve the greater good." He said it with a smile, but there was a hint of something sharp inside it. "Isn't that what you just told Phil?"

PART TWO

10

I couldn't sleep. I got out of bed and went to the kitchen, where I poured myself some whisky and took it out to the back porch. I sipped my drink and listened to the cicadas. I was trying to distract myself, but my mind kept circling back to what had happened in Connecticut. I wondered how long he'd been watching us. I thought he must've known you two were in the house, and that made me feel sick and exposed. I thought about how much I hated having a gun in the house with you. What if it had been one of those nights where one or both of you had decided you couldn't sleep without me in the room? What if I'd misjudged the sound of that man's weight on the floorboard in the hall? I kept imagining having shot one of you by accident, and the thought made me feel like all the blood had suddenly drained out of my body.

At my first FBI posting, in Indiana, I'd earned a reputation for remaining cool under pressure. Really it's that I go into survival mode during an emergency. I'm grateful; if I'd actually been able to feel my terror when that man had been in our house, it would have been lethal for all of us. But now, the emotions I'd been divorced from were finally visiting me and the delay had made them especially ferocious. The physical symptoms were bad: the heart palpitations, the tremors, the cold flashes. The unwelcome thoughts were worse. What I really wanted was to be alone for a few days, to gather myself, but I couldn't do that to you.

Agathe said my name softly before stepping out onto the porch, Poochini just behind her. After I'd told her everything I planned to about that night in Connecticut, she'd taken to doing that—going out of her way not to startle me.

"What are you doing up?" I asked in French.

"This dog of yours snores," she said. "It sounds like there's a man in the house."

"He was sleeping in your room?"

"Yes. I keep pushing him off the bed, but he jumps back up."

"He likes you." I called him over and scratched his back. Poochini had a very expressive face; when he was pleased he looked like he was smiling. She sat on the couch beside me.

"You're always so gentle," she said.

Feeling like her comment meant I'd exposed a vulnerability, I took my hand off the dog. "He's a sweet boy. We got him at the pound. Someone didn't want him so they tied him up and left him in a lot."

As she was about to say something, from somewhere out in the dark came a loud metallic bang. I leaped to my feet, heart racing. My hand went to the gun in the holster on my hip. I hated the thing. It represented the mistakes I'd made that forced a gun to be a necessity in my life. I looked out into the night, trying to find the source of the noise.

"Sometimes coconuts fall off the trees," my mother said. "That sounded like one hitting the chicken coop."

"You stay here with the boys. I'll go make sure."

I took the hurricane lamp off a hook and set out across the pasture behind the house. The smell of burning wood hung in the air. As I padded across the dead grass, my footsteps seemed loud. So did my heart. I approached the chicken coop, circled it. I didn't see any coconuts. I started toward the old stand-alone kitchen and peeked inside. I stood beside it quietly for a moment, listening for footsteps. There was only the sound of insects and the crashing ocean.

My mother looked tense as I stepped up onto the back porch. She was up on her feet and holding Poochini by the collar, so he wouldn't dart out after me. "What was it?"

"I don't know."

"Who'd you think it was?" she asked.

"I don't know."

"Could someone have followed you here?"

"I don't know."

She was annoyed with the way I was answering her. My mother and I have always innately understood the best ways to irritate each other. "I have the right to know if you're still in danger. If we all are."

"As long as I'm here you're safe."

"Marie . . ." We both knew the opposite was true: As long as I was there we were all at risk. "You can't do this. You can't take all this on by yourself."

"What other choice do I have?"

She moved to put her arm around my shoulders, but I was too tense to bear it and stepped out of range of her reach. "I'm all right," I lied. "Don't worry about me."

"I'm your mother. Of course I'm going to worry."

As I sat on the sofa, I thought of you two, asleep in the quiet house. "I want to ask you something."

"What?"

"It's about the boys. You know they love you, right?" You'd warmed up to her, and I felt I could say that sincerely.

She nodded. I said, "If anything happens to me, I want you to take care of them. I have some money saved."

"What's going to happen to you?"

"I don't know."

"What's going on?"

"Nothing."

"That's bullshit!" she shouted.

We both were surprised; it was exceedingly uncharacteristic for her to speak to me as she just had. A few moments passed and she composed herself. "I'm sorry. But you're scaring me. And I feel like I'm in the dark."

Not knowing what to say, I kept quiet.

"You want me to take care of them," she said thoughtfully.

"It's one of the reasons I came here. To ask you."

"They'd have to live here, at least until they go to college."

"I know."

"I mean it. I'm not going back to New York."

"I want them to stay here. They'll be safer out of the country."

She sighed. "I can't say no, can I?"

"Pop would be happy to take them. He's good with them."

"*Your* father?"

"Better than he was with us," I said coolly, and gave her a look: Did she want to call his parenting into question? Was that the thread she really wanted to pull on?

She tensed at the unspoken accusation, then said, "All right. Yes. They can stay with me."

The muscles in my shoulders loosened and relief washed over me. "Thank you, Maman."

She nodded her head once. Curt. "I'm going back in. Good night."

Poochini followed her back into the house. I sat and finished off the last of my drink. Listened to the quiet, and felt reassured. But when I returned to my room, I still couldn't sleep. So I went to the vanity, where I'd hidden this journal and pulled it out. As I was pawing through the odds and ends in the drawer, looking for a pen, I came across Helene's memorial program instead. I sat for a moment and looked at it. I wouldn't have chosen the picture Pop had. It was cropped from a picture of the three of us at Pop's swearing-in ceremony, when he became deputy commissioner. She's wearing a green turtleneck with a flat gold chain, looking away from the camera and smiling stiffly. I missed her then, as acutely as I ever had. I put the program back into the drawer, sat at the vanity, and started to write.

After I got back from my visit to Helene in North Carolina, I decided to let her make the first move. I was confused about what had happened between us in the fitness center; I'd never experienced anything like it in our relationship before. Sometimes I worried that the visit had revealed an animosity she'd always felt that I'd just been oblivious to. At other times, I felt like maybe nothing was wrong, that if things were strange between us it was only because I was making them that way. Three months passed before she finally did call Pop's house, and then it was not to mend fences with me. It was to tell us she'd been assigned to the post on Long Binh.

While she was gone I was obsessed with worry. A silence like the one that had stretched between us demanded analysis, and I thought about it every day of her tour. She wrote me letters, mostly gossip about the other women that worked in the HQ building along with her. She seemed bored. She could've been; I got the sense that the army kept its female personnel cloistered on the post. Or it could've been that maternal instinct made her want to shield me from any horror stories. Or maybe it was that I was mistaking boredom for something else that she was feeling toward me. Anything seemed possible. I felt like I'd been wrong to believe I understood her.

In January 1973, the peace agreement was signed in France, and the United States started pulling personnel out of Vietnam. Her tour cut short, Helene returned to the U.S. safely and called from the Oakland army base. I'd screamed with joy when I heard her voice on the static-filled line. I had a million things I wanted to tell her, but the thoughts crowded my mind, and all I could get out was, "Helene! I've missed the hell out of you!"

"You too." She laughed, and it filled me with so much joy to hear that noise again.

"When will you be back in New York?"

"End of the week. We're driving. I've got some news I want to tell you and Pop in person."

"I can't wait!"

"See you soon," she said.

"Love you," I said, but I think it was to an empty line.

I'm sorry. I had to step away for a moment. This is all as hard for me to write as it is to remember.

Her wake was held in a funeral home in Laurelton, in a large white Colonial that was out of place on an otherwise commercial stretch in Queens. My memories of that day are an unreliable scatter. I think I remember a young attendant in a suit and shoes that were too large for him. I think the halls in the funeral home were carpeted in a vivid, assaulting green. Robbie's sister, Pam, sang a few gospel numbers either that day or at the actual funeral. It's unusual that I can't remember more, and that I'm not sure about what happened when. As you can tell from these pages, my memory is generally exceptional.

I stood with either Pop or my grandfather beside the door, shaking hands with everyone who came in and thanking them. We'd invited just a few of Helene's friends from North Carolina, but thirty or forty showed up, so word must've spread.

When her friend Daniel Slater appeared I shook his hand.

"How are you doing?" he asked.

"Thanks for coming," I answered on autopilot.

"Marie. I'm so sorry," he said, and I nodded at him through the haze of my disassociated perception. "Before I forget, I have something for you. It was on the fridge."

He produced the photo strip that Helene and I had taken in the bar and handed it to me. I looked at it and then up at him. The rush of affection I felt for him then was overwhelming, because it had nothing to do with the gesture and everything to do with my vulnerability.

"Thank you." I hugged him. I clung to him, treating him exactly like what he was, something steady to hang on to to prevent being washed away by a tide. I felt ashamed of having been so lukewarm about him when we'd first met. Helene had liked him. How could I not?

I wanted to talk to him some more; I wanted to crack his head open and scoop from his cerebrum the answers I needed about my relationship with Helene, but Agathe came through the door then and in my grief I was easily distracted.

I hadn't seen her in more than a decade. I put my arms around her and my head into the curve of her neck. As I did, I felt a confusing surge, as happy to see her as I was furious.

"Agathe. Hello," my father said behind me, then turned away. Had I been expecting some sort of revelatory, cathartic exchange between them I would've been disappointed.

"Let's sit," I said to her. I was exhausted. I'd been sleeping for eighteen, twenty hours a day, but there was no amount of rest that was enough. We walked down the aisle together and sat in the pew at the very back. She asked me how I was doing.

I don't remember what I said. I remember staring at the roses on Helene's casket. They were pink. I know that for certain. I hated those awful flowers.

Agathe put her arm around me. I put my head on her shoulder and was surprised that she still smelled familiar, like talcum powder and cigarettes. Matt Testaverde was up front, studying the photos of my sister on display behind her casket.

"I should go up there." She stood. I watched her slowly make her way up the aisle to the casket, and seeing her there, looking down at Helene's face, was what finally made me cry.

The afternoon after the funeral, I drove Agathe to the airport in the Bean Can. Before her flight, we each paid a dime and took the stairs up to the observation deck. Only a handful of other people were up there, some of them watching the taxiing planes at the binocular machines.

Agathe leaned against the guardrail and took out a cigarette. She was wearing the same long-sleeved black dress she'd worn to the funeral, part of the generation that still dressed to fly. She looked out toward Co-op City and pulled hard on her cigarette. I watched, with an echo of the pain I'd felt after she'd first left reverberating along my spine. That pain was defining. It was what childhood felt like for me. I used to imagine her turning up again, just as abruptly as she'd left, sweeping me up in a hug, unpacking her things. Now I imagined her turning to me to say that she'd decided to stay a little longer. That she could tell I needed her. She turned then and did say something that I didn't quite hear over a plane engine that had started screaming on the tarmac.

"What?" I said.

She shook her head and opened her big black purse. Took out a handkerchief. And then, as she wiped her face, I was all at once tipped away from longing into fury. Most of the time I was too frightened by my own rage to lean into it. But at that moment, I felt possessed by Helene's anger. I let go. "Stop it, Agathe. I'm not going to stand here and watch you cry."

"What's the matter?" she said, startled.

"I don't have the energy for this. Don't pretend you just lost her. You lost her when you left her. You left both of us, and I don't remember you crying back then."

"I wish you could understand. You all were better off without me around."

"What kind of mother says that?" I spat out angrily. "What kind of mother are you?"

She let out a small, involuntary noise—like I'd hit her—and tears welled up in her eyes. But I couldn't find any sympathy. I couldn't even look at her, so I turned and started toward the exit.

I didn't talk to my mother again for close to a decade, and didn't see her until I showed up at her farm pregnant with you two. My grief for Helene was so intense because she wasn't the only one I'd lost.

When I got back to Pop's house from the airport I found him sitting at the kitchen table. He was wearing his reading glasses and had been poring over some papers spread out in front of him, but as I came through the door he started to gather them.

"I didn't hear you pull up," he said.

"What's all that?"

"What do you mean?" he asked, playing dumb.

I looked at him and hated how calm he was. Only now do I realize I was mistaking exhaustion for calm, that he was as devastated as I was but couldn't let me see it. I wish he could've been able to grieve with me. I know he was only trying to protect me, but it was worse to be isolated with those feelings. My only glimpse into his emotional life was what I was able to surmise from how little he'd been sleeping and the weird bout of clumsiness he was suffering through—I never noticed his hands shaking, but that must've been the reason he broke as many dishes as he did.

I snatched the first page from the pile he'd gathered. It was a copy of the investigation report for Helene's accident.

"What are you doing with this?" I asked.

"Just looking. Wanting to make sure there was nothing out of the ordinary."

"Is there?"

"No."

I looked into his face. He was torturing himself in his own way and it broke my heart. I didn't know what to do for him. I sheepishly put the page back. "I'm sorry."

He gave a sharp shake of his head and wiped the tears that had sprung to his eyes. As he stood he exhaled deeply. Crossed the kitchen toward his room. His door closed. I paced the avocado tile for a few minutes, then climbed the stairs to my old room. Looked around. I'd been staying there the last few days and had been comforted by how everything was exactly as I'd left it when I'd moved out the year before—even my *Star Wars* poster was still unstuck in one corner. I pressed it back into place knowing it would come loose again, briefly buoyed by that small reminder of my old life.

I crossed to Helene's door and stood in the threshold for a moment. It was also exactly as she'd left it, but the effect there was cruel somehow. How awful that all of her things could still be there waiting for her to walk back in, when she never would.

I opened her window, looked out into the darkening evening. It was early spring—the air was warm and the buds on the maple tree in the backyard were starting to open. Bunny was buried under that tree. I opened her desk drawer—inside were pens, markers, and some change; a strip of photo booth pictures of her and Pam making goofy faces. I opened a pencil case and found a plump dime bag, smiled as I put it back.

I looked in her closet. There were her cheerleading sneakers. She'd loved those things despite the ugly red and white pom-poms growing from their tongues. I used to tell her they looked like tumors.

In one column she was the cheerleader and the girl who grew up making me dinner and checking my homework. In the other she was the boxer, the girl who beat up Rhonda. And then there was a third column: She was the woman who sent me genial, not fully interpretable letters from Long Binh. That was Helene: putting together a puzzle, getting it all finished, then finding a leftover piece in the box.

I always suspected there was a theory of her personality that nicely accommodated the elements I thought were contradictory. And that was who she really was. But I never learned the theory. I never saw that person, and even now, twenty years later, thinking about that is enough to make me want to cry.

Almost a week passed in Martinique. After you'd go to sleep, I'd spend a few hours each evening, writing in this journal and drinking whisky, which relaxed me enough to loosen the grip of my insomnia. I'd started to get enough rest to function.

One morning, while the three of us were playing in the back pasture, I heard tires on the gravel. My heart lifted. I told you not to go farther than the line of lemon trees—so Agathe could keep an eye on you from the kitchen window—then went into the house and out again onto the front porch. Shielding my eyes from the sun, I watched as Robbie appeared from the cab I'd insisted he take from the airport. On the night my mother had told me I couldn't take on everything alone, my only thought had been to call him.

"Hey, dummy!" he called as he came toward me, which made me laugh.

"Hey," I said back as he put his brand-new suitcase down on the porch and his arms around me.

We held each other, swaying slightly, for a few long moments. I immediately felt safe in his company, and I needed that. I grinned up at him; he'd gotten a fresh shape up before he'd come out there, which was an expression of gallantry that I appreciated.

When I'd called, I'd only told him that I needed him because I was in trouble. I said, "I'll tell you everything later. But come in now and say hi to everyone."

I led him into the house where Poochini was waiting for us. I closed the door firmly. "Careful not to let the dog out. He's a runner."

Poochini sniffed at Robbie, which made him tense. I'd forgotten that he doesn't like dogs. He'd never admit it, but he's afraid of them. My mother came into the living room from the kitchen. I said, "Agathe. You remember Robbie?"

"Mrs. Mitchell, ma'am." He took her hand and spoke slowly in his formal voice. "It must be thirty years since I've seen you."

She nodded, and I was shocked to realize he was right. He'd been on Rikers for Helene's funeral. I went out onto the back porch.

"Tommy. William. Come inside. I want you to say hello to someone."

Tommy, you came up onto the porch and darted into the house.

William, you stayed in the pasture. I asked, "You coming?"

"I don't want to!"

You were in a phase where you said no just to say it, even if it was to your detriment. I knew you'd be bored out there by yourself, and that your curiosity about the visitor would get the better of you, so I shrugged.

Back in the living room, Tommy, you were feeling shy. You had your back pressed up against your grandmother's legs and were answering Robbie's pleasantries in a small voice.

"Tommy, this is Uncle Robbie," I said. "You met him once when you were a baby."

William, you raced into the living room then shouted to Robbie, "*Coucou!*"

"Uncle Robbie speaks English," I said.

"Hi!"

"All right, little man." Robbie held his hand out and, William, you slapped him five.

"You tired?" I asked Robbie.

"Nah, I feel good. Slept on the plane."

"Want to go to the beach? It's not very far."

"Yes!" William, you were excited.

"Okay," Robbie said, looking down at you. "I guess we're doing it."

I helped you boys into your suits, got mine on, and went to find my mother in the kitchen. She'd chopped up a couple of mangos and held out the cubes in a Baggie.

Writing about Helene's funeral had made me freshly angry with her—detailed remembering has a lot of power. This might sound petty to you, but if she would just apologize for how much she hurt me at the airport I could deal better with the residual anger. That feels so obvious to me that I start to see something malicious in the fact that she's never done it. I would never bring it up to her. I shouldn't have to.

You two followed me from the kitchen to the living room. I'd set up a cot there for Robbie, which I sat on as we waited for him. You're both oblivious to the tension between Agathe and me. We never argue; ill will just hangs out with us, follows us around, a malignant old friend. I felt like a teenager, which meant I knew I was being petulant. I appreciated Agathe—although I prided myself on my competence, I couldn't have seen you through your infancy on my own. But I would much rather have walked out into the pasture, lain down, and died there, than told her I was upset.

Robbie appeared from the bathroom, and the four of us went out to Agathe's truck. He went around to the driver's-side door.

"I'm driving," I said.

"Let me."

"Why? You know where we're going?"

"No."

"Your license still suspended?"

"Yeah."

"Then you're not driving my kids."

He put his hands up: *fair enough*. As I got behind the wheel I said, "You're losing your edge."

"What do you mean?"

"Five years ago you would've fought me on this. Like if I didn't let you drive you weren't a man. I hated that."

"That's 'cause you take everything I do like I'm trying to control you."

"Aren't you?"

He laughed. "I'm trying to take care of you. I tell you that all the time, but you don't hear me."

"I hear you. I just don't—"

"Believe me, yeah, so I'm trying something different."

"Where's all this coming from?"

"I'm not allowed to grow? It's not coming from no place. I'm just glad you called."

"Hmm." I thought about what I was going to ask him to do. "You say that now."

"So if you want to drive that's fine. You're a good driver."

"That's a nice thing to say."

"It's true."

"I learned from the best. You and Pop."

I smiled over at him. He *had* grown. He wasn't the same man whose proposal had been scattered with sexist, Five Percenter nonsense, like "the woman is the man's field to produce his nation." He had a steady job, doing maintenance work off the books. And he'd managed to keep himself out of jail for the last decade. He'd grown up for the sake of his son, Chris. Robbie and I both wanted to be the best versions of our-selves for our children.

We arrived at the beach. I laid a couple of blankets on the sand, slathered you both in sunblock, handed over your shovel and pail. As I was helping you fill the pail, Robbie exhaled and looked out at the blue water. "Wow. I wish Chris could've come. He would love this."

"How's he doing?"

"Good. He's kinda into some shit I don't really get though." He glanced around, even though there was no way Chris, or anyone who knew him, could possibly have heard.

"What do you mean?"

"Like comics and shit. And cards."

"Baseball cards?"

"Nah, like comic cards. I don't know. I was mad heated with Rosa, like why she letting him do this nerd shit for? I'm not trying to see my son get his ass beat. Now I'm more cool with it. Sort of."

"How's Rosa doing?" I said, asking after Chris's mother. I didn't fully understand the terms of his relationship with her, other than that they'd never been married and that he sometimes lived in the apartment where she was raising their son.

"Good," he said.

"She know where you are?"

"She might."

"Did you tell her?"

"No."

"Then how would she know?"

He shrugged.

"She still letting you stay by her?"

"Not right now."

I nearly laughed at his caginess as I glanced over at him. When we were growing up, we used to call him Pretty Rob, and he's still very good-looking. His skin is a rich brown, and there's a delicacy to his features that contradicts his roughneck affectation. Women have always liked him. Robbie was my first love, and he's my oldest friend. He's one of the most loyal people I've ever known, having stuck with me even after the Feds knocked on his door.

That reminds me: I'd said there was a specific reason that I had very few friends left in New York. The reason was the bureau. Part of their application process was an extensive background check, so a pair of white men in suits—they were obviously Feds—went around the neighborhood interviewing people about me. The same thing happened with my college friends, and it spooked everyone. They knew that if the Feds were asking about me, there were no good reasons for that.

That episode marked me in a way that I couldn't wash off. But I didn't feel sorry for myself. I felt sorry for Helene. It must've been much harder for her to give up the neighborhood after she enlisted than it had been for me.

The one thing that upset me was that while I was being investigated, the little red address book that Helene had brought me back from Martinique disappeared. One day it was just no longer in the desk I'd always kept it in, which made me feel like I was going crazy. I was heartbroken; I had a very strong sentimental attachment to that book. I'm still sorry it's gone.

I looked down at his basketball shorts. "You still don't have a bathing suit?"

"What I need a bathing suit for?"

"You go to the beach. You been to Coney Island."

"Yeah, but not to go in. There's plastic bags in the water and shit. And, like, glass. It's not this."

"The first time Pop took my mom to Jones Beach she wouldn't even step on the sand."

He smiled. "How's he doing?"

"Not too bad."

"Tell him I say hello." Although Pop couldn't stand Robbie, the feeling wasn't mutual.

"I will."

Robbie was looking out at the horizon again. "You know I never left the country before?"

"Maman," you said, William. "I want to go in."

I stood and walked you both to the water's edge. Robbie followed.

As the water lapped your feet, Tommy, you said solemnly, "It's cold."

You took my hand, and we waded farther into the water together. I showed you both how to float. Robbie tried it too, and he sank, then came up coughing and splashing and laughing. Then he tossed you up in the air, William, and you laughed as he caught you.

"Again!" You couldn't get enough roughhousing. He tossed you up in the air again and once more you squealed with laughter.

"You wanna turn?" he asked you, Tommy. You shook your head and paddled toward me. You hadn't quite warmed up to him yet.

Later, back on the sand, I took some pictures of the three of you together—I'd brought an old camera that belonged to your grandmother. I also made sure that Robbie took some of the three of us.

"I'm hungry!" William, you threw yourself into my lap. I went into my tote and held out the Baggie full of mango to you.

"I don't want that."

"I don't have anything else."

You plucked a cube out, popped it into your mouth. "You take one."

I shook my head and smiled. "They're for you and your brother." You pressed a piece against my mouth. "I want to share."

I knew you wanted to take care of me, so I let you tuck the piece of mango between my lips. I laughed. "That tickles!"

I felt Robbie smiling at me. William, you started laughing too. I leaned in and gave you rapid-fire kisses on the cheek that you squirmed against, squealing, showing off a mouthful of mango.

———

Back at home, when Tommy opened the door, Poochini bolted out of the house. I shouted after him as I watched him dart toward the feral sugarcane that separated Agathe's property from the neighbor's farm. I called for my mother to come get you two out of your bathing suits, then went running blindly after him screaming, *Poochini! Poochini!*

I ran into the cane patch, calling his name as I moved through the green stalks. I stood still, hoping to hear him crashing through the cane. It was unnervingly quiet, like standing alone during a snowfall. I looked around. I was lost—I had no idea what direction I'd come from. My back was damp with sweat. I closed my eyes, to try and orient myself, but started to panic. I saw that man. Felt his hands squeezing my throat. When the sugarcane finally expelled me, I was at the edge of the road that led to Agathe's farm. As I started in the direction of the house, I saw my mother's truck approaching. Robbie was behind the wheel.

"Glad I found you. Your mother's been calling around. She says one of your neighbors saw him on his farm. It's just a few miles up."

I got into the truck beside him.

"I need to find him."

"I know."

"I want everything to be normal for my boys."

"I know. Don't worry, it will be."

I was quiet.

"Tell me about that dog. What did you get him for? Protection?"

"Sort of, but he's too sweet. I'm glad he was in the room with the boys that night. When that man . . . That man could've killed him."

"He could've killed you."

"You think I don't know that, Robbie? I can't think about that." It was too late. Tears were welling up in my eyes. Embarrassed to cry in front of him, I looked down at my lap. He stopped the car and when he said my name I leaned into him. He put his arm around me, and I wept with my head against his shoulder, as he rubbed my back. I cried until I was exhausted. Robbie is one of the few people who've seen me cry, which is how I know I love him. He had never let me down, not once. Like when I asked him to come out there and he didn't hesitate. I told him I felt better. He started the truck again.

As we approached the neighbor's property, a tree came into view. Poochini was sitting beneath it with a young man that I knew by face but not name.

"Poochini," I called. He stood. Tired from his adventure, he ambled over slowly and calmly hopped up into the truck. I thanked the young man, who waved back.

Poochini stretched out. His panting filled the cab. As we headed back, I picked sandburs out of his coat and pressed my face into his neck and called the dog an idiot. Robbie laughed. Then he pulled a face.

"What?"

"His breath stinks."

I laughed too. He smiled at me. Then he reached out tentatively and patted the dog between the ears.

11

The first time I saw Thomas Sankara he was laughing.

He was at the front of the General Assembly hall, the small delegation from Burkina grouped around him, everyone else looking serious. He should've been nervous; he was about to deliver a speech at the UN. But, no, he was up there cracking up over something Blaise Compaoré had said.

I'd read about the delegation's members in the case file Ross had given me: Blaise and his wife, Chantal; a security officer named Sam Kinda; a young man named Vincent Traoré, who'd be serving as a translator on the trip.

I was watching from a distance, in the interpreter's booth. A harried UN employee, a member of the chief of protocol's staff whom I'd briefly met for the first time the day before, had asked me to bring a copy of Sankara's speech up there.

I'd gone up some stairs and found a door with *English* engraved in black on a white plaque. When I'd knocked, an interpreter with feathered hair and large round glasses appeared, took the pages from me, and, as she looked them over, absently stood aside to let me in the booth—it seemed like she expected someone in my role to stay and watch the speech from there, so I went inside and crossed to the bank of windows looking down on the hall. Viewed from behind and above, the room's magnitude dwarfed the suit-jacketed backs of the assembly members sitting in the curved rows of seats.

Sankara crossed to the green marble podium, and his delegation sat at a table to the right. The secretary-general and two other UN officials were sitting on the platform above and directly behind Sankara, and on the gilded back wall, presiding over them all, was the enormous UN emblem, two olive branches embracing the world.

He began his speech without any hoopla. I wasn't wearing interpreters' headphones, so I could barely hear him and instead listened to it in the steady voice of the interpreter speaking into her microphone on the honey-brown console. To be honest, I was a little bored.

"Mr. President, Mr. Secretary-General, honorable representatives of the international community, I bring you fraternal greetings from a country whose seven million children, women, and men refuse to die of ignorance and hunger any longer. I come here with the aspiration to speak on behalf of my people, on behalf of 'the disinherited of the world,' those who belong to what's so ironically called the Third World. And to state, though I may not succeed in making them understood, the reasons for our revolt.

"Of our seven million inhabitants, over six million are peasants. And this peasantry, our peasantry, has been subjected to the most intense exploitation at the hands of imperialism and has suffered the most from the ills we inherited from colonial society: illiteracy, obscurantism, pauperization, cruelty in many forms, endemic diseases, and famine."

The interpreter waved an extra set of headphones at me. I took them, not convinced that would improve the experience, but it turned out his voice was pleasing and sonorous. As I listened to it, I felt something warm open inside my chest.

"Imperialism tries to dominate us from both inside and outside our country. Through its multinational corporations, its big capital, its economic power, imperialism tries to control us by influencing our discussions, and influencing national life."

Even from a distance, his posture transmitted confidence and passion and excitement. Despite his natural charisma though, I remained unconvinced by his Communism. Che Guevara had given a similar speech in front of the General Assembly. So had Fidel Castro, I realized, and the similarity sent a cold flush through me. I remembered being seven, the terror of the Cuban Missile Crisis. Curled in bed, the castle-shaped night lamp on our dresser casting its yellow light on the wall, Helene had looked over: "Ça va?" *You okay?*

"Ouais." I squeezed our mother's teddy bear in a headlock—she'd left it behind—and stared up at the play of shadows on the ceiling.

"Sure you're not scared?" she asked in French.

I said no, but she knew I was lying. Helene pulled the quilt off her bed and came to mine. She squeezed in beside me and slung her arm over my body. She soon fell back asleep, but I was too paralyzed by guilt and fear to do the same. I'd spent the previous few days praying for Saint George to help the Americans drop a bomb on Cuba—*to help us kill Castro before he could kill us* was how I'd been putting it in my mind. But then I'd realized how close Martinique was to Cuba and began to fear that what I'd asked for would come true. If my prayers were answered and the bomb killed Agathe, I understood, in the excessively accountable way of nervous children, that it would be my fault.

I respected Thomas Sankara's government for its socialist policies, which stood in stark contrast to those of Reagan, who'd spent the last six years pumping money into the military while slashing funding for domestic programs. He was happily presiding over a gap between the rich and the poor that was yawning wider every year; one that we felt harder than most people. But I couldn't allow myself to be seduced by the ideas of a politician like Sankara, who called himself a Marxist, a fraught word at a tense time.

The problem with the good he was doing was that it made his Communism palatable. He was too charismatic. Although his country was one of the poorest in the world, he had still managed to galvanize support across the continent. It was worrisome when that happened in countries that had recently become independent. Because they were no longer under the control of a colonial power, there were ideological vacuums in those countries. And I understood the fear that Communism would rush in and fill those voids.

I thought Communism was dangerous. That opinion could've been the product of propaganda—as Sankara would've argued—or it could've been because I'd grown up watching it fail again and again around the world. Watching people die because of that failure. Reaganomics was an unpleasant little philosophy too, and when you added the punitive character of our country to it, we emerged as a breeding ground for a really virulent strain of cruelty. But the alternative was worse.

Sankara finished his speech, and it was met with muffled applause. I turned to the interpreter who said, "That wasn't too bad."

"Yeah. Not too bad at all," I agreed with a nod as I put the headphones back on the console.

I went downstairs. My assignment that day was straightforward if not exactly simple: I was to guide his delegation around the UN and eat lunch with them after his speech. I was to be present, charming, and familiar so that he would feel comfortable with me, and I could gather my intel.

It was my first undercover assignment, but I felt strangely confident; slipping into a false identity had proven to be easy for me. I'd had a lot of informal practice with performing different versions of myself to please other people: The good version of me that Mr. Ali knew, the good version of me that had attended City College, the good girl who'd grown up in Queens.

I found Sankara and his delegation gathered around a UN staffer I'd met the day before. The staffer introduced me in French by the alias Ross had assigned me and told the delegation that I was from the chief of protocol's office. Up close, Sam Kinda was tall and broad—I would've guessed he was a member of the president's security force even if I hadn't read it. Compaoré was also tall, a head above Sankara, a lanky and youthful man wearing black slacks and a gray tunic with a pattern of white diamonds around the shoulders and neck. Chantal Compaoré was attractively ample and looked elegant in a gold brocade dress, matching head wrap and large, hammered-gold earrings that dangled on both sides of her wide, square face. Vincent Traoré had a short Afro, was wearing black plastic eyeglass frames, and couldn't have been more than twenty.

And then there was Thomas Sankara himself. He was very handsome in person, and had a magnetism that the photographs I'd seen of him couldn't capture. He was wearing his captain's uniform and red beret, and was very commanding in them. When I put out my hand to shake his, he took it in his own warm, rough one and held on to it for just a moment longer than was appropriate.

"It's an honor to meet you, Mr. President," I said in French.

When he smiled at me, I felt like I recognized him. I knew the gentle strength of his voice before I heard it and the liveliness of his dark eyes, the sweep of pink in his lower lip. All that sounds sentimental. And silly, I guess, or even incomprehensible. But that's what it was like when I met your father.

The staffer told Sankara that the two Diplomatic Security Service agents—they knew I was undercover—and I would accompany his delegation for the rest of the day. Then he started in on an excessive amount of instruction about our lunch in the delegates' dining room.

Enough to be condescending, but I tried to believe it was how he'd been trained to deal with all dignitaries: cover the bases. Sankara, who was increasingly getting annoyed, finally put up his hand. "That's enough. If I have any questions I'll ask Ms. . . ." he said with a gesture toward me as he referred to me by my alias. The staffer took the cue and as he made to leave he said, "Well, Mr. President, it truly was an honor."

Sankara gave him a curt nod in answer, evidently unmoved by the platitude when it came from someone else.

We started toward the secretary-general's office, Sankara charging ahead, although I wasn't entirely convinced he knew where he was going, me and the rest of the delegation following behind him. I caught up to him and said in French, "You're a fast walker. I'm supposed to be leading the group."

He slowed down, which I suspected was a concession that he wouldn't extend to everyone. As I strode by his side, I could feel that sublime energy of his. I don't mean that in a mystical way, more as a comment on the strength of his will. He smelled like soap, like his uniform had been freshly laundered. Three gold stars studded his orange shoulder boards; his wedding band was also gold.

I felt him staring at me and glanced over. "You look familiar. Do you hear that a lot?"

"Not really."

"Maybe you remind me of someone."

"Maybe," I said. "Is this your first visit to the UN, sir?"

"My third, and I'll tell you something: I don't plan to be back. I don't like it here. Just look at him." He pointed to a man in a suit. "Look at his face. The people here are way too serious."

"But you don't even know him," I challenged with a smile. To soften it I added, "Mr. President."

"Call me Thomas."

"You don't even know him, Thomas."

"I know plenty of men like him. And I know you have to avoid becoming one of the rats in the UN corridors."

"What do you mean?"

"You don't know? You must be new here," he said.

"I am."

"Well, be careful or you'll become like these men. You'll get too in your head, and you'll forget all about the world outside of this place. You'll become a rat, who reduces the real problems in the world to abstract subjects to bicker over."

"At least the world's problems are discussed here. A lot of people won't even do that."

"But it's not enough just to discuss things. We are the elites. We can't just talk about human rights, while we conveniently forget that we condemn thousands of children to die because we couldn't agree on the best policy to help. Or in my government, if we can't agree on a pay cut so that a little clinic out in the country can be built. Those kinds of choices make us part of the international complicity of men of good conscience."

"What a sound-bite-ready speech. You've said it before."

"I have," he said with a bright laugh. "But I mean it."

"I believe you do, sir. And I'm sorry. I don't mean to be rude."

"No, it's good. Stay sharp. Keep me and everyone else here on their toes. If you do, there might be hope for you yet."

We were at the secretary-general's office. I showed the delegation inside, then watched the handshaking, the pleasantry exchanging, the secretary-general handing Thomas a gift—a book, something large and decorative that I didn't catch the title of—while a UN photographer documented the moment.

Once the pageantry was over, we went to the delegates' dining room. Its two most striking elements were the expansive river view the floor-to-ceiling windows offered and, after the speech on global inequality Thomas had just given, the massive buffet in the center of the room. I sat across the table from Thomas, between Chantal Compaoré, who didn't say a word to me, and Vincent Traoré, who spoke steadily throughout the meal, using the opportunity to practice his English. He spoke it well despite the fact that he'd never been to an English-speaking country before. He talked mostly about his membership in the Committee for the Defense of the Revolution at the university, of which he was very proud. He explained that the Committee was a local governing body run by average people. According to him, it promoted participatory democracy and the popular revolution, having replaced the corrupt and reactionary officials who'd governed before Thomas had come to power. While I was suspicious of his government—of any government—being the only ones allowed to dictate who was reactionary and who revolutionary, I said nothing.

As I was looking at Thomas, who was staring down at the small portion of food he'd taken from the buffet, he looked up; I let him catch me watching him. As he smiled, warmth washed over me, starting as a gentle tingling at the base of my skull. I urged myself to remember that feeling. I was happy, I'd liked him immediately, and it had been so long since I'd had such feelings that they seemed like a novelty.

I wasn't able to speak to him again until the meal was over. He was standing beside the window with Sam Kinda and Vincent Traoré, and as I approached, I heard that he was talking to them both about the New International Economic Order, a set of proposals designed to replace the Bretton Woods Agreement as the international monetary system. The leadership of several developing countries had proposed it about a decade earlier but, as Thomas saw it, the NIEO had gone nowhere because the status quo, Bretton Woods, too heavily favored the powerful countries that had created it for there to be any change. He was saying that it had gotten no traction because western Europe and the United States kept railroading its adoption.

"Maybe your comments today will spark some interest in it again," I offered.

He shook his head. "They invited me here to speak because they only want words. No action. The right to a fair international economic order is like the other rights of the people: They won't be given to us. We must conquer them in struggle."

Vincent nodded in strong agreement.

"So why did you accept the invitation to speak?" I asked. "For the free trip to New York?"

He smiled. "Yes. I'd like to spend some time in Harlem on this trip."

"Really?" I was genuinely surprised. I assumed a foreign dignitary would prefer to spend his time in an upscale neighborhood, like Midtown.

"I know people think of the place as a dump, as a place to suffocate. But I believe Harlem will give the African soul its true dimension. That's where our White House is, among the black people of Harlem. I should see it while I can."

"You were serious then? This will really be your last visit to New York?"

He nodded. "When I first became president, I thought it was necessary to come to the UN. Now, while I do feel a duty to represent the interests of the nonaligned countries, I know I can do so more effectively other places. The UN is too much of an echo chamber, one manipulated by a few powerful drummers."

"Well. We should make it count. I could show you around if you want." I was standing too close to him.

He hesitated, and I worried that I sounded forward. "Do you mean tomorrow? After the rally?"

"Yes. I live up there. I could give you a tour of my neighborhood afterward if you'd like. Take you for lunch."

"Did you grow up in Harlem?" he asked, still not responding to my invitation.

"No. My father did though. Actually, I grew up over there." I pressed my fingertip against the window, and we both looked out at the shore. "In Queens. In a little house out in the suburbs."

We were alone. Vincent and Sam had moved a few paces away to one of the other windows. I touched his arm then; there was no real reason for me to do it other than that I wanted to. He looked at me, and in his gaze I suddenly felt very transparent. I knew I had a solid cover; everything I'd told him was based in truth, which is where the best covers are formed. I knew I could be an effective spy. But in that moment, it felt like he was looking into me, and it made me unsure of myself. I didn't know if I was more worried that he could tell my flirtatiousness was manufactured or that he could tell it was real.

"All of us?"

"Excuse me?"

"Is the entire delegation invited on your tour?"

"Oh. Yes, if that's what you want. It's up to you."

Before he could answer, a voice called his name. Blaise and Chantal Compaoré were crossing the room toward us. Chantal and I stood quietly to the side as Thomas and her husband spoke in a foreign language—Mooré, I guessed from what I'd read. I assumed they were talking about business or politics, until Thomas said something that made Compaoré laugh. Mirth made his distinctive features even more striking. His eyes turned down, and when he smiled the crease that ran across the bridge of his broad triangular nose deepened. They were not only political allies but close friends, and observing their dynamic confirmed that. When they were finished, Compaoré turned to me. He asked me to remind him of my name, and when I did, he repeated it with deliberate eye contact—a move out of the slick politician's playbook. He asked, "No dessert?"

"I don't have much of a sweet tooth," I answered.

"How about you, Thomas?" As he gestured grandly to the buffet tables, it was obvious he was joking.

Thomas shook his head, clearly repulsed by the idea. He said to Compaoré: "We were talking about the tour she was going to take us on tomorrow. She lives in Harlem."

"Where exactly?" Compaoré asked.

"Not very far from where they're holding the rally, 128th Street." "So we'll pick you up," Compaoré said. "Give your address to Sam. But we should go now, Thomas." He steered the president toward the exit, Chantal following in their wake. And I watched them, genuinely sad to see Thomas go, before catching myself. Then I went to Sam and wrote down my address.

12

The next day, I waited for Thomas and his delegation to arrive while sitting at my living room window. Below me, a pleasant fall day was unfolding on Lenox.

I was eager to see the president again. I admired him. Even so, I saw no reason why that had to get in the way of my work. This was the case that could start me on the path toward my goal: becoming a special agent in charge. And Daniel Slater had recommended me; he was somewhere waiting in the wings, trying to give my professional life a boost. It felt like a gift being given on behalf of Helene.

A black town car pulled up in front of my building. When Thomas stepped out from the passenger side, I called down to him and waved. Said that I would be there in just a minute. I met him on the sidewalk, and kissed him on both cheeks. He was wearing his captain's uniform again and took off his beret in a show of gallantry. The driver got out of the car in a panic. He said in English, "Miss, you've got to talk to them. They want to walk."

Vincent explained as he unfolded from the backseat. "The PF

doesn't want to show up to the rally in a chauffeured car," he said, using a nickname for the *president of Faso*. He was wearing a busy polyester shirt with a wide collar and looked like he hadn't slept well.

"I don't need you to speak for me," Thomas snapped. He seemed irritated, his mood apparently as bad as mine was good, which made me think the political tension that Ross had mentioned must've broken to the surface in Burkina somehow. By then Sam had joined the group on the sidewalk.

"I can't let them just disappear on me," the driver said. "Please, miss. If anyone finds out, I'll lose my job."

I told him there was nothing I could do: If a president says he wants to walk, it seems to me that he'll be walking. I didn't know why he was so worried. The DSS agents I'd met the day before were surely nearby. Maybe he thought they'd snitch on him.

We started in the direction of the school. As we walked along Lenox, one of the DSS agents stepped from a car. He was very conspicuous as he followed us, just a few paces behind.

"Where are the vice president and Mrs. Compaoré?" I asked Sam. "They've gone," was his curt response.

"Vice President Compaoré is heading back to Burkina this afternoon," Vincent elaborated. "His wife is still here though. She'll be going to Paris in a few days with their son."

Sam said something to him in Mooré as he glanced at me. I had the impression that it was about me, perhaps a warning. Sam had been immediately distrustful of me, and had no problem showing it.

I led our group with Vincent at my side, who kept yawning.

"Couldn't sleep?" I asked.

"I was up until three with Thomas taking notes on phone meetings. I think he must've called every politician in Ouagadougou."

"Is something going on?" I said casually, as if saying it coolly enough would prod Vincent into a spontaneous itemization of the intel I was after: bullet points outlining precisely what Thomas knew about how much my government was meddling in his. No dice. It's much harder to subtly coax information out of people than the movies let on.

What happened instead was that I was greeted with silence, and we continued toward Harriet Tubman elementary. It was as institutional as any other New York City public school, the finger paintings taped up behind the barred windows giving it the appearance of a prison for children.

The Patrice Lumumba Coalition's director, Aisha's uncle, who was a bald man wearing glasses on a chain around his neck, was waiting in the lobby with a few other men to greet Thomas's delegation. He led us into the auditorium where two hundred or so people were waiting, many of them standing. As we passed down the aisle toward the reserved seats in the front, I saw Aisha with Marlon in her lap. When she recognized me she quickly looked away.

We sat. The director went up onstage, and as he talked about how pleased he was to have Thomas speak, I looked around and took in the excitement of the crowd. Both DSS agents were waiting by the exit, and I saw a special agent there too, one I knew by face, not name. He was wearing a black suit and looked as much like a Fed as it was possible to look, a standard intimidation tactic that no one in the room seemed particularly intimidated by. I was surprised. Ross hadn't told me that another agent would be present.

Vincent went up to the stage first and spoke into the microphone attached to the podium there. I expected him to be nervous, but he was composed. He talked about how exciting it was to be in New York before shifting his focus to Thomas and the work his government, the CNR, was doing in Burkina Faso. The people around us began to clap as Vincent looked down toward Thomas and said in French: "Comrade President? Your audience is ready for you."

Thomas stood. He strode briskly toward the stage and climbed the steps on a sea swell of applause. He waited there, looking out at us serenely, all of his earlier irritation having apparently dissolved.

The crowd quieted. He let a few more moments pass before he gripped the podium with both hands and leaned toward the microphone. His voice barely audible, he said: "L'impérialisme."

"À bas!" a few French speakers in the crowd said back. *Down with it.*

"Le néocolonialisme." There was a smooth tranquillity to his voice that provoked excitement in the crowd.

"À bas!" more voices shouted.

"Le racisme!"

"À bas!" the voices in the auditorium thundered.

"La patrie ou la mort, nous vaincrons." *Homeland or death, we will win.* "*Merci,* comrades." He paused for a moment. When he spoke it was with Vincent translating for him. "We feel that the fight we're waging in Africa, principally in Burkina Faso, is the same fight you're waging in Harlem. Even if you have greater material wealth than we do, you have misery in your hearts. The misery of the ghetto, for example, and the brutality with which your police treat its citizens, the misery associated with the inhuman life created here because of the power of money, because of the power of capital."

The audience around me erupted into applause once more, and I realized I was as captivated as everyone else in the crowd. This was so different from the speech at the UN, which had been interesting but not galvanizing. It might've been because I was sitting closer or because of the engaged people around me; either way his passion felt sincere and was being amplified by the crowd. And yet it was intimate, like he was talking directly to me and only me. Everyone probably felt that way, I understood that, but it was still intoxicating.

"It is also a fact that any American, whatever his wealth, is like a pawn on a chessboard, a pawn who is moved around, who is manipulated, who isn't told one-tenth of the realities of the world. The American people can't be proud of the fact that, wherever they go, others look at them and see behind them the CIA, see behind them the attacks, the weapons, and so forth. I understand that black Americans also want their freedom. But don't confuse real freedom with the freedom of the few to exploit the rest."

I wondered then if his Pan-Africanism was too idealistic. While it was generous in its inclusion of me and other black Americans, at the end of the day, the very imperialism that he resisted was being enacted in our names too.

"You can't be proud that your brothers are treated with suspicion. You can't be proud that while we are here discussing things, while we are here talking to each other as Africans, your government regards you with such suspicion that they send spies who are here in order to make a report tomorrow morning."

His gaze landed on me briefly then, and I felt like he was looking into me again. And that time I felt afraid. Not of having my cover blown, but because I feared I was on the verge of losing control. It was intense fear, and in that way made me feel like when as a child I'd broken something or been caught pawing through the metal desk in my father's room and was about to find myself in serious trouble.

His eyes moved out behind me into the crowd, presumably toward the special agent standing beside the exit. "We say to them that they don't need to bring secret microphones. Even if television cameras were here, we'd be saying the same thing: We are ready to fight imperialism. Imperialism is the cause of your misery. The fight against it is our common fight."

Thomas banged his fist against the podium. He'd reached the apex of his speech and folks were near hysterical, calling out *yes* and *preach*, applause breaking out in all quarters of the gym. Although I recognized his words as propaganda, it was impossible to be in that room, full of energized people, and not feel electrified. I looked around and found myself wanting to believe, as they seemed to, that he meant what he was saying.

He unbuckled the pistol from his belt and held it up. "I want to show you that I'm ready for the fight. Please believe me, this isn't a toy. These bullets are real, and when we fire them it will be against imperialism. It will be on behalf of all black people. It will be on behalf of everyone who suffers domination. It will be on behalf of those white people who are our genuine brothers."

Applause began again, but he raised his hand and said over it, "I want you to stand. Stand because you represent the people, and wherever you stand up, imperialism trembles. I want you to repeat that: When the people stand up, imperialism trembles!"

"When the people stand up, imperialism trembles!" People all around me screamed as they stood. I got on my feet too.

"Again!"

"When the people stand up, imperialism trembles!"

"Imperialism!" he called.

"Down with it!"

"Puppet regimes!"

"Down with them!"

"Racism!"

"Down with it!"

"Neocolonialism!"

"Down with it!"

"Dignity!"

"To the people!"

"Health!"

"To the people!"

"Power!"

"To the people!"

"La patrie ou la mort, nous vaincrons!" he called. "La patrie ou la mort, nous vaincrons!"

"La patrie ou la mort, nous vaincrons!" voices around me called back at him. *Homeland or death, we will win!*

"Merci, comrades," he said, and left the podium. He was smiling as he came down the stage stairs, and as he closed the distance between us, I stared at him, captivated, clapping, pleasure radiating in and out of me in overwhelming waves as applause crashed around us.

Outside, Sam and the DSS agent forged a path through the crowd, Thomas following directly behind them, shaking as many of the hands extended to him as he could. He briefly stopped to talk in careful English to a girl of seven or so who was with her mother. I watched as he smiled down on the child, who had a beautiful head of hair: Her twists, adorned with hair bobbles and closed with white plastic barrettes, reminded me of the way my mother, and later Helene, used to do mine.

The second we were away from the crowd though, Thomas's mood collapsed in on itself. We were on the other side of the street where the high-rises of the St. Nick projects unspooled along the whole block.

"Leave us in peace!" he said to the DSS agent, clearly looking to take his anger out on someone. His petulant streak was unpleasant; it burst the idealized vision of him I'd been cultivating during the speech. The agent ignored him.

When we arrived back to my block, the driver was parked at a hydrant in front of my building. Vincent opened the car door.

"We're not going back yet," Thomas firmly reminded him. "The tour."

Vincent was obviously exhausted and I felt sorry for him. "You can rest in my apartment for a little bit before we start."

Thomas looked at him. "Are you tired?"

"I'm fine," Vincent said with a shake of his head.

"You look like you're going to pass out," the DSS agent said, speaking for the first time. "I can take you back to the hotel." I wondered if he was trying to help me with my assignment.

"Yes, Vincent, go back. Sam, you go with Vincent."

Sam said something in Mooré—it must've been an objection, because Thomas said, "I don't want security hovering over my shoulder. The same goes for him." He pointed at the DSS agent. "That isn't the way I want to see this place."

"I have to stay with you," the agent said. "But I'll keep my distance."

Sam nodded at that, pacified. He opened the car door, removed a bag from the backseat, and gave it to Thomas. Then he and Vincent got into the car. Thomas started toward my stoop. I lagged behind for a second to tell the agent that I'd bring my automatic and a radio, and if there were any problems I'd call him.

"I'm hungry," Thomas called from the sidewalk. "Are you ready?"

13

The bag Sam had given Thomas held a change of clothes. I was glad. He would've been absurdly conspicuous walking around Harlem in his uniform. He pulled the clothes from the bag and brought them with him toward the bathroom. As I waited for him in the living room, my eyes fell on the bag he'd left behind, sitting near a sofa leg. I went to it and glanced inside. I was hoping to find an itinerary. I wanted to know who he'd been meeting with in New York, but other than a small box, it was empty.

By all accounts, Thomas was a man of principle. When I'd suggested that we stay in my apartment, that I could cook for him, he must've heard a sexual subtext, because he'd quickly shook his head. I didn't know how I'd meant the invitation, to be honest. It was a confusing situation: While I was attracted to him, I knew it was wrong to try and seduce him, because it was so clear to me that Ross wanted me to do so.

Returning to my seat, I called to him through the bathroom door and asked if he liked his hotel. He said he did and told me the name of the place he was staying downtown.

"Nice," I said.

"The UN is paying for it," he called back. "I wouldn't have chosen a place so expensive. All of the CNR ministers are kept to a strict travel allowance of fifteen thousand CFA francs a day."

I did some quick calculations—that was about thirty-six bucks. I asked, "Don't they resent it?"

"They see the result. When the CNR came to power, we had a deficit of 695 million CFA francs. Two years later, in our first quarter, we had a surplus of a billion. That surplus is what I'm proudest of. My ministers might resent it, and the newspapers might attack me. But the men who do that don't go out to the countryside and ask the six million peasants out there if they're happy because of the new road we built, or the new school in their village, or the new clinic, or the new well."

"And you stick to that allowance too?"

"I do," he said, his voice getting louder as he stepped back into the living room. He looked great, wearing a pair of black pants and a high-collared cream-colored tunic.

"That's a nice shirt," I said, reducing the overwhelming thoughts crowding my mind to a compliment that seemed appropriate.

"It's *faso dan fani*," he said and added that the phrase translated roughly from Jula as *handwoven cloth of the homeland*. Wearing it was a way of supporting the local economy and embracing Burkinabè culture, he said, and he required the civil servants in his government to wear it at work. As he spoke, I felt like he was giving me a speech, and an authoritarian one at that—I understood the political purpose of the uniform, but in practice the idea rankled my American sense of personal freedom. And I was hoping I would've made more headway with him by then, but he was sermonizing to me just as he had the day before.

"Soft," I said, and touched the fabric. I was buoyed by the fact that he let me do it for a little too long. If I was going to get anywhere with him, I would need to bypass the ideologue.

"What are we going to eat?" he asked after a few moments.

It was a good question. He seemed to want an *authentic* tour, a desire that, ironically enough, immediately makes whatever you're going to show a person something of a performance.

Even though I knew it was a little ridiculous, I took him to Pan Pan.

We sat at a table beside the window. As he looked around, taking it all in, I worried that I'd made the wrong choice. I was relieved when he said he liked it. The waitress approached and put our menus down, and he glanced at his only briefly before tucking it between the condiments and asking me to order for him. I did. Once she'd gone, he spoke first: "I'm glad you called my attention to how tired Vincent was."

"He seems like a nice kid."

"He is."

"You were a little rough on him."

"He knows I expect a lot of him because he's talented. He can take it. He's my nephew. I've always been proud of him."

"How did you like my speech today?" he added. "Did you learn something?"

I laughed. It was clear he wanted to argue and I was game—getting him to disagree with me might loosen him up.

"I already know all I need to about Communism."

"You sound scared of it."

"I used to be when I was a kid. Fidel was like the bogeyman. Now I just think it's a proven failure."

"After talking to you yesterday, I started to believe you weren't as brainwashed as other Americans. Was I wrong?"

"I suppose so, if being brainwashed means having no memory of recent historical events."

"There's nothing inherently wrong with Communism. When it has failed it's done so because the forces of imperialism were undermining it."

I shrugged calmly. "That's bullshit."

He sat up, apparently about to object, but the waitress returned to our table then and put plates of food down. I'd ordered a couple of dishes for us to share.

"Thank you," he said in English, his whole face lighting up. He'd only spoken two words, but they'd manage to arrest her. She smiled brightly.

"That's no problem," she said, and I knew what she was feeling because I'd felt it too.

It wasn't enough to call what he had magnetism. The way he could make you feel. It was like he saw a version of you that was superior to the version you saw of yourself. It was very generous. And it was inspiring, that reminder of the better angels of your nature.

"How do you like it?" I asked as he tried the waffles.

"Most of this food is too rich." He pointed to a plate with his spoon. "But I like this one."

"The grits," I said, and he nodded, repeating the word in English. We chatted more, mostly about the neighborhood, and he started to relax. I felt like he was finally talking to me and not an audience. When we finished our meal, the waitress returned to the table.

"Who's this?" she said to me as she put our check down.

"A friend."

"Mm-hmm." Speaking to Thomas she added, "I see her in here a lot, but I don't never see her laughing like that."

I wasn't happy that she'd recognized me. But when I translated what she'd said he beamed at her—I was surprised by how pleased the comment made him. Still, I wanted to leave quickly. I shrugged on my jacket, and we exited the restaurant.

As we walked along Lenox I watched him take in the ramshackle beauty of the tenement buildings around us. We past the Schomburg Center and I thought of Phillip. I'd learned a lot about him in our short literary conversation, so I asked Thomas if he'd read any good books lately. He smiled at the cliché and said, "I can't tell you."

"Are you serious?"

He laughed. "I don't like to say what I've read. That's how you disclose the most about yourself. I never make notes in a book or underline passages either. That's even more revealing."

"Thomas . . ."

"Yes."

"I think you might be a little out of your mind."

He laughed again, a sharp, honest noise. "You're very funny."

"Glad you think so."

"You have a very American sense of humor."

"What's that mean?"

"Sarcastic."

"Is that a compliment?"

He smiled and walked on without answering.

"Fair enough," I said to his silence. I don't know if it's true that I'm funny. But I do feel sometimes like I've been trapped in an absurdist's fever dream, and that if I couldn't find a way to see humor in our lives, I wouldn't be able to get out of bed.

"Is everyone in your cabinet as paranoid as you are?" I asked him. "Does Blaise also keep his books locked up?"

He shook his head. "Blaise and I have our differences."

"Is that why he didn't come to the rally?"

"What?"

"You seemed upset earlier, and he wasn't there today. I thought maybe you'd had an argument."

"I asked him to return to Ouaga early to attend to some business."

"What kind?"

"Why are you asking?" he said, suddenly curt.

"I'm sorry. I didn't mean to be intrusive."

He softened. "Blaise and I don't see eye to eye all the time. We spar. But it's all right. I need him because he's honest with me. And even though we don't agree, we always speak to each other from a place of respect."

"Like brothers," I said.

"Exactly. He *is* my brother. He used to come with me to my parents' house for family dinners, at least once a week, and they love him like he's one of their own."

We continued south. The leaves were turning and the street was busy. I watched Thomas observe the scene around him and glance at two elderly women at a bus stop, both of them wearing dresses and matching hats. We walked west on 125th Street, where I pointed out the Apollo and my gym, and on the corner of Adam Clayton Powell Boulevard, I led us in the direction of the Hotel Theresa. I said, "This is where Castro was staying."

"When?"

"What do you mean when?" We exchanged a look. "When he gave the speech you quoted yesterday. The UN had organized a block of rooms for Castro and his delegation in a luxury hotel in Midtown, the Shelbourne. At the last minute he decided to come up here instead."

"Why?"

"My father says it was because he wanted to be up here, around Latino and black people. People who looked like Cubans. He thought he'd be treated better. But I've also heard that the Shelbourne's management asked him to pay cash up front, expecting the delegation to cause damage. And that made him angry. He thought the UN had talked them into it to harass him."

We stood side by side on the sidewalk, looking up at the marquee. I glanced over and saw that he was smiling. Maybe he was picturing it: Castro waving down at a sea of cheering New Yorkers, many of them black.

"A lot of people knew he was up here. He came out on the balcony a few times to wave hello."

He turned to face me and looked into my eyes. "Do you remember that? You must've been young."

"No, but I heard the story a lot when I was growing up. My father worked crowd control in front of the hotel."

"He's a cop?"

"He was. Retired now."

"Why'd he become one?"

"People ask me that all the time. A lot more than they would if he was white, that's for sure."

"Of course. There are two systems of law in your country, and the one designed for black people was created to oppress them. It's reasonable to ask why a black man would want to support that."

I nodded.

"It must be hard to be a black cop in this country. Most of them probably wonder at some point if they're fighting for the right thing."

"Most of them probably do. He never forgot he was black though. I think if you asked him he'd tell you he tried to do right by us while working within the system." The words were out of my mouth before I could catch myself. I was being more truthful about my own motivations than I'd meant to be.

"Did he actually change anything?"

"No. He kept trying to so they forced him to retire."

I'd said it as if I were joking, but it was true, more or less; he understood that and laughed bitterly.

"It made sense for him. He became a cop because he was a soldier. And because more than color was at issue."

"Like what?"

"Like family. Like the obligation he had to us. It was a good middle-class job for a black man to come back home to after the air force." Obligation. I thought of the promise I'd made Helene.

"What did your grandfather do?"

"He was a grocer."

"Why didn't your father follow him into that business?"

I thought for a moment. "I don't know. But my father made the right choice. We grew up with a little money, and that put us . . . not exactly ahead, but it put us *somewhere*. And on top of that I was lucky. I know some people who had really bad luck. I think Pop was right to take the job he did."

"He could've raised a family on a grocer's salary."

"I know," I said, a little testily.

"I don't mean to attack you, or the way you grew up. I'm asking because my father did the same thing, and I've never been able to understand it."

"He was a soldier?"

Thomas nodded. "In the Second World War. He fought on behalf of the Mossi chief of Tema, in place of his son."

"Why?"

"Because his family was allied with the chief."

I nodded despite not understanding what that meant. "When mine enlisted, his recruiter told him there wouldn't be another war, not after World War II. He fought in Korea. He was a radio operator."

"Was he really?"

"What? Yes."

The question made me wonder if he thought I was making up a biography that aligned with his. We really did have a lot in common though, odd synchronicities that a part of me now wants to believe had a deeper meaning. He was a Catholic, like Agathe. I very nearly blew my cover when I learned he had a sister named Marie and that we shared a birthday, having forgotten for a moment that he knew me by an alias.

"Did the chief give him anything? For fighting on his behalf?"

"Yes. He was given the chief's last name. Ouédraogo, which is Mossi. They're the ethnic majority in Burkina; they have the most money and social privilege and political power. I'm Silmi-Mossi. Historically, we've been on the bottom rung of society. Sankara is a Silmi-Mossi name. I reclaimed it when I was in high school. So he got a name and a minor appointment in the colonial government. My father was an auxiliary gendarme in Gaoua, the town where I grew up."

"Do you take after him?"

"Not politically, no. Our conversations about politics are more like confrontations. The Germans captured him, so his attitude has always been that things could be much worse. But I want change. I want things to improve. I don't believe anyone will hand that to us. We have to force it to happen. And I don't understand why he was a gendarme. How could he enforce the laws of white men when they applied them so unjustly?"

"For personal gain. You just said the posting was a reward. He was like my father: He wanted to ensure a better future for his children. That makes sense to me."

"But the fact that he was a gendarme didn't protect him or us. He was tossed in prison twice because of things my siblings and I did when we were kids."

"What did you do?"

"Why is that your question? To decide if he deserved the punishment?"

"No. I—"

"In Gaoua the school had a French principal. Once one of my younger sisters threw some stones up into a tree to knock fruit out of it. She was hungry. The stones fell on the principal's roof, and his wife, who was inside taking a nap at the time, said that the sound disturbed her rest. So they came to our house and arrested my father."

A couple of kids on bikes were approaching us from behind; I hooked my arm around his and pulled him close to me. I could tell he was confused until the bikers sped past us.

"Tell me about the second time."

"Did you see them coming?" he answered, avoiding the question.

"Heard them."

"I couldn't pick them out from all the other noise. This is a very loud city."

"I don't notice it anymore."

The way I was holding him must've made him nervous, because he gently unhooked my arm from his as he said, "I can't imagine growing up in a place like this. What was it like?"

"A little boring. Especially in Queens."

"That's it?"

I thought for a moment. "There was a lot of competition. If you wanted something you had to figure out a strategy to get it. No one was going to hand you anything. Ever."

"What was your strategy?"

"I was the best. I worked the hardest. I wanted to leave the neighborhood. I wanted more than it could give me." I thought of Helene, who'd been motivated in the same way. But I'd taken it as a personal rejection.

"You had to be exceptional just to leave."

"Yeah, like my grandfather. He immigrated here from Barbados and he was—I'm talking a lot about my family," I said, interrupting myself.

"Are you?"

"More than I'm used to. I don't like to talk too much about them. It's like you and your books. I reveal too much about myself when I talk about them. They're the people that formed me."

"And I'm the paranoid one," he said.

I smiled. A black car with the DSS agents inside passed by slowly. We'd walked in a large loop and were headed back toward my apartment by way of the long, narrow, and strangely steep park where I'd first approached Aisha. I told Thomas that there was a wood house in the park that had belonged to Alexander Hamilton. And I said that farther up the hill was the college I'd attended. He said he wanted to see it, but the sun was starting to set and I thought we should turn back. I said, "I want to take you one last place before you go back downtown."

I was taking him to the Lenox Lounge. Although it was close to my apartment, I'd only been there once or twice, but I thought he'd like it because there'd be live music playing. Plus the bar was beautiful, or at least, you could tell it once had been. Strictly speaking it was a dive, but there was bold geometry in its Art Deco design.

When the bartender looked up he did a double take. As he stood at attention and saluted, I noticed a tattoo on the inside of his arm: a heavy 89B. It must've been his army MOS—his job code.

"Captain Sankara. This is an honor."

Thomas saluted back.

"I was at the rally," the bartender said, and I translated.

"We're here for the music," I told him. I'd thought Thomas would like to see the show because he used to have a band, Tout-à-Coup Jazz.

"What can I get you?" the bartender said.

"Do you drink?" I asked Thomas.

"Only occasionally. I like dolo," he said, referring to a millet beer. "You don't have that here though."

I had no idea what dolo tasted like, so I ordered us both a beer I liked and hoped for the best as the bartender poured it. When Thomas tried to pay, the bartender put up his hand. "No charge, Captain."

He dried his hands on a bar rag and picked up a camera. "Do you mind?"

Thomas said it was no problem and I took a picture of them together, assuming the bartender would add it to the mirror behind the bottles that was studded with photos. As I handed back the camera, I noticed a copy of *The Spook Who Sat By the Door* near the register. I'd read it; we'd had to at Quantico. Very deliberately, with a raise of my eyebrows, I asked him his opinion on it, planning to force Thomas into our conversation about books.

"It's great," the bartender answered. "Really got me inspired."

Thomas knew what I was up to. Humoring me, he asked, "Have you read *The Devil's Alternative?*"

The bartender shook his head. "He a black writer?"

"No, but you might like it. It reveals some of the hypocrisy of the major world powers."

"And what about Burkinabè novels. Any you'd recommend?"

"I don't like African fiction in general. The books I've read have been disappointing. It's always the same story: A young African goes to Paris, suffers, and when he returns he's out of touch with tradition." Thomas watched me as I translated for him. Once I'd finished he said as an aside to me, "You didn't like that criticism."

I was flustered. He'd known exactly what I was thinking, and it surprised me. I often heard I was hard to read.

"Well?" he pushed.

"It sounds like you're only describing one book in particular. He'll take that generalization more seriously than you do."

"I prefer African writers who write about real problems, not just for literary effect."

"That's fine. You just can't say it to him."

"I *can't?*"

"Don't ask my opinion if you don't want it."

Thomas opened his mouth to argue but I turned back to the bartender and picked up my drink. "Nous vaincrons."

He smiled and repeated the phrase, tripping over the French a bit.

"It means *we will win*," I said.

Thomas and I started toward the small room at the back of the bar.

"You revealed a title you've read," I said as we walked, trying to shift the conversation back to its earlier tone. "Now I know everything."

"Me too. You told me about your family."

I hadn't mentioned Helene. I'd been more careful than he realized. As we sat together on zebra print seats he said, "Blaise would like this place."

"I'm sorry he couldn't make it to the rally."

"He had to take care of an emergency. Our government, the CNR, has voted to ban multiparty elections."

I believed that a single-party system was a dictatorship, no matter how much good that party did for its citizens. But I didn't say that. He was upset, and for the first time in our conversation I didn't want to push.

"There'll be a lot of backlash facing me when I return. People are starting to accuse me of authoritarianism, but that's not fair. The truth is that we can't just re-create a system of Western democracy in our country. Corrupt politicians hide out in parties; they become men who use their power to undermine the revolution and *true* democracy. Participatory democracy. Take members of the so-called ULCR."

"What is that?" I asked.

"A political group. They'd like to form their own party. Any chance they get they vote en masse to block my campaigns. The last instance was about whether or not they support trade unions. They voted to support them in order to force my hand. I had to ban them."

"But why are you opposed to the trade unions?"

"That's not the point! The ULCR are reactionaries. They don't even care about whether trade unions are legal or not. They want to frustrate me at every turn as a political tactic. It's obvious. And self-serving." He angrily took a sip of his beer.

"Why are they doing that?"

He looked at me steadily for a moment before he spoke. "I told you already. Because they're reactionaries."

I nodded. I thought I had my answer to Ross's question. Although it's hard to prove what someone *doesn't* know, I thought that if he knew the ULCR was under CIA control he would've made an accusation about my government directed toward me, an American. That seemed in keeping with how he'd been speaking.

By then a few other couples had arrived to the dark, smoky lounge. The band started the early show set: upbeat, brass-driven jazz. I watched Thomas more than I did the musicians. He had an expressive face, and was enraptured; I noticed that the music had quickly improved his mood. While the band was playing a slower number he caught me looking at him. I was overwhelmed by how intense it was to look in his eyes.

When the show ended, Thomas got to his feet and enthusiastically applauded. He was the only one standing. The bartender came into the back room then. He went up on the stage and whispered something into the guitarist's ear as he pointed over at us. As most of the other people filed out of the room, the guitarist waved Thomas over.

He went up onstage, where the guitarist handed over his instrument to Thomas and said the name of a standard. He nodded—he knew the song—they began to play. It was a pleasure to watch him because his enjoyment was so sincere. His anger from earlier was long gone, and he looked truly happy.

When the song finished, I clapped and whistled. He thanked the band, who each took care to shake his hand, then came back toward the table, his face flushed and ecstatic.

"You were excellent," I said as he dropped onto the bench beside me.

"Thanks. For everything, I mean." He took a small box out of his bag, the one I'd seen earlier. "Do you already know what's in this?"

"How could I?" I said with a smile. He couldn't prove I'd looked inside his bag—that I'd fallen for the trap he'd apparently laid for me. He handed me the box, which I opened. Inside were copper bracelets. Taking them out, he slipped them up my arm.

"They're beautiful," I said. "Did you bring them from home?"

"I saw them in a shop yesterday and asked Sam to go buy them for you. Copper is a powerful metal."

"Thank you."

I wanted him to kiss me then—for my work or just because, it didn't matter. I leaned slightly toward him. Once again he knew what I was thinking and stood. "I should go."

At the front of the bar there was music playing on the jukebox and far more people crowded in the space than there had been when we first arrived. By the door I said, "Wait. Thomas. Don't go back downtown yet. Come back to my place for a nightcap."

He smiled and took my hand. Pumped it twice. "I'm glad I met you. Maybe not everyone at the UN is a hallway rat." He leaned close to me and said into my ear, "But you have to understand. I can't do anything wrong. You see?"

I nodded. "I can give you a ride downtown."

"I'll get one with the agents who've been following us. They weren't very subtle, were they?"

"Not at all." He kissed me on the cheek and I watched him leave.

Once he was out of sight, I went immediately to the bar and ordered one whisky and then another. What I felt was confusing—although I'd gotten the intel Ross had asked me for, I still felt like I'd failed. I was ashamed and disappointed in myself.

After my second drink, I started back toward my apartment, even though I hadn't yet hit on the magic amount of liquor that could chase my humiliation away.

As I approached my building, I noticed a white van idling out front.

My heart picked up speed as I got closer; it seemed so out of place, and so much like the surveillance vehicles we used at the bureau. I knew immediately that it was there to capture images of Thomas and me. I went up my stoop and let myself inside.

In my bedroom, I looked over to the window across the street, the same one where I saw the girl reading sometimes. I felt unsettled. Although the window was dark I could've sworn I was being watched.

I spent a few days sunken in a mire of self-loathing, scolding myself, although for what I didn't actually know. I'd done what Ross had asked—if he thought I hadn't that was his fault for being so vague. Still, when he summoned me for a lunch debriefing at a diner downtown, I arrived with my stomach in knots.

When I told him that I didn't believe Thomas knew about the CIA's involvement in the ULCR, he nodded and said, "Were you able to get him alone?"

"No," I said, assuming he was asking if I'd slept with him.

"Never once?"

"Only for a few minutes when he changed his clothes at my place."

He opened his briefcase and handed me an envelope. "That's half the amount we talked about."

I didn't have to ask why. After seeing the surveillance van I finally understood why Ross wanted me to sleep with him. It wasn't for the sake of intel. It was only obvious in retrospect: SQLR was about using me to blackmail Thomas. They wanted photos of us together. And Thomas had known that was a possibility even when I didn't—that's why he'd slipped my arm out of his and said what he had at the lounge.

I tucked the money into my purse. "When can I talk to Daniel Slater?"

He shook his head. "He's not in New York."

"We had a deal."

"Did we?" he said.

"Maybe I could speak to him on the phone, or go to him. I just want to ask him a question or two about Helene."

I was leaning forward, practically begging.

"I'm sorry," he said, not sounding at all contrite. I hadn't given him what he'd wanted and he was punishing me. It was an ugly side of him.

After the meeting, I returned to the field office. I'd thrown myself into my work at the bureau, even though my days were still filled mostly with paperwork, and seemed especially gray after the flashy excitement on an undercover assignment.

When Rick Gold called me to his office in the late afternoon, I had the uncharacteristically optimistic idea that it was because he'd noticed my hard work and was going to put me on the surveillance squad monitoring the suspected spy in the Foreign Mission.

Gold's office smelled like brand-new carpet and was garishly decorated with a number of gold-colored accessories on the walls and shelves (the man wasn't the most original thinker I'd ever met). To my surprise, Mr. Ali was there. I tried to catch his eye but couldn't.

The SAC, my boss's boss, was there too, clutching a paper cup of coffee. I'd never exchanged more than a few words with him; he wasn't a particularly friendly man.

"Close the door," he said to start the meeting. "You understand why you're here today, don't you?"

"No," I said truthfully, with a small shake of my head.

The SAC frowned at Gold before he turned to me. "Your ASAC informs me that you've been falsifying paperwork. Is that true?"

Gold had laid out a few forms on his desk: Aisha's termination papers.

"I'll need you to sign off on the disciplinary report," the SAC said. Gold handed me the paperwork, which I glanced over. I looked up at him.

"You're suspending me?"

I glanced at Mr. Ali for help, but he was still studying a spot on the carpet. When I'd first walked in, I'd wrongly assumed his presence there served no other purpose than to humiliate us both. But no. They were setting me up and he'd helped them.

"This is ridiculous. I'm not signing that." If I didn't, they'd have to give me a formal hearing. I stood. "I've always maintained a strict standard of professionalism as a member of law enforcement. My performance reviews here and in Indiana all attest to that. If Gold has some ax to grind—"

"Ax to grind?" he said. "You've been *falsifying reports*. Who knows how many."

"I'm not signing anything." I stood and left the office. At my desk, I gathered my purse and suit jacket; while headed to the elevator, I heard Mr. Ali call my name. I ignored him and kept walking, but he caught up with me at the elevator bank.

"Marie, let me explain—"

"Don't bother." I pressed the call button.

"I thought you didn't forge any paperwork," he said. "You told me you didn't."

"So then why'd you tell them I did?"

He shook his head. "I didn't."

I didn't believe him, and he read it in my face.

"This is what happened: Gold said he had a hunch that you were breaking rules. I told him I knew that wasn't true. You're the most principled agent we have."

"And then?"

"I told him about our lunch. I said that if you were even thinking about taking paper clips out of this place that you'd talk with me about it first. When he said he'd found something while investigating you, I told him I thought he was making it up."

"So you threw me under the bus."

"That wasn't my intention."

"What does it matter if you meant to do it? That's what happened."

He shook his head. "Fight the suspension. I've never seen anyone get sidelined for so long over something this minor."

The elevator dinged and the doors opened. I didn't step inside. My anger had ebbed, and I was suddenly very tired. I turned back toward Gold's office, leaving Mr. Ali behind me at the elevator bank. My SAC had left. I closed the door behind me and asked Gold why he was gunning for me.

"Gunning for you? Don't flatter yourself."

"That's what it looks like. Seems like you want me out of here."

"Let me ask you a question. When the CIA came here, sought you out for your help, why didn't you give it to them?"

It was an impossible question to answer. He spoke into my silence. "I'll tell you why: You don't play ball. If I don't think you fit in here, it's only because you refuse to try."

I was too tired to defend myself. I took in the smug look he was giving me, took stock of the scorn I felt, and wondered why I was holding on to a relationship with that place. They hated me for thinking I was fine the way I was. I'd been so afraid of repeating my mother's mistakes that just leaving had stopped feeling like an option.

But it was. I sat across from Gold, pulled the disciplinary report toward me, and signed it.

"Good," he said as he watched. "That makes it easier on everyone. If you want my advice, take some time to figure out what you want. Whether or not you want to be at this field office. If you do, see if you can find a way to be more approachable. It wouldn't kill you to have a smile on your face sometimes. You don't have to act like you hate everything about this place."

"I'll see what I can do," I said, and if he didn't hear my sarcasm, it was because he chose not to. I stood and left his office.

14

I took a seat at the bar in the Lenox Lounge, and as I waited for the bartender, glanced at my face in the mirror above the line of bottles. I looked tired.

He came over, called me by my alias, and said it was good to see me. After my suspension I'd gone there almost every evening—without being asked, he poured me some of my brand of whisky. I'd been spending too much time at the lounge, but it beat the doom-filled quiet of my apartment. Given my suspension, because I couldn't distract myself with work, the fact of my deep loneliness had come into sharp focus. I was already too familiar with the regulars there. I thought sometimes about drinking at home to avoid having interactions at the Lenox, but that impulse was a depressing one.

The photo I'd taken of him and Thomas had been framed and hung on the wall beside the mirror. I kept gravitating toward that place—the good feelings associated with the time I'd spent with Thomas must've outweighed what came after.

The lounge was most pleasant when it was almost empty, as it was that evening. There was only me, the bartender, a pair of old-timers in driving caps who'd both greeted me when I'd walked in, and a woman in a shiny wig and skintight dress, who sat alone in one of the red booths, already drunk.

I lifted the drink to my lips; the copper bangles Thomas had given me fell down my arm with a jingle. I wore them almost every day and smiled as I put them on, even though I found it more than a little mortifying to be a woman in her thirties wearing jewelry given to her by a hopeless crush.

The bartender started to tell the old-timers about Thomas playing the guitar, embellishing in parts; they'd heard the story before but smiled and pretended they hadn't.

After that, and serving another round for them, the bartender went back to reading *The Devil's Alternative*. I glanced at my watch. I was supposed to be meeting Ross, who'd called and said he wanted to talk to me. Because of how our debriefing had gone, I'd been surprised to hear from him again.

It was with a measure of perversity that I'd insisted he meet me at the Lenox Lounge and was surprised when he'd agreed. I'd grown up feeling like whenever I left my neighborhood in Queens, or my grandfather's in Brooklyn, or the East Village, I was entering hostile territory. It wasn't until college that I started going into those parts of the city that didn't belong to me, and then only because I was compelled to do so for my classes. Maybe part of me had insisted Ross come uptown because I hoped he'd experience that feeling.

Finally, the blood-red door to the lounge swung open in my peripheral vision, and Ross appeared. He sat down on the stool beside mine. "Nice place you picked here."

The bartender came over, and Ross ordered a drink. When it came we moved to a booth. He asked how I was doing.

"Not too bad."

"Really?" The question was pointed. He must've heard about my suspension.

"Really," I said, lying. I was upset. The worst thing was that although Mr. Ali had been instrumental in my suspension, Pop wouldn't take my side over his. So the way he'd betrayed me had also managed to tarnish my relationship with my father.

"How long are you out for?"

"Forty-five days."

He nodded. "You don't deserve it. What they're trying to do to you."

"How do you know about it?" I was wary of him. The last time we'd seen each other, he'd revealed a poisonous side to his nature.

"I make it my business to know things."

Anger flared up in me then. I was furious at everybody, and that kind of vague answer wasn't going to improve that state of affairs. "What do you want, Ross?"

"I've been thinking a lot about that conversation the three of us had—you, me, and Phil. About the agency's blind spots. It does us a big disservice not to give female officers a fair chance, because there are so many places in the world where it would never occur to the locals that there are women working for us. There's no better cover than one that depends on someone else's prejudices. I know that from personal experience." He paused and sipped his drink. "One place that might be a great example of that is Burkina Faso."

I'd been wondering if he was working to a point, but when it arrived it still managed to surprise me. "You want to send me out there?"

"Dan does. He asked me to reach out to you. He wants you to contract for us again. He's in the field in Ouaga."

"So I'd be working with him."

"Yes."

I tried to disguise my excitement.

"We give female officers a hard time," he continued. "We hold women to an unfair double standard. The bureau probably does too."

"Yeah. No shit." Hearing him explain it in theoretical terms when I'd lived it caused me a specific type of maddening anger.

"CIA policy reflects a lot of fear. The administration is afraid of female officers finding husbands and leaving, which would be a waste of the money it costs to train them. The bigger waste is dismissing effective personnel for made-up reasons. They're too old-fashioned. And they're overlooking the potential advantages of female officers."

"This is all very progressive of you."

"That's not what I'm trying to get at. I'm just pointing out that the CIA has its weaknesses. More modern-thinking, nimbler firms are possible."

I nodded, even though I had no idea if he was talking specifically or in general. He said, "We'd treat this like an extension of your previous contract. The terms are the same. We'll pay you the second installment when you get back." A few moments passed. "Well? What do you think?"

I looked around me. The woman in the booth was drunkenly laughing to herself, and one of the old-timers had his head propped up on his hand and was starting to nod.

"All right," I said. "I'll go."

I wanted to see Slater. And I wanted to work. I needed to.

"Fantastic," he said, drawing out the word. "Come by the office I have up here on Thursday, so we can talk about the logistics of the assignment."

I agreed.

He said, "Back to Africa. You excited?"

I frowned. "I'm not going as a tourist."

"Still."

"Ross, come on. Black Americans don't have a great track record with going to West Africa to push neocolonialism."

"What do you mean? Liberia?"

"Yes."

"Is that how you see what we're doing? Pushing neocolonialism?"

"Well—"

"You're a very cynical person, aren't you? Which isn't a bad thing, by the way. No, that's not what we're doing. Get that clear in your mind. With everything that's happening in Iran right now, the way that country is exporting terror, the United States can't just sit by. We have to be proactive and prepared for what's coming."

"I thought it was Communism that we're fighting."

"What?"

"Not terrorism."

He frowned at me and spoke slowly, as if he believed I'd been struck suddenly with stupidity. "It's both of them. It's everything. That's the world we live in today."

He paused, struggling. "For me—listen, it doesn't matter. I'll be fine. I've spent my whole life compartmentalizing. But Phillip. One of the things that scares me about the Soviets is what they would do to him if they got the chance."

"Fair enough." I sympathized with how he felt: He was saying Phillip couldn't pass and it frightened him. But I couldn't be bothered to hide how skeptical I was about his ideology.

"Marie, I'm going to put my cards on the table."

"Go ahead."

"Let me ask you something."

"Okay."

"One of the things I love about Phil is the way he cuts right through the bull. He really knows how to ask the sixty-four-thousand-dollar question."

"That's not a question."

"Why did you become a Fed?"

I'd become a Fed because of my sister, which made it a shame that I'd realized too late that from a certain angle, it looked like I'd greedily mined my life out of her death. I'd felt bad at my first posting in Indiana when I'd liked my job too much. After Helene died, it was impossible to escape my gutting, awful sorrow; there's a year of my life that I lost to it, which I'd rather not detail. Sometimes I felt like I deserved to feel as bad as I did then. In a certain sense, the New York office was better for me because it was so punishing.

"I'm very excited," I answered with a sigh.

"What?"

"To visit Africa. It's going to be a lot of fun getting back to my roots." I raised a fist.

"Okay." He nodded, having understood that I wasn't going to answer the question. "Well, it's definitely an experience."

After that we moved on to more general conversation about politics. I had the sense he was probing for something about my perspective, information that I instinctively didn't want to give. By the time we left the bar, the night had come on in earnest. He strolled out of the lounge before me, as at home as he'd been in Midtown.

"Want a ride?"

I looked off in the direction of my apartment. "I'll walk."

"You sure that's safe?"

"Yes."

"Don't get mugged."

"Have a good night, Ross."

As I walked home I thought about Daniel Slater. I wanted to talk to him about my sister. I thought of Helene, how she'd wanted to travel with the CIA. And now I was going to do precisely that, and I couldn't help feeling like I'd taken something from her.

When I was sixteen, I couldn't understand that desire of hers as more than a whim. I'd thought: What would it have earned her? Pop had defended American interests abroad. He'd been in the air force, had flown to the other side of the planet to fight for our country and come back to his base in Biloxi, where they'd made him sit at the back of the city bus in his uniform. He'd expanded himself to come back to a place full of small people with rules that could run him over. How much smaller must they have looked to him then; how ridiculous and arbitrary those rules must've seemed. And how much more dangerous that place was for him once he was fully aware of its pettiness.

The address Ross had given me belonged to a nondescript office building in Midtown. Inside, I found a deserted lobby that only featured ways out of it: an old menu board that listed the firms in the building, a door that was propped open to reveal a staircase, and an elevator with stainless steel doors.

I rode the shuddering elevator up to the fourth floor, toward Helene's dream of heading into a CIA office, and stepped out into a hall with a single door at its far end. There was an intercom there, and when I pressed it, a security camera swiveled toward me. I held up my credentials. After a few moments, a startlingly loud buzzer sounded, and I let myself into a little antechamber with a shabby gray carpet where an officer was sitting at a small desk beside another door. Young, white, and fair-haired, he was exactly what you'd expect.

He stood. Stuck a perforated card into the slot, pressed his finger against a reader beside the door, and after a much more subtle beep than the one out in the hall, pulled open the unlocked door. He led me down a quiet hall. At the end of it was a small office, and inside I found Ross speaking Arabic into a beige phone. He gestured for me to sit. I did. I looked around. There was a grime-covered window behind him and fluorescent lighting overhead. A flimsy bookshelf stood in the corner, gasping under the weight of dusty binders. In other words, it looked like what it was—a government office. I should've known better than to expect something out of a movie, but I admit I was disappointed that the design was not at all futuristic and there were no high-tech gadgets lying around.

"Sorry about that," he said as he hung up the phone. "Want some coffee?"

I told him I did and he left me alone for a moment, then returned with two cups. As he handed me one I looked around and asked what exactly this place was.

"Just an off-site. One of the Company's satellite offices. They let me use a desk and a phone here when I come up from Langley." He sat. "So. Let's talk about your assignment. Have you been keeping up with news from Burkina Faso?"

"A little bit. Only what I've seen in *Le Monde*."

"Sankara's becoming more of a dictator every day."

I nodded. The news wasn't plentiful, but there'd been enough to make me aware that the CNR was flailing. To combat the push for multiparty elections, it seemed like Thomas was relying on increasingly authoritarian tactics. A few weeks after returning to Ouagadougou from New York, he'd fired hundreds of striking teachers in the country because, encouraged by the ULCR, they were trying to unionize. There were already too few teachers in the country; the termination of so many would have a serious effect. He was also being accused of suppressing a free press.

"Well. I guess it was inevitable." I said it lightly, although inwardly, I was disappointed to hear Ross confirm what I'd been reading.

"It always happens this way with Communist governments. The quick pace though, I'll admit that surprised me. Communism is just like a disease. Luckily, I think we can handle this outbreak before it gets out of hand."

"Why this one? Isn't Ghana the bigger problem? Rawlings's government has a lot more money."

"Rawlings is also a problem, sure. We're running operations in Ghana designed to keep him in check too. But don't underestimate Sankara's appeal. His government may not have much financial influence, but he has a lot of political power, especially considering he's only been president a few years. They already love him in South Africa. And in Angola, which is a resource-rich country that we can't afford to lose to Communism. Imagine the economic disaster and the humanitarian crisis that Angola would face if they nationalized their mines. Imagine it under a socialist regime, with a heavily centralized state-run system. It would fall to ruins."

I nodded, hoping to hurry him along. His ideological stock phrases were having the opposite of their desired effect. I kept informed enough about global politics to know that Angola wasn't a good country to use as an example of the gloom and doom Ross was describing. They were already facing a humanitarian crisis—civil war had been raging there since the mid-seventies, and I understood it to be a proxy war between the Soviet Union and the United States. I assumed he knew the situation was more complicated than how he presented it, but was banking on my ignorance of the rest of the world to make his point.

But I wasn't as uninformed as he'd hoped. I knew we'd been fighting the Cold War in Africa since I was a child. In the Congo, in the 1960s, Patrice Lumumba was assassinated by firing squad. Both the Belgians and the CIA were in on the plot —there's a rumor that Eisenhower signed an order for a scientist to slip him poisoned toothpaste, which sounds so ridiculous and far-fetched that I'm sure it happened.

After a brief détente in the seventies, Ronald Reagan took office, and expressed a set of foreign policy goals that seemed ludicrously improbable at the time. Not only did he want to turn the Cold War around in our favor, he wanted to win it.

In the pursuit of that goal, he'd returned us to an era of fear and vitriol. Reagan wasn't nearly as sneaky as Eisenhower had been—his presidency was characterized by open hostility toward the Libyan president, Muammar Gaddafi.

Personally, I thought Gaddafi was an unhinged maniac, but in everything I'd read about Lumumba, he emerged as sensible and thoughtful. He believed Communism and colonialism were equally destructive, which I agreed with in theory. Still in practice, I thought Ross was correct when he'd said that Thomas's government would eventually run out of money and his socialist policies would come to an end. And what after that? He'd fall back on retaining power like a tyrant. We were seeing that happen all over the world.

"As I'm sure you remember we're involved in the ULCR. CIA funds it and one of our agents leads it. The party's agenda is to undermine Sankara's government."

I nodded. "He told me he believed as much."

"We don't just want to create multiple parties, we want to use the ULCR to splinter the government and weaken it. Of course, Sankara's livid about this and trying to prevent it. He's calling for a series of meetings to dissolve the different parties and reunite the government around the CNR's guiding philosophies. He wants a dozen of the most valued politicians in the government to sign a joint declaration. It's basically a loyalty pledge"—he looked down and read from the papers in front of him—"'to overcome our respective ideologies with a view to the construction of one political organization.' We're sending you out there to help make sure he can't strong-arm the politicians back into line. So the goal in Ouaga is the same as it was here: to get you close to Sankara."

"Ross, why don't you level with me?"

"Meaning?"

"I saw your surveillance van, the one parked in front of my building. I know this is a blackmail operation. You want to prove that he's unfaithful."

He thought for a few moments before he spoke. "I keep forgetting how smart you are."

I preened.

"Yes, Dan's going to ask for a few intimate photos of you with Sankara. We want you in the country after the revelations come out so the press can have access to you. Much of his support is based on his reputation as an honorable man; you're going to help us discredit him. Reveal him as a hypocrite."

"Why do you have to rig the election? Isn't there a chance that your agent in the ULCR might be elected?"

"The country's still a few years from voting in its best interest. We're installing a candidate now to open the door to true democracy later. And it could be worse. There's a contingent in the military that wants to have him executed and to install a general as president."

"Does that align with what CIA wants?"

"No."

I wasn't sure I believed him and said as much.

"Really," Ross said. "We don't want to raise a single eyebrow in the international community."

"The station office doesn't want any blowback."

"Yes."

"What does Slater do out there exactly? What's his title?"

"He's our operations officer. He'll fill you in on anything else he'll need when you get there. Or at least whatever's need to know. Dan has an office set up in an American NGO. You'll be doing most of your work there, so the house you'll be staying in is close by."

I asked him the name of the nongovernmental organization and he said it in such terrible French that I asked him to write it down for me.

"*Le Havre des Femmes*," I read. "Haven for Women. Is it a shelter?"

"Yeah. Apparently they house women who've been accused of witchcraft."

"Really?"

"Uh-huh. Sounds like you'll have to prepare yourself for a bit of a culture shock."

"You've never been to Burkina?" I asked.

He shook his head. "The closest I ever got was to Tamale in the north of Ghana. There are a lot of bikes up there, and I hear it's the same in Ouagadougou. Other than that though the countries seem like they're worlds apart."

"When do I go?"

"The first CNR reunification meeting is scheduled for next week. We want you in Ouagadougou for it."

"How long will I be out there?"

"No more than a couple of weeks. And you start back at the bureau when? First week of November?"

"Yeah."

"You'll be back before then." He pulled open a drawer and reached inside his desk for a large interoffice envelope.

"Even though you won't be at the embassy, I'm sure you'll meet the station chief and everyone else at the station office, so I had an ID made for you."

I looked inside and pulled out a plane ticket. It also held two passports, one of them with the alias I'd been using, the other a backup with another identity, and the embassy employee identification he'd mentioned. I looked them all over: He'd managed to get his hands on the photo of me that the bureau had on file.

There were a few more items in the envelope: African francs and new francs, several maps of Burkina Faso, and a State Department guide to the country. I looked up at him. "Anything else?"

"Like what?"

I shrugged even though I knew exactly what I'd meant: In all the time I worked as a contractor for Ross, he never actually gave me a contract to sign. Coming from the FBI, I was very aware that there was no paper trail, and none of the legitimacy that such a trail would've lent the operation.

I stood, took the envelope, and thanked him for the opportunity. He wished me good luck. "I'll see you in a few weeks."

I left the office. As I walked to my car, my mind wandered to my time at Quantico, to a class called Defensive Tactics that I'd taken there. We had to rotate sparring partners, and in one of our last classes before graduation, my partner was much bigger than I was. Although I knew he could beat me in any fight, I was confident that we were better matched than we looked because of my speed and good form.

I started off all right. Then his fist connected with my headgear, and as lights burst around my eyes, I struggled to stay on my feet. I shot a couple of jabs his way, and he sent me back a stunning wallop to the chest that made it hard to breathe.

In the locker room after class, I took off my headgear in front of the mirror. I have to admit, boys—I'm more fragile than your average hero: My face was bruised, the redness and swelling on my temple was already starting to deepen to purple in places. I was going to have a black eye.

Our graduation ceremony was two days later. I sat beside my roommate, Peggy, who was from Wisconsin. I'd been surprised to find I liked her. Before Quantico, she'd been a contract lawyer for a corporation, and on our first night in the dorms she said she'd joined the FBI because she hated being afraid. She'd applied to the bureau to make the world a place where no one had to live in fear of nuclear war.

Because I'd scored highest in the class in academics, I'd been asked to speak at the ceremony. I remember Peggy giving my arm a squeeze of reassurance as the program director called me up to the podium. And standing there, looking out at the crowd, absolutely humiliated because my face was still a mess, I thought of my sparring partner, thought I could feel him gloating. He'd scored second highest in academics, and I'd heard that he'd asked to see some of my exam results to make sure I'd really beaten him.

Pop was there with Mr. Ali, who'd present me with my badge and credentials during that part of the ceremony. The point of the story— the thing that reminds me of the way I felt after Ross laid out his plans to use me, and how I reconciled my choice to let him—was a memory I have of my father from that day. He'd seen my face earlier, before I'd gone up onstage, and told me if I didn't want to speak I didn't have to. He said, "You don't owe them anything. You give them what you want to give them. But it's easier if they think you're one of them. It's easier to work from the inside. That's what I try to do. I've been a spy in this country for as long as I can remember."

I didn't know what side I was on. While I knew I couldn't trust Ross, I didn't know if it would benefit me to let Thomas in on their plans. But I'd get what I wanted. My meeting with Slater. And I knew too that I'd only give them what I wanted to give, once I figured it out.

I thought of Pop sitting toward the front of the amphitheater at the end of the aisle, his old Minolta up to his face. I'd decided to present my speech even though he said it wouldn't disappoint him if I didn't. We were twin spies. That thought tamped down my embarrassment. I smiled at him, cleared my throat, and began to speak.

PART THREE

15

After dinner tonight, I got you two into your pajamas, then set up a VHS tape for you, some paper and crayons. While you lounged on the floor of the living room, I sat beside Robbie on the sofa and wrote in this journal. Tommy, you sat up on your knees and turned toward me on the sofa, "Maman! Look."

You held up your picture.

"Come show me."

Standing beside me—on my foot, to be more precise; you lovingly treat me like a piece of furniture—we looked at your drawing. I pointed at one of the people. "It's beautiful! Who is this? Is it me?"

"Uh-huh."

"And who's that?"

"Uncle Robbie."

Robbie looked over from the cartoons on the screen, a smile lighting up his face.

"Will you take it? On your trip?" you asked.

"Of course."

"I want to come."

"I want you to too. But only grown-ups allowed." I kissed you on the top of your head. "It's bedtime. You too, William."

"No!" you said, even though you were half asleep.

"Yes," I said, and scooped you up from the floor.

By the time I'd finally managed to get you tucked in, and got you both water, and read a story, it was later than I'd hoped. I poked my head into Agathe's room and told her Robbie and I were headed out. I was no longer as angry with her—not because anything had changed, but because it was too tiring to stay mad. She wished me a good night. If she wanted to ask me any questions, she didn't show it.

I hid this journal in my room. Your grandmother hasn't asked me what I'm writing, and she won't. There are oceans of silence between us. I trust her not to read it, which I resent in a way because I believe it's mostly out of a lack of interest. Still, I stuck it in the very back of the drawer under some sweaters whenever I went out.

Robbie was still on the sofa. He was trying to lift the corner of his passport with his fingernail, testing its resiliency I guess. It was a fake he'd traveled to Martinique on, which Mr. Ali had grudgingly had made and dropped off for him. Mr. Ali didn't like having to supply a passport for Robbie, but I didn't care. He'd helped stitch me up. At the very least, he owed me and my associates federal-quality fake identification for the rest of my life.

"Stop messing with that," I told Robbie.

"You stay talking to me like I'm one of your kids."

"That's 'cause you stay *acting* like one."

"All right, bet," he said. But he was being sarcastic, and when he put the passport on the coffee table it was with a look to let me know he was doing it just to humor me.

I felt a little better with him around. During the day, we bickered a lot, which occupied my mind, sometimes keeping me distracted from the frightening, intrusive thoughts I had about killing that man. The nights were still bad though.

We took Agathe's old truck toward downtown Sainte-Anne, on a road that curved along the coast and passed the picturesque cemetery on the outskirts of town. The mausoleums there were white tile, as were the tombs, which were aboveground—out of necessity, I assumed, because the land was too close to the coast to be very deep.

Although it was dark, I knew the vases near each grave held vivid artificial flowers that were so uniformly distributed I believed the town was responsible for them, and that they were the tokens of a civil servant's aesthetic vision and not of collective loss. Just beyond the cemetery, several hundred feet below it was the still bay, dark, the sailboats docked there that seemed so cheerful during the day were now gray.

I thought about that cemetery a lot, mostly because I wondered if they still buried people there. If there were any practical requirements like having to be notable and from Sainte-Anne. I was neither, but thought it would be a beautiful place to be dead.

At the restaurant we sat outside on the patio, ordered a couple of beers and some food. The night was warm; it smelled like the sea and the citronella candles on each table. Robbie sipped from his bottle and waited quietly for me to start talking. I'd given him the broad strokes about that night in Connecticut, having told him that a man had broken into our house and tried to kill me. Of course he'd had follow-up questions, and I'd felt overwhelmed by having to think about all that had happened, and told him that I wanted to wait just a few more days before we talked about it. Now was that time.

"The man who came to my house was hired to do it," I began. "There's another man who thinks I wronged him."

"Why?"

"I hurt a friend of his," I said, choosing my words carefully. "He'll send someone else. Unless I go after him, my kids will never be safe. So that's what I want to do. I wanted you to come out here to ask for your help, but I understand if you can't give it. I know you've got your son to think about."

"I'll help."

"Wait a second. I want you to think about it. This man is dangerous. He's CIA."

He exhaled. "How'd you tick someone like that off?"

"I was working for them. The Company sent me to West Africa."

"The answer's still yes."

"Really?"

"Marie. Haven't I always been there for you?"

"You have," I said, and was overwhelmed with gratitude for that fact. And frustratingly I wanted to dissect it: Why would he put his life at risk for me? There was so much I lacked, so much about me that was broken and had been that way for so long that I wasn't even trying to find a fix. I didn't deserve his loyalty.

"I'll need a weapon," he said.

"I have one for you."

"You do?" he said, and I watched his eyes light up.

I'd gotten a package from Mr. Ali the day before. I hadn't opened it yet, but I knew the 9mms I'd asked him to send were inside.

Robbie and I disagreed about guns. He believed that owning one was his right as an American, which he must've picked up when the Panthers out in Oakland were arming themselves. That was screamingly funny when I thought about it: a black man, one who'd been locked up twice, clinging to the Second Amendment. The strongest gun laws the country had ever passed were to prevent the men who'd inspired him, the Oakland Panthers, from having guns. If he'd been a little more intentional about his stance, it would have been subversive. But he wasn't. He owned a gun because he liked them, and thought he was entitled to do so.

Pop raised me to believe that guns weren't for civilians. I think that stance was too soft; I think he shouldn't have taught us how to shoot. It wasn't a beneficial skill, or even a neutral one. It was knowledge that had attracted and bred the violence in my life.

Even if your uncle Robbie and I were able to do what we had to, I wasn't sure it would remove me from the cycle. But I'd remove you. Pop was under strict orders never to teach you how to shoot a gun.

I looked into his eyes. "Robbie. Thank you."

"Sure."

"No. I mean it. And I just want to say—I do see it. When you try to take care of me."

"What?" he said.

"The day you showed up you said something about trying to take care of me. I know that you try. And I appreciate it." I looked down at the table, embarrassed by my sincerity. "It's not that I can't see it. I have trouble *trusting* it." Almost everyone who made me feel that way when I was a kid left.

"But I trust you," I added. "That's what I'm trying to say."

He put his hand on mine and squeezed it. A part of me still loves Robbie, but I can't tell him that—he'd take it as an invitation. I can only confess that to you two, here in these pages. To tell anyone else how I feel about him is to blow my cover. Throughout my life, the most consistent way I've revealed who I really am is through whom I've chosen to love.

16

I woke with a start and lay still in bed for a moment as my disorientation receded. It was my third full day in Ouagadougou, and realizing where I was still excited me. As I sat up I glanced around the room in the house I'd been provided with. The décor was pleasing: a blue *kplé-kplé* mask hung from the wall, and the mosquito net dangling from the vaulted ceiling was also blue to match. The black handwoven cotton comforter was patterned with diamonds and matched the curtain fluttering over the small window.

I would finally be meeting with Daniel Slater that afternoon, and I was nervous.

After my shower I returned to the bedroom. There was a large wardrobe in the corner beside the window that I crossed to. As I was choosing the clothes I'd wear, my eyes fell on the locked case tucked in beside a pair of heels. At the last second, I'd decided to bring my service automatic with me to Ouagadougou. I had a license, a hard case for the gun, and was a federal agent—they'd tucked it in alongside the other checked baggage with no problem.

I locked the bedroom behind me and went to the kitchen—the cook, Djeneba, was there, squatting beside a range that was a couple of feet off the floor, waiting for water to boil. We were around the same age. She had a round, dimpled face, microbraids, and was wearing a plain white T-shirt and a colorful wrapper around her waist.

"Hello."

"Good morning," she answered as crisply as she always spoke to me. "Wait outside, please. I'm almost finished here with your breakfast."

I smiled. Other than when Djeneba was meeting my cordiality with instructions, she'd barely spoken to me in the time that I'd been there. But I knew she wasn't shy. Women stopped in all day to chat with her in Mooré; I'd heard her loud, distinctive laugh many times, just never when she was speaking in French with me. Her attitude didn't seem like rudeness, obsequiousness, or timidity—it seemed to reflect a sincere and complete lack of interest in me. I respected that.

I took a large bottle of water from the fridge and drank lustily from it as I strode through the living room. Whoever had furnished it had good taste—or rather, they had taste that appealed to my American sensibilities. It was a large, pleasant space with the same vaulted white ceilings that were in the bedroom; a worn Senufo bed functioned as a coffee table and as such was spread with glossy magazines. Above the sofa was a large abstract painting of a brightly colored fish on a bicycle that made me think of Gloria Steinem.

I strode out onto the covered patio, to the plastic table and three lawn chairs there. A calico cat was curled up in one of the chairs. She glanced up at me, blinking slowly. I don't think she belonged to anyone and seemed to consider the house hers, so she was as entitled a cat as any other.

I looked out at the garden, which by its very existence communicated American extravagance. It was a dry, dusty city; I'd yet to have been anyplace else in Ouaga that was quite so green. Privet bushes guarded the patio, and a group of small shrubs huddled in one corner of the shaggy lawn. There was a carissa tree, and a bougainvillea with yellow flowers in bloom on it, one so tall that its pom-pom top could be seen above the vine-covered adobe wall that enclosed the yard.

Jean, the guard, was sitting in a lawn chair on the other side of the garden, beside the black metal gate. His presence was a convention of the city—every place that was populated by the wealthy or foreign had a guard stationed by its gate. He waved and asked if I needed the bike.

"Not yet," I called back. He was balding and had a wiry build, and I guessed he was only in his forties, despite the deep lines the sun had baked into his face. Whenever we made small talk, I could tell that his patter had been specially generated for me as an American.

Djeneba appeared on the porch with a heavy tray, which she set down on the table before going back into the house. Breakfast was a baguette, a homemade croissant, half a papaya on a blue ceramic plate. A French press was filled with dark, rich-looking coffee.

I ate quickly. Went back into the house to get a second bottle of water, then descended the patio steps and crossed toward the green motorcycle waiting in the shade of the bougainvillea. It was a Yamaha XS1 according to the brand plate, one with a rusted flank, but it had quickly revealed itself as a powerful, reliable machine. I loved it. When Jean noticed me approaching the bike, he jogged over to it and quickly wiped it down with a dry rag. Then he put it in neutral, pushed it through the gate and out into the street.

I looked around as I kick-started the engine. My temporary neighborhood, Zone du Bois, was a suburb in the south of Ouagadougou, and everything about it suggested relative wealth. The lots were large, the roads were paved, and while most of the houses there were hidden behind walls, the ones I could glimpse were much bigger than they were in other neighborhoods.

Between the houses, neem trees and plump bushes waved almost imperceptibly in what passed for a breeze. People persisted in telling me that the neighborhood was one of the coolest, temperature-wise, in the city, because of the nearby reservoir and park, but I'd only been in the direct sun for a few minutes and I already felt brutalized by the heat.

It was embarrassing how poorly equipped for it I was. On my first day there, I'd tried to go for a walk, but had only managed to get a few blocks before feeling like I might pass out.

It wasn't that I was surprised it was hot in equatorial Africa—your mother wasn't a complete fool—it was the *nature* of the heat. It was heat you could feel crawling around in your organs, trying to squeeze them to a stop.

The engine roared awake, and I started toward Haven for Women. Although the NGO was in walking distance of the house, I thought it best to take the motorcycle. I sped across the red-dust-covered Avenue de la Croix Rouge, which featured one of the rare street signs in the neighborhood, a nefariously subtle blue plaque. I'd later learn from my first trip to Paris that the style was a French import. There was a mechanic's garage on the corner, and a young man was already out front in a sleeveless US Army shirt pressing a homemade barbell—a pole that he'd made two disks for out of concrete. He waved at me as I passed. I was conspicuously foreign in Ouaga, but people didn't guess I was American until they heard my accent. Until they heard me speak, they assumed my father was French.

I rode through Zogona, the neighborhood adjacent to my own. On the day I'd gone for my one and only walk, I'd gotten as far as Zogona before having to turn back. A second example of the obviousness of my foreignness: As I'd passed a group of children playing in the street, they'd all stopped at the sight of me. Then one little girl—a tiny, self-appointed dignitary—had detached herself from the group, come over, stiffly shook my hand, and said *bonjour* before returning to the game.

The sky was bright and full of clouds. I rode along a commercial stretch in Zogona, where there were several kiosks set up in the street. I passed a woman who was leaning into the open window of one, wearing a wrapper, a T-shirt, and a scarf on her head. At the level of her waist was a shelf crowded with bottles of what I thought might be cooking oil. I couldn't tell you what the shop sold though; portions of the oil if I had to guess. I note this to point out precisely how lost I was when it came to commercial interactions in Ouagadougou. My ability to buy things, or in some cases, to even recognize a building as a place

of commerce, was a surprisingly accurate indicator of the overwhelming Americanness that made it difficult for me to navigate this new
place.

As I rode I thought of Thomas. I was looking forward to seeing him
again, in the flesh, for reasons that were personal as much as professional. It was hard not to think of him in Ouaga: His face was a common sight in the newspaper, silk-screened on T-shirts, and on billboards.
My favorite was the enormous one facing the airport to welcome visitors: Bienvenue au Burkina Faso, tombeau de l'impérialisme! *Welcome
to Burkina Faso, the tomb of imperialism!* It featured a photograph of
Thomas, and in a cutout in the center of the billboard was a Coke logo.

I turned onto a red dirt street busy with pedestrians, bicyclists, people on mopeds. Up ahead was an intersection with a tower of four or
five tires in the center, presumably to indicate that it was a two-way
street, and on that corner stood a man in front of a corrugated tin kiosk,
listening to a radio and flipping meat with tongs on a sizzling grill. I
turned right there, as I'd been instructed to do when I called HDF the
day before, and found myself on yet another residential street.

The map I'd looked at before I'd left hadn't indicated that the street
I was on would narrow like it did as it came to its end. I had to cross
over a weathered piece of plywood laid over the sewer to get out into
the wide intersection—I watched the woman on the moped ahead of
me do it, but I pulled up short at the last second, afraid that the weight
of my XS1 would land me in the sewer. A man and his young son were
laying the foundation for a house nearby. I felt them both watching
with amusement as I made a graceless ten-point turn.

I passed the man at the grill again and turned up the next street, in-
correctly assuming that it ran parallel to the one I'd been told to take to
HDF. It ran diagonal. Frustrated, I took the first road it intersected
with, and was on it for a while before realizing it wasn't going to take
me anywhere close to where I needed to be.

My panic was starting to rise. It had rained the night before, and
there wasn't any drainage on the dirt roads, so some puddles were quite
deep. I rode down an incline, going slowly to avoid them, then came

around a bend. A camel was there, tied up and sitting in the shade of a tree. They are bizarre-looking creatures if you aren't used to them, and I found the thing so surprising that I took my eyes off the road for just enough time to speed right into a deep puddle.

I cursed as I backed out of it and pulled over near the camel. My dress clothes were splattered with mud. I noticed a couple of teenagers sitting on a low wall on the other side of the street; they'd stopped chatting and were watching me. I reached into the small saddlebag attached to my motorcycle, took out the bottle of water and a map. As I was trying to make sense of it, I was startled by a voice talking into a megaphone and looked up for the source. A truck flew past and through the puddle, sending mud up into the air and more onto me. I wanted to scream. Despite my cynicism, I must've had an idealized vision of West Africa in my head—in it travel wasn't nearly so frustrating.

A man was standing in the truck bed, littering leaflets behind the vehicle. A second was shouting into a megaphone in French: "Support fair elections or suffer under Blaise Compaoré, the schizophrenic despot! Blaise Compaoré, the shadow manipulator!"

The man repeated the slogans in two other languages: Mooré, I assumed, and maybe Jula, before the truck was out of earshot. I quickly picked up one of the leaflets, which was stamped with *Democratic Defenders*. At the top was a drawing of Compaoré with his lips pushed into a grotesque kiss. I skimmed the page:

Chronic schizophrenia is characterized by:

- Neurotic sex drive.
- Phantasms in the subject's consciousness that cause him to seek to live his dream life detached from external realities. Which explains why Blaise believes himself able to sleep with all the beautiful women of Burkina and in the Ivory Coast when he visits his father-in-law, the president, Papa Houphouët. Without fair elections, the shadow leader will force us toward the brink of destruction.

Believing the flyers to be an indication of the serious dissent facing the CNR, I folded the leaflet into my pocket to look at later, then turned back to the map Ross had given me. It wasn't remotely accurate, and I gave up on it after a minute or two. Worried and annoyed and already tired from the heat, I crossed the street to the teenagers and asked for directions. All three greeted the request with silence and blank stares. I wondered for a moment if it was because they couldn't understand me, but then one of the boys hopped down off the wall. He said something to his friends that made them laugh. I thought he was making fun of me, which was irritating. Any fondness I had for the city was quickly waning.

Still, the boy threw a leg over his moped and gestured for me to follow him. He started in the opposite direction of the one I'd been planning on from the map, then turned sharply into some foliage. There was a narrow road hidden there. As I rode behind him, I thought of the afternoon in New York I'd spent with Thomas, the way he'd been surprised when we were in the park and those kids on bikes had whizzed around us. He'd sounded embarrassed when he'd said he'd been unable to pick out the bikes from the ambient city noise, and now with a teenager practically leading me through Ouaga by the hand, I thought I understood why. It is humbling to have your social fluency, your sense of yourself as a competent, independent person, upended by a foreign city.

The boy led me through a network of streets to the mouth of the one I was looking for, nodded, and went on his way. I glanced down it. Walls visually dominated the architecture, some of them mud brick, others concrete. Because there were no kiosks here, the effect was of severe uniformity. I rode down the street and pulled up beside a gray 4x4, parked in front of Haven for Women. To distinguish it from the other homes, someone had painted its black metal gate with a woman on a rearing horse grasping a spear.

I shut the engine off, and although I was late, sat for a moment with my eyes closed, trying to mentally prepare myself for the meeting. It was quiet; all I could hear was the buzz of the slack power lines above my head. I was worried about the mud, what a bad first impression I was about to make, but took a breath, got off the ticking bike, and passed through the gate.

I was standing in a red dirt courtyard with what looked like an open-air dining area in one corner and a few buildings laid out in a half circle in front of me. The ones to my immediate left were an outhouse and—I assumed because it was the largest building—the dormitory. Two older women were sitting together on the ground of its shaded porch, and a third was resting, curled up on her side, with her eyes closed. The dining area was on the far right; all it amounted to were a few benches haphazardly sitting beneath a blue tarp and a fire pit, where a woman was squatting to cook. I went toward the center building, thinking it might be the office, and stuck my head through the doorway. "Bonjour."

A woman sitting at a plastic table looked up from her work and greeted me. She was in her early twenties, had dark, smooth skin and long box braids up in a high bun. She was wearing a white collared shirt and a white midi skirt—the color suited her complexion well, and the outfit was miraculously crisp considering the heat and red dust in the air.

Her appearance made me freshly embarrassed of my own. I'd spent a lot of time choosing my outfit that morning, wanting to be appropriate and inoffensive. According to the guidebook I'd read, women weren't supposed to show much of their legs. Because of that, and because I knew I'd be taking the motorcycle, I'd opted for gray wide-legged pants. I'd paired them with a white silk collared shirt and an oversized belt. I was also wearing my favorite sunglasses, which were large and literally rose-colored. Despite the care I'd taken, I looked as messy as she did neat.

As I got closer she noticed the state of my clothing. "Oh my god! What happened?"

"The bridge was out," I said. "I went another way and got lost."

"It was out? But I went over it this morning."

"Someone had put something temporary there. Some plywood."

She was confused. "Yeah, the bridge."

She spoke French in a way that's tricky for me to re-create on paper, peppered with English, elongating her words that reminded me of the cadence of a Valley girl, but didn't imply (for me anyway) the usual American materialism and vapidity. Plus, what she said was filtered through a culture as divorced from Southern California as it was possible to be. The result was beguiling. And slightly jarring.

It was clear from the way she spoke that she consumed a lot of American movies and music. I would later hear the word *disquette* used to describe a particular type of Burkinabè girl—one who was as thin as a floppy disk, because that was what appealed to the French men they hoped to marry. One who wore chic, Western clothes, spoke fluent French and maybe even a little English. She could easily have been dismissed as a disquette. But it was a lazy characterization of any woman, and I would come to realize that was especially so in the case of Nicole Ouédraogo.

She was beautiful; the only aspect of her appearance that might've been called an imperfection was the broken front tooth that revealed itself when she smiled.

She handed me some tissues and laughed gently as she quickly helped me with the mud stains; her amusement was good-natured and made me feel better. She said, "It's a cute outfit though."

I looked around the single-room office, which was sweltering despite the industrial fan working in the corner. On the table there were a few bottles of water and some stacks of paper. On the far wall was an open door that led to a backyard.

Nicole followed my gaze. She said, "His office is out back. You want some water before you meet him?"

"Please." I thanked her as she handed me a bottle. "I can't get used to this heat."

"He totally used to say the same thing."

"What's he like?" I asked as she led me out into a small backyard where there was a second outhouse and a small hut. I'd been a little worried about seeing Daniel Slater again. A lot of time had passed, and I was guessing he'd become a cynical Thomas Fowler type.

"Oh my god, so nice. You'll love him."

She knocked on the hut's door, and a voice from inside called for us to come in. She turned and said she'd see me later.

I opened the door. The office was dim and cool, air-conditioning running at full blast. There were cartons of cigarettes stacked on the desk as well as several bottles of Scotch. In the far corner was a handbill press. International news poured from the radio. Daniel Slater was sitting behind the plastic desk with a phone receiver up to his ear; he was wearing jeans, a dress shirt, and wraparound sunglasses on his head. He had a new belly pushing against his shirt and a heavier jowl than I remembered. His hair was flecked with gray and thin at the temples.

When he finally put the phone down he smiled at me and said in English, "I'd forgotten how much you look like your sister."

17

He introduced himself with an alias then turned off the radio and said, "She was always late. You can't be though, not while we're working together."

"I won't," I said, feeling taken off guard. I mumbled an apology for the delay and my appearance; he dismissed my concerns with a gesture.

"Late. All the time. It was the one thing about Helene that drove me nuts."

His eyes were as piercing as I'd remembered. I was glad that he spoke in English. I liked to speak in French because it had an element of nostalgia to it—I was reminded of whispering through the wall to my sister. But I felt foreign to myself in Ouaga, which was so different from New York. I was glad for any opportunity I could get to cling to the familiar.

"Sit. Let me walk you through your next few days here." He looked at his watch. "We only have a few minutes; one of my agents will be here soon. Did you meet Nicole?"

"Yes."

"She was a secretary at the embassy, until I offered her this job. Stole her away. Efficient little thing. She handles everything related to HDF, all the charity stuff. She's great. Without her, we wouldn't be able to focus on our real work."

"Can I ask a question? I know we're in a rush."

"Go ahead."

"Is it unusual for you to be working out of an NGO?"

"A little. But this one's administered by the US embassy, which means that as the director here I'm considered an embassy employee."

"Meaning?"

"I still qualify for diplomatic immunity. I can explain later when we have more time. For now, let's talk first steps of SQLR. The palace is hosting a national conference on the environment tomorrow afternoon. A number of politicians will be attending. I want you to use the opportunity to reconnect with Thomas."

"You call him Thomas?" I asked.

"Everyone does," he said brusquely. That seemed true so far. I saw him referred to by his first name or TomSank in the newspapers, and couldn't tell if it was because of the informality of the CNR or the smallness of the ruling class in the city—many people working in the government, at the embassy, and for the newspapers knew him personally.

"Charm him. Set the groundwork for an invitation back to the house, but don't ask yet. Make him think he's asking you. How do you like it, by the way?"

"What?" I said.

"The house. I stayed there too when I first arrived. Thought it would be a better place to be able to head back to than a hotel."

"Oh. Yeah."

He put his hand on the radio. "I want you to take this. It's a camera. The antenna's a spring motor; if you push it down it takes a picture every few seconds."

He unplugged it, took off the faceplate and showed me where the viewfinder was, then unscrewed the back and told me how to change the film. I nodded, delighted by the novelty of the gadget.

"Set it up in your bedroom before he shows up. I have a journalist on my payroll who'll write the story and help distribute the pictures. We're trying to erode his support. Proving that Thomas is a hypocrite will help do so with all but the most loyal in his base."

The phone rang then, interrupting him. He picked it up, spoke angrily in a mix of Mooré and French, then slammed it down.

"Excuse me a moment," he said. I watched him dial another number, but no one answered. He hung up with a heavy sigh and stood. "I have to go."

He handed over the radio to me.

"What's happening?" I asked.

"There's an emergency with one of the projects I'm overseeing. I have to head out of the city for a little bit now to check on things. Can you do me a favor? I know running errands for me is not strictly what you came out here for, but—"

"Yeah, sure. I can help."

"Did Ross tell you about the ULCR?" Before I could answer, he continued: "It's a political party, and our strongest challenge to the single-party government that Thomas has created. It's led by one of our agents. Once we can set up elections here, he'll be our candidate. We think we can make him president. There's a ULCR meeting happening in twenty minutes, at an agent's house. He was supposed to have been here already to pick up these pamphlets. I just called—I couldn't get in touch with him. Can you bring them over?"

"Like this?" I said, referring to the mud on my clothes.

"Don't worry about it. The agent's name is Issa. Give them to him or his brother, Amid. Only to one of them."

He wrote down directions to the house, then picked up the pamphlets lying on the handbill press and handed them to me. They were stamped with Democratic Defenders in the corner, just as the flyer I'd seen in the street had been.

"I saw a truck distributing these earlier."

"That's us," he said. "My operation targets Thomas Sankara and the leaders of the major political parties who are trying to emerge. Even our candidate in the ULCR. By publishing attacks on everyone, it looks like no one in the government can trust anyone. Creating that perception is much more important than whatever rumor we're spreading about their sex lives. Any questions?"

"No. I just wanted to say . . . I remember seeing you at the funeral. Why didn't we talk more then?"

He softened for the first time. "Oh. I know that was a hard day for y'all. I couldn't intrude."

"I don't know if I thanked you for the pictures you gave me. But I still have them."

"Good," he said. "I'm glad you're out here, Marie."

"Me too," I said as I followed him out to the backyard. "And I don't want to let you down."

We walked through the main office together, where Nicole was working at her desk. She smiled up at us as we passed.

He got into the 4x4 that I was parked beside. From the driver's seat he said, "Do you mind doing one more thing for me? When you go to the palace tomorrow. It's easy."

"Sure."

"One of my cutouts will give you a package for me," he said, referring to the intermediary between the agent (meaning the spy, asset, or snitch) and the officer. "Bring it back here after the meeting at the palace. And you can tell me what Thomas was like. Help me gauge what the next steps of SQLR should be."

"You don't know already?"

He shook his head. "Not my style to keep everything totally structured. I like to play some things by ear."

"How will I find your cutout?"

"He'll find you," he said as he started up the engine. "See you tomorrow."

I watched him peel off, then went to my motorcycle. I felt like I had to take a moment to catch my breath. It had been such a disorienting, whirlwind of a meeting. Nothing like what I'd expected.

I tried to fit the radio in the saddlebag, but it was so long that half of it jutted out of the top. I rode toward the address Slater had given me. I smelled the smoke in the air well before I arrived.

The street was blocked off by an ancient red fire truck with its own water tank. Several firemen in green military uniforms idled nearby. I left my bike where it was, squeezed around the truck, and started down the street.

There were puddles in the road. A fireman stepped out through a set of open gates and I went through them. It was a compound-style home—a side of one of the buildings there was black, apparently having been licked at by flame. Another was completely destroyed.

A man was sitting in a lawn chair in the yard, with his head in his hands. I asked, "Are you Issa?"

When he didn't answer or look up, I cleared my throat and repeated the question. He looked up, dazed, and nodded.

"I think these are for you," I said, and pushed the pamphlets into his lap.

The next day, as I rounded a bend on my motorcycle, I got my first glimpse of the presidential palace, which came into view above a line of palm trees. It was a surprisingly accessible building in the heart of the city, standing behind a simple green gate with only one guardhouse. It wasn't a large building. It consisted of three attached sand-colored columns, the one in the center the tallest, a perfect rectangle with slats carved into its face instead of windows. A Burkinabè flag flapped on the roof. Modest, egalitarian—the building was a reflection of Thomas's governing style.

I pictured him at work inside, Sam Kinda standing guard at the door with a clutch of other uniformed bodyguards. I showed identification (false, of course) to a baby-faced soldier in fatigues who checked my name against a list on a clipboard. Instead of lifting the barrier he ducked briefly into the guardhouse and handed me a large padded envelope. I realized he was Slater's cutout. I slipped the envelope into my purse next to a few of the photos I had of Helene, which I'd brought with me in anticipation of my meeting later with Slater. I then rode onto the grounds, parked, and was directed upstairs to a conference room on the second floor.

It was a close, hot room, ripe with body odor. A dozen or so people, mostly men, were already sitting in the small audience. As I took a plastic chair at the back near the exit, I looked around. Thomas wasn't there.

The first speaker stood at the front of the room. He started his speech: "Imperialism is the arsonist setting fire to our forest and savannas. . . ."

As he droned on, I looked around, bored and disappointed. I only had a week and a half before I headed back to New York.

When the speaker finished he was met with light applause. A second presenter went to the front of the room. He began, "While the effects of our environment's destruction will be felt by everyone, it will be much more lethal, by orders of magnitude, for our world's poorest. . . ."

I glanced at the exit, trying to gauge the best way to make my escape. Thomas was there, leaning in the doorway, listening attentively. He was dressed casually in black pants and a striped shirt and was wearing his pearl-handled pistol in a holster. I looked at him until he turned toward me.

He didn't acknowledge me in any way, but he'd clearly recognized me, and after a few minutes disappeared back into the hall. I got up and pushed my way through the crowded room toward the exit. By the time I got out to the hall, Thomas wasn't there—it was empty except for a soldier in a fatigue uniform standing guard at one end. But he couldn't have gone far. I moved down the hallway methodically trying doors. When I opened the last one, I found Thomas standing in a small room, his back to me as he looked out at the courtyard. He must've been waiting for me. I said his name as I went toward him.

"The American." He turned to me. "I thought that was you."

I'd buried my desire in the lead-up to this trip, but once he was standing in front of me again, it plucked at my belly. His pull on me was even more intense than it had been when we'd first met.

"Why'd you leave the desertification conference?" he asked. The corners of his mouth twitched up as he added, "Do you find the topic too dry?"

"Thomas." I rolled my eyes at the silliness of the joke but was charmed by it. I could tell he was pleased with himself.

Although only a couple of months had passed, there were signs of exhaustion in his face that I thought must be new, not just blotted out by the polite censorship of memory.

Then he said, his question surprisingly harsh, "What are you doing here?"

"I'm working on a project for the embassy," I stammered. "I'll be here for a few weeks."

His tone had made me aware of my mistake. I'd thought I would be able to play my appearance in Ouagadougou as a coincidence, but I'd been so worried about being recognized as a spy and a honeypot, it hadn't occurred to me that he might think my appearance in the city was crazy. That I was stalking him.

"I'm here for *work*," I emphasized. "My office sent me because I was your liaison at the UN."

Although he didn't look like he believed me, I felt that desire larger now, and thrumming between us. I stepped closer to him.

"You should go back to the forum," he said. "Aren't you worried you'll miss something important?"

"Not really."

"I need to get back to work." He stayed where he was.

I'd never felt an attraction like that to anyone before. It was undeniably intense. He felt it too, I could tell. I touched the buttons on the front of his tunic, then slid my hand to the warm back of his neck. His eyes closed for just an instant before he took my hand in his and gently removed it. He said the name I'd given him. We stood where we were.

After a few more moments, I spoke. "If you need to go back to work I'm not stopping you from leaving."

He nodded and stepped around me. I watched him open the door and slip out into the hall.

18

I went immediately to HDF, and as I approached Slater's office I heard raised voices. I knocked on the door and went inside. Issa was there, with a second man who must've been his brother.

"Should I come back?"

"No. We're going now," Amid said.

"I'll take care of the situation," Slater promised as they left.

"Issa was telling me about the fire." For just an instant I saw reckless fury in his face, then it was gone just as quickly as it had appeared.

"Do you have a lot of agents?"

He nodded. "They're everywhere you can think of: in the CNR, the trade unions, the student unions, the university, a cutout at the palace, and another at our embassy. The one I had at the Soviet embassy disappeared."

"Dead?" I sat.

He shook his head. "I think he's hiding."

I took this information in. I appreciated that Slater was less cagey with me than Ross, who'd never answered any of my questions so directly.

"I have your package," I said, and put the envelope on Slater's desk.

"Did you look inside?"

"It's none of my business," I said, even though I'd peeked at it of course—it contained a spiral notebook.

"Good answer." He took it out of the envelope. "Do you know what this is?"

When I told him he shook his head.

"It's a copy camera. I had an agent at the palace using it to take picture documents."

He tucked it into one of his drawers.

"Tell me about Thomas," he said. "Did you get him alone?"

Ross had asked the same strange question. "For a few minutes, yes."

"Did you?" He sounded surprised. "No bodyguards around?"

"Yes."

"That's good. Very good."

"Are you sure I shouldn't invite him for dinner?"

He shook his head. "He's going to invite himself. I promise."

"Okay," I said, but it was clear I didn't believe it.

"I promise. He'll come because he's exhausted. All you need to do is be around. You'll have a second opportunity. There'll be an election in two days at the university, and Thomas will be there. They'll be voting for the new head of the university's Committee for the Defense of the Revolution, and one of Thomas's nephews was the incumbent. Vincent Traoré."

"I met him in New York," I said.

"Oh yes. That's right. The election has the added benefit of giving you a sense of the work the station office has done to undermine the CNR. Traoré won't win because the members of the committee understand that he's a Sankara proxy. Six months ago that would've guaranteed him victory."

"So my assignment is just to attend."

"We're getting you close to him. We're getting him used to you."

I nodded, accepting this. And because he'd answered my question about his agents, I thought he might be receptive to another. "I know you are involved in propaganda. With the Democratic Defenders. What else do you do exactly?"

"*Exactly?* I can't tell you. But I will say that I'm in charge of about a dozen operations out here. I work hard. Too hard. Our goal could be accomplished in one shot, with SQLR. Which is why I asked for approval to bring you out here. I have a lot of faith in you."

"Thanks."

"You're a Mitchell, right? You girls never give up."

I took that as an opportunity to take the photos from my purse. "I didn't get to talk to Helene as much I would've liked when she was in North Carolina."

"Where'd you get these?"

"They were at my dad's house."

"Huh." He looked at a picture. "Oh, this is a good one. I took it."

I pointed to the man holding the beer. "Who is that?"

"Ray. He's a friend of mine."

"Did you meet Helene through him?"

"No. I sought her out because she was in intelligence and I'd heard she might have some information I needed."

"So you met her at Fort Bragg."

He nodded. "She was working in a little office, and the second I saw her—even in that fluorescent light, even in her uniform—it was love at first sight. She was so beautiful. I felt like I had to have her."

"Did she help you?"

He smiled. "No. I even took her out for a drink to get her to lower her guard, but she knew what I was trying and wasn't having it. She wouldn't tell me a thing."

"That sounds about right," I said.

He nodded. "Yeah, well. It was sensitive information. I guess I was asking her to bend some rules."

I shook my head, feeling overwhelmed. Even now, I feel hard-pressed to explain why the anecdote meant so much to me. Sure, I could call up someone like Robbie to talk about old times with Helene. But this was totally different—this was new information from the time when she'd been closed to me. He knew things about her that I didn't. The more of it I could get, I thought, the closer I could get to the truth about what had happened.

On the day of the CDR election, I was up early, confident and determined to succeed. The bulk of the past two days had been taken up with a few more little tasks like the ones Slater assigned me on my first day. Nothing particularly big or interesting, just small errands that I'm sure ate up a lot of his time. As I crossed the yard, my guard, Jean, made his usual show of wiping the motorcycle down with a rag, then pushed the heavy bike out into the street for me. I thanked him; I'd adjusted to having a staff disconcertingly quickly.

Ouagadougou was scattered with ghoulish signs begging the population to wear helmets, but the only person I saw with one was a Frenchman who told me he'd brought it from home. I told Jean about this and—once I'd made it clear that the request wasn't a joke—he managed to scare one up for me.

I put on the helmet, which hid my face entirely if the plastic visor was down. I kept it flipped up, because it was so yellowed with age and the assault of red dust that it would have obscured my vision, but even so it changed my whole appearance. Although it was hot, I wore it because I was so conspicuously American in Ouaga—or at least so conspicuously foreign—and the helmet made me feel like I was in disguise, even if practically speaking it probably called more attention to me.

I got on the bike. It was quiet as usual on my street, the only activity being an old man clearing away brush and pruning neems, throwing the limbs into a wooden cart yoked to a patient donkey. I started up the engine, shattering that peace.

The university wasn't very far from the house. I passed Thomas's face on a nearby billboard, rounded a dump site scattered with chickens pecking at the debris, crossed a wide street, and sped onto a dirt lane where a ten-foot pile of every imaginable auto-body part sat in front of a garage: engines and doors, truck panels, even a giant bright yellow piece that I guessed was a school bus hood. A mechanic in orange flip-flops was standing beside it, his arms crossed as he laughed with another man.

I wasn't often happy in Ouaga and was frequently sick—early on in my trip I had a run-in with a bit of lettuce from which I never fully recovered—but I did find it beautiful. I've never been anywhere before or since that had the capacity to surprise me with its sights like that city did.

I passed an empty guard booth and rode onto campus. The road was smooth and lined with trees. Groups of students walked on the side, most of them young men who were conservatively dressed in collared shirts and slacks.

That Committee election was an important one because the university was a seat of political activity and power. So much so that a few months earlier, students protesting the trade union ban had clashed with police on campus and the result was an abrupt school closing that had thrown the academic calendar out of whack. It had since reopened, and classes resumed, but some programs of study were permanently out of sync.

Following Slater's instructions, I rode over a short footbridge, turned off the road and onto a dirt embankment that ran alongside a narrow, dried-out canal. After a short time I came to a slope and parked my bike beside a few mopeds at the bottom of it. At the top of the slope was a rare sight—a copse of tall leafy trees and ample shade. I started up.

A handful of chalkboards were peppered beneath the trees. There was writing on some of them, math equations mostly, and low benches in front of each board—the space must've served as an outdoor class-room. About a dozen students were waiting there for the election to start. A man broke away from a group of students and approached me. Because the university was a locus for political activity and the professors were paid notoriously poorly, Slater had recruited several of them as agents. He'd asked one to attend the election with me—he was a professor and also a member of the CDR.

I was glad Slater had sent his agent, who was only a few years older than I was and had a pleasant face for a snitch. I was the only woman in the crowd and would've been far more conspicuous alone. We returned to the group where he introduced me and said I was an American who worked for the UN, there to observe the election. One of the candidates, Jonas Somé, was standing in the group. He was short and had a heavy brow.

The agent asked Somé if he felt confident. He smiled and said he did, as his friends chimed in with assurances. Somé explained his position to me: He supported the ULCR and believed that the country should adopt a multiparty system. He believed the CDR was weak because of its current leadership; if he was elected, he would do his best to once more make the group a strong political force.

As a pair of young men began setting up a table and a box for the votes to be cast in, I heard the sound of motors; a new group had arrived at the bottom of the slope. I'd hoped it was Thomas. Instead, three young men came toward us, Vincent Traoré among them.

I left Somé and approached Vincent. He was wearing a starched pink shirt tucked into blue pants and looked nervous. He remembered me from New York and spoke to me in English, asking me niceties about my family; it seemed like he wanted to keep his mind off the election. He had far fewer friends in the crowd than Somé—only two young men came over and joined us.

Suddenly Thomas appeared at the top of the hill, just a few paces away, Sam Kinda and a second uniformed soldier with him. He was dressed casually and just as handsome as usual. An excited pulse went through the crowd—I think that Slater's agent, Vincent, and I were the only ones who'd had any indication that he might show up.

Vincent and the young men who were standing with us began to clap and cheer, and the rest of the crowd soon joined in. I was just as excited as everyone else, experiencing that same sea swell under my heart that I had when I'd first shook his hand, the personal physical connection. And there was the second kind of excitement too, although it had waned some from the day I saw him speak at Harriet Tubman school, the charismatic draw that a large crowd intensified.

Thomas came over to us. He greeted everyone, then wished Vincent good luck. Up close, his trademark vigor looked like it had been wrung out of him—he seemed as exhausted as he had at the palace. Vincent left our group to circulate in the crowd, as Somé was doing, leaving me alone with Thomas and his guards. I brushed off the nervousness I felt and said, "I hope he wins."

Thomas smiled at me. His glance landed on the copper bangles on my wrist, which I'd deliberately put on that morning. I said, "The bartender read that Frederick Forsyth book you recommended. He still asks about you, you know. And whenever I go to the lounge, he tells that story about you playing guitar. I swear you get better at it every time." I looked around. "It seems like you're too busy for music these days."

"That's true," he agreed solemnly. He told Sam and his other bodyguard to give us some privacy, which they did grudgingly, but didn't go far. I could feel both of them watching as I spoke to Thomas.

"You look exhausted," I said.

"That's kind of you."

"Was that sarcasm?"

He smiled again. "I am tired. We're still getting things done, but I have to push a lot harder these days."

"Even you need to rest though."

He nodded. "How do you like Ouaga so far?"

"I love it," I said, telling a genial lie.

"Where are you staying?"

"In Zone du Bois. The American embassy owns a house there."

"I know the place. I'll come by one day soon."

I hid my surprise about the fact that Slater was right. He'd invited himself. "If you want to. We can talk about Harlem. Or music. Or books. Anything, really, except politics."

I looked into his face. His eyes were beautiful: His pupils were large despite the light, the ring of his irises warm brown.

"That sounds nice." Then he did something that was hard to decipher: He called a young man over, greeted him, and asked, "Comrade, why do you wear that shirt?"

The young man looked down at the emblem on his white T-shirt. Thomas continued: "It's free advertising for Converse. I always say it: We grow cotton here. We can make clothing here. We can be self-sufficient." He glanced at me sharply. "We can be successful despite the intervention of foreign powers."

At first I was a little relieved, if I'm honest, a strange way for a spy to react to being made. But the alternative—Thomas believing that I was a lunatic who had traveled across the world because I was obsessed with him—was much harder on my pride. I still believed that he would come to the house though, which made me wonder about his motivations.

He turned back to me and seemed about to say something, but was interrupted by one of the students at the table, who declared the voting open. As students got in line to vote, Thomas went toward a low bench and climbed up on it to address the larger group. "I came here to thank you for being good comrades. Participating in democracy is the only way it will function. I'd like to say a few words before you cast your votes. I want to remind you that everyone who talks about the fight against corruption isn't necessarily innocent. There are those who pretend to be revolutionary to participate in the committee, but their goal is to undermine your power. They talk loud because they are afraid of you. They call this committee useless and ineffective; they say that to devalue the regime and its leaders. They are doing everything to ensure that you don't act. So you must act."

He stepped down off the bench to notably light applause— apparently not very many of the young men in the crowd had liked what he'd had to say. The mood seemed to support what Slater had told me: Thomas was losing support in certain quarters. Ironically, I was feeling more convinced by him than ever.

Thomas, Sam, and the third presidential guard started toward the slope to leave. As they passed, Thomas glanced at me. His exhaustion, which had seemed to dissipate while he spoke, was back. I gave him a supportive smile and he nodded, then Sam ushered him down the hill.

I joined the agent and stood to the side as the students cast their ballots. Vincent and Somé lingered as well, even standing together and chatting for a little bit. I wasn't obligated to stay so long, but did because I was more interested in the election than I had been in the conference. I'd never seen democracy practiced that way before; the only thing that was similar to what I was used to was the partisan scrabbling that had dominated it.

The whole process took hours, but eventually, after a long period of deliberation, one of the students at the table declared Jonas Somé the winner. His supporters burst into cheers; someone in the crowd called for a recount. Vincent shook his head at the idea, and as a signal of concession he went over to shake Somé's hand.

19

I rode back to the house and took a quick shower to cool down. There was a guesthouse owned by a Frenchman nearby that I planned to walk over to for dinner. Like all cities, Ouagadougou was segregated by class, and I stuck to the handful of places where the wealthy hung out, which were always crawling with foreigners. I had no anxiety about that as I would've at home. After just a few days, my idealized vision of Africa had given way to the realities of Ouaga: I'd accepted that there were streets I wouldn't ride my motorcycle on because they were too chaotic. Restaurants—and this was most of them—I didn't want to eat in because there was neither running water nor real toilets in their bathrooms. Every day I spent in Burkina Faso was a reminder of how American I was.

And although I found it difficult to be there, I thought it was good for me too, because it took me out of my usual context. There was the language, the new culture, the fact that in the United States I thought of myself as black before I thought of myself as American. In Ouagadougou, routinely, those designations were reversed: People saw me as American first. *The* American. I can't say I preferred it that way, but it gave me a new perspective.

I pulled my gate closed behind me. As I approached the guesthouse, a hand on the small of my back startled me, and I turned to find Slater beaming at me. We didn't have plans together; he was just there, apparently having been waiting for me. I chased away the paranoid thought that he'd set me up at that house to bug it or to keep tabs on me through one of the employees.

"What happened today?" he asked.

"You were right. He invited himself to the house. I expect him to visit me within the next few days."

"Told you so. Excellent work. Do you know when?"

"No."

He shrugged. "Par for the course. Expect him at a weird time. It'll be whenever it fits into his schedule."

"What are you doing here?" I asked, trying not to sound as put off by it as I felt.

"I thought we should get dinner. Talk about more personal things if you want. And we can celebrate your success."

I nodded. "I'd like that."

There was a whitewashed wall built around the guesthouse, which was stenciled with a heron-like bird and the name of the place in green: Bénou Lodge. A guard sitting on a wooden bench beside the gate stood as we approached and opened it for us.

Wooden patio tables scattered the grass at the center of the garden, which served as an open-air dining room. We sat at one of the tables, and I looked toward the waiter, who was showing a couple a chalkboard menu. The only other patron was a Chinese businessman at the bar, who was holding a hand-rolled cigarette. His tie was loose, and his face was red from alcohol flush.

"I've been busy too," he said.

"I bet. Did you find out who set the fire?"

"Not yet, but I have a few theories. I have a Soviet counterpart here, and his agents are ruthless when it comes to sabotage. I'm sure one of them did it, but which one is hard to say."

"I'm glad no one was killed."

He shrugged, which was a strangely noncommittal response.

The waiter approached with the chalkboard menu and rested it in a vacant chair. We ordered drinks.

"What did you think of the election?" he asked.

"We won," I said. "And it was interesting to watch."

"Yeah. Too bad Thomas imported the idea from Cuba without learning any of the lessons from the Cuban model that he should've."

"Such as?"

"Most of the CDR leaders in Cuba have been corrupted by the power. They keep files on their neighbors, and depend on colleagues and friends to rat each other out. You can't give young people—or inexperienced people—power like that. In some towns here in Burkina, now, the CDRs have become flat-out vigilante groups. Thomas is a dictator, and CDRs, in practice, just wind up reinforcing that."

The waiter returned with wine for me and Scotch for him. He tapped his glass to mine. "To you. To your success with your mission."

He took a sip and said of the Scotch: "It's hard to get this brand here, so I have cases of the stuff at home. I hand them out to important men."

I nodded.

"Helene liked this brand."

"Really? I can't imagine her drinking Scotch."

"I turned her on to it." A smile burst onto his face. "I'd forgotten how much you remind me of her. You laugh like her and your gestures—that thing you just did, rubbing your chin like she did. You know, she talked about you all the time."

"Really?"

He nodded. "She always said how much like her you were."

I wasn't as insistent as he was that we *were* alike—not just looked alike. But I liked thinking of her saying that, even if I didn't know if I believed it was true. "Well, she raised me."

"She was something else, your sister. Most of the time I felt like I understood her perfectly. But every once in a while I saw a glimpse of something that made me feel like there was part of her that I couldn't see, that she was hiding from me."

"I felt that way sometimes too," I said, even though I heard something different in his words than what I'd felt. The way he'd said it was like he believed there was some malice there. That she was hiding on purpose.

"Yeah? I'm glad to hear it. Makes me feel a little better."

The waiter put down our entrées and Slater ordered another round of drinks for us. Once we were alone he asked, "Did you know that your sister wanted to start her own intelligence agency?"

"Yeah," I said. "She wanted me to be part of it."

"Me too. While she was on the post, I was in North Carolina helping her gather contacts. And money."

"Really?" That was a wonderful shock. What he'd said supported the fantasy I'd been maintaining.

"Yeah. But after she died I lost my nerve. I only came back to the idea recently. After I talked about it with Ross. He agreed it's a good idea. He thinks we can create a modern-thinking, nimbler firm."

I thought back to what Ross had been saying at the Lenox. He'd used the exact same phrase. Now it made more sense. "The kind of firm that's *crucial*. And I'll tell you why. How much do you know about the Battle of Kolwezi?"

"Only a little," I said, which was true.

"It was mostly Zaire's and Belgium's fight, but France was also involved. So were a couple of Americans from the 82nd Airborne. Like me. I was chosen for tactical airlift support because I spoke French."

He explained with an ironic smile that his team was "beating back the Communists." He told me that rebels had captured Kolwezi, hoping to establish it as a people's republic loyal to the Soviet Union. They took three thousand hostages and eventually began killing them. He said, "It was terrible, but the opposition didn't have much moral high ground. The president, Mobutu Sese Seko, ordered his soldiers to pa-

rade the bodies of the Europeans massacred by the rebels in the streets
to prompt the French and Belgians into action. All that bothered me."

I'd thought he meant the casual desecration of human life, but Slater
explained that the fact that the battle had even happened was what
bothered him. Because the Soviets had started buying up all the cobalt
on the free market, he thought that anyone who was paying attention
should've known something was about to affect a major source of it.
And he thought the rebels should've been stopped before they ever got
to Kolwezi because they'd come through Zambia from Angola.

"The United States has one of the most complicated intelligence
networks on the planet," he said. "But somehow four thousand rebels
crossed two international borders on *bicycles* without anybody picking
up on it. If I was in charge, things would never have gone that far."

"You sound confident," I limited myself to saying. This was the
Cold War he was talking about. It was so complicated and the stakes
were so high that humanity had been brought to the brink of nuclear
war. But Slater believed that had he been able to insert himself into the
early planning stages of something that became an international conflict, that conflict would have been avoided. I thought of something
Helene had said a long time ago, about CIA officers thinking they were
all tactical geniuses. I wondered if this streak of his had ever bothered
her.

"My experience in Kolwezi is why I joined the Company. If France's
intelligence agencies had been better informed, we could've avoided
the whole mess. I thought that by working with the CIA, I could end
battles before they started, but it's not agile enough. So Ross and I are
forming our own private military company," he said. "Security Solu-
tions International. SSI's won a few military contracts, enough money
to start the firm in earnest. We've got two projects we're working on
here."

"What are they?"

"You'll see."

Wanting to know more, I tried a different approach. "Was there a
tactical reason that you chose this country to start in?"

He shook his head. "We started here because I was already assigned to this station office."

"So you launched your firm when Ross was still in the field. Did he ever come up here from Ghana?"

"Of course. It would've been impossible to organize things otherwise."

I realized that Ross had said he'd never been to Burkina, which meant he'd lied to my face. And although I prided myself on my ability to detect deceit, I hadn't picked up on it.

The waiter cleared our plates and started toward the kitchen. I glanced across the table at Slater.

"I'm leaving the Company," he blurted suddenly.

I nodded, not wanting to commit to any reaction to the news.

"But they're not threatened by SSI. They're happy because we have the same goal. It'll be a big help to them that we can creatively stop problems before they escalate into something too large for either organization to control."

I thought about this, and realized I didn't believe it. What he'd said about the Company not being agile enough made it sound like he was unhappy with them, so I doubted he was leaving on good terms. I was sure the Company viewed him as a threat. I asked him suddenly, "Is SQLR something you came up with through SSI? Is that one of your projects?"

He looked surprised. "What makes you think that?"

"If the CIA knows you're leaving, I doubt they'd give you permission to bring someone new out here." They would have no reason to grant him any concessions, particularly if his departure was making them unhappy, which it sounded like it was. I said, "I haven't been working for the CIA at all, have I?"

He let out a nervous giggle and hunched into himself in a mannerism that was surprising on a former soldier of the 82nd. "Ross warned me that it would be hard to hide things from you. Not technically, no."

I was annoyed to learn this, but mostly at myself for not paying attention well enough to have figured it out earlier.

"The Company would never think to hire you," he said. "Or use you like we plan to."

"Was that a job offer?"

"Yes, SQLR is a test run. To see if you like the way we work and to see if the way you work suits us. It has so far and I hope it continues to. I think Helene would've wanted you to join us. And I owe her memory a lot, more than I could ever explain."

I didn't know if it would be a good fit for me, but I had no problem pretending I thought it was. "Would I have to live here in Ouaga full-time?"

"No. We'll be overseeing projects all over the continent. You'd be able to keep New York as your home base and fly out to where we are whenever we need you."

"If my experience so far means anything I'd be happy to join SSI," I said, lying to keep my options open. My suspension from the FBI had felt like the last straw—I was considering resigning, but wasn't entirely sure what I wanted.

He was pleased. "Good. That way I can look out for you, which I think your sister would've appreciated. And I bet she would've been happy to see us working together."

He ordered another round of drinks for us and paid the check. He was three Scotches in and it was starting to show in his body and gestures. He said, "There's something else I need to tell you. Just to clear the air. I don't want there to be any secrets between us. Helene and I were married. When we were driving back from California we stopped in Vegas and did it there."

I stared at him, too astonished to respond, my mind reeling. I couldn't believe it. She'd been married and hadn't told me. Hadn't invited me. He studied my face for a moment, trying to read it. "Are you all right?"

"I would've liked to have been there," I said as expressionlessly as I could.

"We were going to have a reception in New York. But then the accident happened . . ."

I stood. "I have to go."

"I hope this doesn't change anything between us. Or your feelings about the job."

"No. It's just a lot for me to think about."

I left the guest house, headed back to Zone du Bois, with my mind turning over the news he'd given me. The way he'd delivered it had taken my breath away, but I wanted to forgive him for that. He'd married my sister, whom he'd loved powerfully, and she'd died a couple of hours later. I didn't know how someone copes with something like that.

20

I spent the next afternoon at the house in Zone du Bois waiting to hear from Thomas. I had lunch out on the patio, where I liked to eat my meals while listening to the radio or reading the newspaper. Jean was, as usual, sitting in a plastic chair by the gate, near the motorcycle. I looked up to see him letting a young man into the yard, where he began cutting the grass with a machete. It made me nervous to watch him work—I was afraid he'd lop off a finger in service to the greenery at the American house.

There was an announcement on the radio: The CNR had imposed compulsory physical education events and Thomas was attending one being held in Ouaga.

As I listened to the hollow *thock* of the machete hacking against leaves and branches, I imagined him at the event, the center of attention—the star—surrounded by admirers, shaking hands, smiling, exhausted, and terribly lonely.

The phone rang, but of course it wasn't him. It was Slater. "I hope you're not still upset about that news I gave you."

"I wasn't upset. Just surprised."

"Really?" he said.

"Really," I lied.

"Good. Listen, I assume you haven't heard from Thomas."

"Not yet."

"I want you to do something for me."

"What if he shows up here while I'm out?"

"He won't. I promise. Not in the middle of the afternoon."

"What do you need?"

"There's a dead-drop location near the market close to the house. I want you to pick up the film that's in it and bring it to me at the embassy."

I agreed and hung up. I was excited about the assignment, in the sense that it was something proactive to do, which beat waiting around. The market was only a ten-minute walk from where I was, but I took the motorcycle. I'd been there once already to exchange money, because an Algerian there had a better rate for a cheaper commission than the Société Générale. It was one of the many markets in Ouaga, and I can't say that I ever visited one I liked. I've never enjoyed crowds or haggling, and the alternative, overpaying, wasn't exactly a thrill either. The dead-drop location was on a desolate stretch of road about a hundred feet past the mosque with green trim that stood at the market's northwest corner.

My heart was pumping fast as I approached it. I looked around, and once I was sure no one was watching, retrieved the metal spike stuck in the ground and quickly grabbed the film.

As I headed back, I thought of Helene and me in our Soviet café. The temperature was wrong but the heart-pumping thrill of the mission was what I'd always imagined. As I was cutting through the market, I was suddenly aware that I was being followed; when I turned to look I saw a young soldier a few paces behind me. I walked faster. He did too.

The muezzin's droning call started. Vendors started to leave their stalls, headed toward the mosque, and in so doing, created a bottleneck

at the top of the street. I felt trapped. Someone tapped my shoulder, and
thinking it was the soldier, I tensed. Although the dead-drop location
was already some distance away, I was worried that he was following
me because he'd seen me retrieving the spike. I turned. I saw that the
soldier was still a few paces back, also caught in the crush of bodies.
The person who wanted my attention was a man in wraparound shades.
He asked if I was French.

"American," I told him.

"You'll like this." He pushed a flyer into my hand. On it, there was
a caricature of Thomas—his head was bandaged and he was wearing a
straitjacket—and there was a Democratic Defenders emblem in the
bottom corner. I imagined Slater in his office, cranking out flyers at his
handbill press.

> Every weekend Sankara sends emissaries to every corner of
> the country, and God help the chief whose hallway or staircase
> the President of Faso deems excessively noisy. This confirms the
> findings of two French doctors: Sankara is mentally deranged.
> That also explains why both his domestic and foreign policy are
> totally incoherent and dramatic failures at all levels. Fellow citi-
> zens, we are being governed by an individual who is already in
> an advanced stage of madness!

I looked up from the flyer to the sound of overlapping voices mount-
ing into an argument. There was a second man in the market handing
out the same flyers, and he and one of the vendors were shouting at
each other. The vendor tore the flyer into pieces.

He shouted in a mix of French and Mooré, and I managed to gather
that he was calling the flyers foreign-produced garbage. He wasn't the
first person I'd heard suggest that the Democratic Defenders flyers
were propaganda produced outside of the country. People seemed to
suspect the Ivory Coast though, not the United States. Ironically, the
flyers that criticized Blaise's relationship to Houphouët, Ivory Coast's
president and Chantal Compaoré's father, were the ones that made

people most suspicious of their involvement—the flyers were thought to be a false flag.

Several of the men who'd been on their way to the mosque intervened in the argument. They tried to calm the vendor down.

"The president is a dictator!" one of the Democratic Defenders yelled as they left the market. "And you're all reactionaries! Pay attention! The PF is a dictator! He came for the striking teachers and the trade unionists. Next it'll be you!"

The American embassy was way on the other side of town, in a suburb in the north of the city. As I rode, the soldier was a steady presence in my mirror. I was rattled. Had Thomas sent him, wanting to know what I was up to before he came to the house? The neighborhood was like my own, wealthy and isolated, the building a low, adobe-colored box lousy with gleaming windows. I stopped and showed the guard posted at the boom gate the embassy identification Ross had given me. I turned to watch the soldier continue straight past the embassy. The guard let me through with a smile.

I parked and crossed through the lot in the shadow of an indecorously large American flag. A marine was exiting the embassy as I reached the steps; he held the door open for me. I remembered that there was a marine attachment on the grounds—after the bombing in Beirut all of the American embassies were getting them.

I took off my sunglasses and looked around the reception area. The artificial cool and the English spoken by the employees lent it the insular feel of an American satellite. The walls were cornmeal colored, and one featured a large mural of a welcoming woman wearing a head wrap and holding out a bowl of fruit.

Slater was already there, flirting with a secretary wearing her hair in a cornrow bun, bright red lipstick, and a striped blazer. He had on a gray suit, which the secretary complimented; he thanked her, took her hand in his, and asked: "Awa, darling. Any mail for me back there?"

"*Eh!* Do you think I would not tell you?"

It was interesting to watch him with her—to me the charm he was using was obviously manufactured. It was mesmerizing to be able to see through it and also to see it work. Had Helene really found this man compelling? A doubt cropped up that I pushed away; she was a better judge of character than I was.

Releasing the woman's hand, Slater gestured to me, and I followed him down a brightly sunlit hall lined on one side with courtyard-facing windows and on the other with office doors. I held out the film to him. "Hang on to it. I'll show you where the darkroom is. You know how to develop film, right?"

"Yes."

Another marine appeared from one of the doors—apparently the embassy was crawling with them. Slater clapped him on the back in greeting.

"We missed you at movie night," the marine said.

"Next time," Slater said. He introduced me, and the marine said with a nod, "It's a pleasure, ma'am." He continued on.

"I saw a soldier in the market. I think he was following me."

"I doubt it," he said.

"You're probably right," I said with a nod, even though I was annoyed that he'd dismissed me.

"Welcome to the show," he said as I followed him into the political section. The room was small but held a half-dozen large gray filing cabinets, so overly full that they gave the impression of being on the verge of comic explosion. There were two doors with frosted glass that must've led to internal offices and a telex machine standing against the far wall beneath several shelves lined with black binders. A cardboard-backed photo of Reagan was taped on one of them.

An unremarkable mustachioed man in his fifties was talking to a clerk who was sitting at one of the desks in the center of the room, taking papers out of a tiered letter tray.

"That's the station chief," Slater said. "He knows we're old friends, in case you're wondering."

I nodded. That seemed a little strong—*friends*—but I was willing to go with it. Slater approached, greeted his boss warmly, and introduced me. He also introduced the clerk and explained that he worked for the State Department. The two men nodded at me, but the interaction was a tense one.

"Where's Dave?" Slater asked, seemingly oblivious. "Out lighting fires under his agents again?" He let out that strange giggle of his. I wasn't sure what he meant, but he was making a joke that made me think of the arson at the ULCR meeting. I wondered if it had been set out of revenge for something someone at the station office had done.

"What are you doing here?" the station chief said, his tone undeniably hostile. The cold reception we were getting forced me to rethink something Slater had told me: He said he'd chosen to work at HDF. Now I wondered if he'd been banished there. That made just as much sense to me as what he'd said.

"I still have a right to use the facilities here," he said.

As we went toward the back office, I felt the station chief's eyes following us. Slater opened a door and flipped on the red light inside. We were in a small darkroom. There was a table with developing trays on it, a string for drying photos, and a sink in the corner. It smelled overpoweringly like photo chemicals. Slater closed the door behind us, forcing us close together.

"I've given the Company ten years of loyal service. They should be happy for me." I guess he must've forgotten that he'd told me they were.

I looked up at him in the red light. He'd closed his eyes and had his fingertips to his temples, was breathing in and out heavily.

"This is the best the Company can do: a messy office with a dusty little bureaucrat in charge. This is why our government needs more private firms."

"He might be able to hear you."

"So what!" he roared. "Sorry, sorry," he said with shake of his head and that giggle. "Can you develop film?"

Although I'd already told him so, I didn't want to upset him more and was quick to nod again. "Black and white. I had some training during my class on investigative photography at Quantico and took an art class in college. I might be a little rusty though."

His anger had seemed murderous and then it was totally gone—his changeability caused my stomach to clench. I'd taken a step back, feeling frightened. I wondered if he'd ever made my sister feel that way.

"Good. Next time you'll come here alone. I shouldn't have to deal with any hostility. Instructions," he said as he tapped them on the wall.

"Hey," I said. "Are you embarrassed?"

He didn't answer.

"You don't have to be," I added. "Not in front of me."

He stared at me as if *I* were the unbalanced one, the one who'd been swinging so wildly between intense emotional states. Then he burst into a grin.

"Just like your sister. Right from the beginning it felt like she could see me so clearly." He spoke slowly, carefully measuring his words. "No one had ever made me feel that way before. Never thought I'd feel that way again."

He was beaming, the menace that had been in his face before totally gone. He reached out as if to touch me on the cheek, but thought better of it. He looked at the clock on the wall. "I have to go. Bring those pictures to HDF when you're done. I might not be there. Just leave them on my desk."

After he left I started to relax. He made me tense, which was a realization that I pushed away so I could focus on developing the film. As I hung the photos up to dry, clipping them on the line with clothespins, I saw that they were all of internal government documents: a memo indicating that a meeting to reunify the CNR had gone poorly, a handwritten note from Thomas asking that a member of his cabinet visit a chief in Tenkodogo who'd been accused of corruption. When Slater had said he had agents everywhere he wasn't exaggerating: Whoever this source was, they must've been very high up in the government.

One of the notes was about electoral reform and the different candidates who were anticipated to run in each party. I was stunned when I read the name of the ULCR candidate. It was Blaise Compaoré. I couldn't believe it. Thomas's closest friend was collaborating with the CIA to betray him.

I left the embassy parking lot and was on the road toward downtown when I noticed the soldier behind me again—he was obvious because the street was otherwise almost empty. How had he found me? I followed the major boulevard that led into the heart of the city, commuters on scooters and bicycles speeding along beside me in the outer lane, went through a roundabout with a statue of Yennenga on her rearing horse in its center (she was a legendary warrior princess, the mother of the Mossi empires, so her image was ubiquitous), and into downtown Ouagadougou. As I idled in traffic, vendors crisscrossed the street selling bagged limes and small electronic gadgets.

There my defensive driving training kicked in, and I made a sharp turn against the light and stopped in front of a café that lay between a dirt access road and the busy two-way boulevard. Unable to make the same maneuver, the soldier kept going. He hadn't been very good at tailing me, so I thought I was supposed to know he was there. Maybe it was a threat. I pushed the XS1 along the access road, rolling over a Democratic Defenders flyer in the dirt, then parked it beside a tree with a weathered foosball table chained there to attract the neighborhood kids. The café was essentially a giant table with a square cut out from the center. It stood beneath a canvas roof and had a few tall metal stools bellied up against it. I sat and looked out at the boulevard, which was strung with one-room ateliers belonging to men selling potted plants, using sewing machines, building cabinets.

A waiter, who looked like he was ten or so, was kneeling on one of the stools, rubbing the tabletop with a rag. I asked him for a bottle of water, and when he didn't understand, I pantomimed drinking from a glass. He went under the bar to the fridge there and put a bottle of Coke on the counter in front of me. I took it.

I'd never thought of myself as having much of a sweet tooth—it was through feeling like I was going through withdrawal in Ouagadou-gou that I discovered I was completely addicted to sugar. I walked around desperate for it, practically shaking, and celebrated when I stumbled upon a *boulangerie* within walking distance of the house, only to be devastated when I found that the closest thing they had to cookies were tiny bready wafers that I found inedible.

A man came toward the café with a radio in hand. He went under the bar, popped up in the gap, put the radio down beside the micro-fridge, and introduced himself as Asalfo. He was an energetic man in his late twenties with a round face and small pointy ears, who it turned out owned the place. He seemed very happy to chat with me during the morning lull. After hearing me speak he asked if I was American. I nodded and said I was from New York.

"I have a cousin there. He lives in the Bronx."

I nodded again and looked toward the street, keeping an eye out for the soldier. A group of boys appeared, and two began to play a game of foosball; the waiter went over to watch. Asalfo pointed to the radio and told me that it had been broken for a while, but he'd finally gotten it fixed for the anniversary of the Political Orientation Speech. Thomas had given the orientation speech a few months after the CNR came to power, and because it had outlined the guiding philosophy for the revo-lution, it had taken on symbolic importance.

Fiddling with the radio dial, Asalfo found the station he was looking for and turned it up to full volume. A reporter explained that he was broadcasting live from Tenkodogo—a town a few hours north of Ouagadougou—and that Thomas would soon speak. Asalfo called for the young waiter to return to the bar. He told me that he wanted to make sure the boy, his cousin, heard Thomas's speech.

The voice on the radio introduced Jonas Somé: He was speaking not only in his capacity as the leader of the university's CDR, but as the president of the National Student Union. I listened to him praise the country's Committees for the Defense of the Revolution for putting political power back into the hands of common people. He added, "I believe we should establish a more advanced political organization in the country, our multiparty system; we don't simply have to imitate a foreign system of revolution. That's what the CNR does now. That's why their revolution is built on evil spirits and unhealthiness!"

Asalfo began to boo the radio. "He's calling the PF a stooge for the Soviets! Do you see, Ms. America! These are tricky, poisonous people! Somé is a reactionary, which is why the ULCR supports him. The party is full of selfish, corrupt men who are threatened by a real revolutionary."

Somé finished his speech and was greeted with some light applause. When Thomas's voice came on the air, Asalfo snapped his fingers and hissed to the boys playing foosball, presumably telling them to be quiet. As I listened to Thomas I felt that same sensation, now familiar, of something opening up, that I had when I'd first heard his voice at the UN.

Today we celebrate the fourth anniversary of our guide to revolutionary action and ideology—the Political Orientation Speech. It's the collective achievement of the Burkinabè, of all who are a conscious part of making the democratic and popular revolution. Our revolution is not a public speaking tournament. Our revolution is not a battle of fine phrases. Our revolution is, and should continue to be, the collective effort of revolutionaries to transform reality, to improve the concrete situation of the masses of our country. Our revolution will be worthwhile only if, in looking back, in looking around, in looking ahead, we can say that the Burkinabè are, thanks to the revolution, a little happier. Happier because they have clean water to drink, because they have abundant, sufficient food, because they're in excellent health, because they have education, because they have decent housing, because they are better dressed, because they have the right to leisure, because they have enjoyed more freedom, more democracy, more dignity. Our revolution will have a reason to exist only if it can respond concretely to these questions.

When he finished his speech, Asalfo applauded the radio and the boy joined him. Once more, it was impossible to ignore the effect of sitting with people who saw in Thomas a capacity for a brighter future. I felt buoyed by his words, and felt myself turning toward him and his revolution.

"Homeland or death!" Asalfo shouted.

"We will win!" the boy responded in thickly accented French. "Homeland or death!"

"We will win!"

"The PF is a great man!" Asalfo was smiling at me, his eyes shining. "Do they know that in your country, Ms. America?"

He obviously wanted me to say yes, so I did as military music began to pour out of the radio. I picked up my helmet and pushed the guilt away. I started up my bike, and headed toward HDF.

21

When I showed up, I found Nicole sitting on the dormitory steps with one of the women who lived at the shelter. In the dining area I could see the cooks squatting near the metal pots resting on a grate above the fire pit. One of them was stirring a pot. The women often had *bouillie de mil,* a type of porridge.

Nicole waved at me and I waved back as I started in the direction of Slater's office.

"He's not here," she called after me.

"I know," I said. I went to his office and put the photos on his desk as he'd asked—even though I thought that was a wildly insecure way to deal with sensitive intel—and returned to the front yard. As I was leaving, Nicole called to me. She said, "I'm glad you're here. I want to talk to you."

"Can it wait?" I wanted to get back to the house. Although I knew Thomas was in Tenkodogo—which was four hours away—I was still worried about missing a phone call from him.

"No. I wanna know: Are you, like, in love with Daniel?" she said, but instead of calling him by his real name, she used his alias.

I laughed because of the sheer unexpectedness of the question. "No. We're colleagues."

From where I was standing I could see into the dorm. It looked like just one large room with a bunch of mattresses on the floor. It seemed clean, but also horribly cramped and dark.

"You can be honest. He already told me the truth." She narrowed her eyes. "I don't care. Really. I mean I care, but not for my sake."

"Nicole. I have to get back to the house."

The woman next to her said something in Mooré that made Nicole smile. She said, "This is Fatimata. She says hello. She's only got here yesterday, which is why I'm hanging out with her."

"Tell her I said it's nice to meet her."

Nicole did so, then turned back to me. "I want her to know she's totally welcome here. Even though we didn't really have the room I couldn't turn her away. She made such a difficult journey. And, like, imagine having to leave your house 'cause your neighbors think you're a witch."

Fatimata spoke again quickly. She was clearly upset, and Nicole translated her response into French: "She said her cousin accused her because she made him angry. So, like, Fatimata told his wife that he'd secretly married another woman. Which was true! But he managed to turn the whole village against her. They ran her off."

I gave Nicole my full attention, resigning myself to the fact that I was being held hostage in the conversation.

"It's crazy. All he had to say is that her eyes are red." She shook her head. "But she's an old lady, and she's spent her whole life cooking over a fire, with smoke and everything getting into them. Of course her eyes are red. Her cousin is a bully. I wish I knew this man." Fury flashed across her face.

One of the cooks started to clang the dinner bell. Nicole and Fatimata stood as women emerged from the dorm. As they went down the stairs, most of them warmly greeted Nicole. I watched as women crossed toward the blue tarp.

"All of these women are, like, grandma age, you see that? Maybe their husbands died. Their children are gone. For some reason they were left vulnerable in their village, and some family member decided to take advantage of it. I'd bet a million dollars that Fatimata's cousin is living in her house now. And I just think: What if that was my grandma, you know? It kills me. I work hard for these women. And if someone were to take Daniel away from this place, they'd ruin everything I've tried to build here. And that person would really piss me off."

She looked solemnly into my face. I wouldn't have said I was afraid of her, but she was suddenly more menacing than I thought she was capable of being. She looked toward Fatimata and brightened. Then they both went down the steps and started in the direction of the dining area.

I returned to an empty house—Djeneba must've gone to the market. I wondered sometimes about the fate of the people who'd stayed in the house before I had, the operations they might've been involved in.

I crossed the tiny white tiles of the living room floor toward the sofa-styled bench, sat, and went back to waiting for Thomas to call.

I picked up one of the magazines from the coffee table and flipped through it. The cat found me there and curled up next to my thigh. Then Djeneba returned with several bags full of grain, oranges, and a wriggling straw bag that I assumed contained a chicken. She greeted me perfunctorily as she headed to the kitchen. I went to the bedroom. The radio camera was exactly where I'd left it. After dinner, I listened to the news on the radio for a few hours and went to bed early.

A loud noise woke me up sharply at four thirty. It was heavy banging on the gate, presumably to wake up the night guard. His watch was from 6 P.M. to 6 A.M., but after a certain point in the evening he was only guarding the inside of his eyelids.

I got out of bed. Quickly pulling on clothes, I left the room for the

patio. The night guard was having a hushed conversation with someone at the gate. Then footsteps crossed the pitch-black yard. Three men
came up onto the porch: the night guard, Sam, and Thomas. The guard
looked perplexed and excited. I greeted them, but Sam pushed past me
into the living room without a word. He searched the room. He went to
an open cabinet and quickly pawed through it, then held up the Mont-
blanc my father had given me when I'd graduated from college. I
watched him pull the top off and examine it.

"What is this?"

"What do you think it is?" I said testily. "It's a pen."

"Did you think it was a poison dart, Sam?" Thomas asked as he
came into the living room. "You watch too many movies."

The room clear, Thomas dismissed Sam and the night guard. We
were alone.

"Did I wake you?"

"The sun's not up yet."

"I've been up for hours."

"Well, we can't all be like you."

"Do you know what your problem is? You've internalized the lazy
conventionalism of the petite bourgeoisie."

He'd meant it to be funny—he was making fun of himself as much
as he was making fun of me—so I laughed. But it was clear he was in a
strange mood. I stood closer to him and saw the violently dark circles
under his eyes. He seemed a little manic as his gaze darted around the
room. When he finally spoke, he asked, "Have you been to Bangr
Weogo yet?"

"Not yet." He was talking about a nearby park, the *bois* that gave
Zone du Bois its name.

"We're going there now for a bike ride. Morning exercise is one of
the few pleasures I have left."

I watched him move through the living room, still examining it.
"I've been here before," he added. That didn't surprise me. From what
I'd gathered, the embassy used it for visitors or as temporary housing

for new employees. He could easily have gone there to visit any one of them.

"I'm glad you're here now." I sat on the sofa.

"I had the impulse to see you." There was something defeated in his voice and his posture. "I know what you are, and I know I can't trust you. But I can't trust anyone. At least you're beautiful. And we have a good time together."

"What am I?" he said.

"Relief, maybe. But Sam is here."

I wasn't sure what he meant. He approached the sofa. Sat beside me with a yawn—it seemed he'd spent all of his manic energy. I glanced at him in profile: His earnestness had been surprising and sad and flattering. I put a pillow in my lap and patted it as an invitation. He smiled a little before putting his head against it. I ran my fingers in his soft hair and touched his cheek. We were fully clothed but it was intimate—I'd never seen such a powerful, energetic man in such a quiet moment. I closed my eyes too. In the silence between us the overhead fan worked loudly. I listened to it and to the quiet night and the steadiness of his breath. The cat appeared from the kitchen, jumped up, and flopped beside my thigh on the cushion. I scratched her roughly between the shoulder blades.

He rested silently for a few minutes before I spoke. "I saw your friend yesterday."

"Who do you mean?"

"The soldier you sent to follow me." I wasn't sure that was true. I was testing a theory.

He lifted his head and looked me in the eye. "I would never waste government resources like that."

I believed him. "You look tired. Do you want to rest in my bed?"

He agreed and I took his hand. He followed me to my room, where I clicked the radio and sat beside him on the bed.

When I leaned forward to kiss him he pulled back slightly. "You know I know what you are," he said softly.

"I don't know any such thing."

He leaned over to kiss me on the cheek, then whispered in my ear. "What's your agenda here?"

"I'm working on a project for the embassy."

He kissed my cheek softly again and repeated the question.

I laughed lightly. Not mockingly, but because it was unexpected. "You're trying to charm information out of me."

"Do you have information to give?"

"I do."

"And what's that?" He kissed my neck.

"The United States believes that suppressing political parties is dangerous. You can't create real democracy in such a situation."

"Do you have allies in the country?"

"No."

"Who in my government works for yours?"

"No one."

He kissed me. He was gentle at first, contained, but in the press of his body, I could feel the strength of it humming off him.

"Who in my government works for yours?" he repeated.

"No one," I said again, lying as I looked deep into his eyes. The memo from Compaoré flashed through my mind. I felt complicit in his betrayal—I knew his closest friend was working with us to rob him of the presidency.

His entire demeanor changed, and he stood abruptly. "You don't understand this place, but you think you know what's right for it. Democracy isn't a thing that you conform a society to. We can't just import a system from the West. Real democracy has to develop in response to the needs of that society."

"Thomas." He was already at the door, but turned to me. "Have fun on your bike ride," I said.

He opened the door. Sam was there, apparently having come back in from the garden. They left the house together.

22

I ate the breakfast Djeneba made for me then went to take a shower. I was in a good mood, humming beneath the spray of water as I planned my day: I'd bring the film to HDF. I imagined Slater congratulating me—surely my photos would be incriminating enough to use in whatever propaganda operation they were planning.

I wrapped myself in a towel and crossed the living room to my bedroom. When I opened the door I found Slater there. He was lying on the bed, lazily batting the knotted mosquito net.

"I was hoping you'd still be asleep," he said. "You snore. You're not a beautiful sleeper, which I like. That's how Helene was too."

"Good morning," I said. Obviously, I was terrified but I refused to show it.

"I heard Thomas was here," he said as he sat up. He'd removed the film from the radio and was now holding it up.

"We're kissing. That should be good enough for your journalist to use."

"Journalist. What are you talking about?" He paused to think for a moment before he said: "Oh yeah, that's right. You think this is about blackmail."

A maniacal smile leaped onto his face, and he got to his feet.

"You know what my big problem is?"

"No." Yes: He was out of his mind. I was still in a towel, and considering how anxious I was about him being there, it was a real struggle not to show it.

"I need to learn to trust. Everyone says that. The analyst they sent me to after I came back from Kolwezi. Ed. It's true. I need to learn to trust. So I think it's time to tell you everything."

"All right."

"You know SQLR is one of our projects. I want to show you the other."

"All right," I said again.

"All right," he mimicked.

"Do you mean now?"

"Of course."

"Can I get changed first?" I gestured toward the door.

"Oh, sorry," he said as he left. "I'll be in the car."

As I dressed quickly, I considered going out the window. I'd have to climb over the wall into the neighbor's yard. I settled for bringing the gun; for the first time since I'd been in Ouaga, I pulled it out of the hard case and tucked it into a holster that I strapped on under my blouse.

I went out into the street and found him wearing shades in the driver's seat of his 4x4. I climbed up into it, examining the idling vehicle's interior. There was a tiny Burkinabè flag on the dash, and red dust ground into the grooves of the black window crank and every other nook into which it could possibly be ground.

I'm still in the habit of running my finger along the underside of the seat before I start up my car or your grandmother's truck. The behavior is residual paranoia from working with the division's tech squad at the bureau. They'd install listening devices in a suspect's car, home, or business that I'd later analyze at the field office. It's a minor compulsion, like going back to the door to try the knob, even though I know

I've locked it, or checking and rechecking the seatbelts on your car seats. If there were any bugs hiding, they would require at least a screwdriver to uncover them.

It was unlikely the CNR would spend money to bug Slater's vehicle, but other foreign agencies were active in the country. Our allies of course—the French—but there was also a Soviet embassy that hosted as a station office for its own intelligence officers. But I didn't know who I was most suspicious of: Slater or a Soviet agent.

"How far are we going?" I asked as we drove through Zogona.

"It's just a few miles outside of the city." When we stopped at a light, I considered jumping out of the car, but dismissed doing so as hysterical overreaction. And where would I go if I did? I looked out and saw a daisy chain of boys on horseback at the side of the road. They were in earshot, but I didn't call for help, although I considered it until the very last one, who was barefoot and sitting tall on a square of yellowed Styrofoam, disappeared from view.

We left the city limits and stopped at a *péage,* a tollbooth. Two soldiers were there, and we waited for a while as they decided how much they were going to charge us. My eyes wandered to white graffiti on the walls of a municipal building: THE PF IS SCHIZOPHRENIC! Three more soldiers were sitting in the back of a truck parked in front of the building, laughing and joking. I didn't think I could ask any of them for help either—for all I knew they were Slater's agents.

We continued. After a little while Slater spoke. "Since you got here, I've been thinking about Helene nonstop. You remind me so much of her." He reached out and put his hand on my knee as he drove. I suppressed the desire to jerk away.

"I want you to know that I did what I could. When we were on our road trip. In Vegas, I mean."

Was he saying he'd been in the car when Helene had been in her accident? I felt like the wind had been knocked out of me. I didn't respond, afraid that if he learned he was telling me something I didn't know he'd stop talking.

"Say something," he demanded. "You're always so quiet."

"So after she got back from Long Binh, you met her in California."

"Yeah. I drove that old brown car she had out there."

"Chocolate Chip."

"Yes." He smiled. "We wanted to get married in Vegas; it was this really crazy, spur-of-the-moment thing. I remember we were in Arizona and it was so hot . . . I thought she was fooling around," he said. "The steering was wandering. Like this." He jerked the wheel so that the 4x4 swerved on the road and I nearly screamed. I looked away from him, out the window at the passing savanna.

"We were nearly to the motel when we just swerved off the road and hit, uh, this rock formation, I guess is what you'd call it. We weren't even going that fast, but she wasn't wearing a seatbelt. Worn ball joints," he said. "That's what they told me caused it. It really messed me up. If I'd been driving, maybe it wouldn't have happened. Or maybe . . ."

He'd seen her die. I hadn't realized that. Maybe he could've done something differently. Maybe he could've prevented it. We were crawling up an incline. I looked ahead and saw the glimmering dome of a Quonset hut. We crested the hill, rode past a yellow truck and a large roll of metal fencing, around the hut where several soldiers were at work.

On the other side of it were two small buildings that were under construction: One was complete, while only the foundations had been poured on the other. Slater got out of the car.

"Coming?" he asked, seemingly oblivious to the effect what he'd just said had on me.

"I need a minute," I said.

I waited until he was safely inside one of the buildings before I started to weep. I cried until I was empty, did my best to compose myself, then climbed out of the car.

As I walked toward the building, I heard a humming generator. A soldier was standing in the corner of the sweltering room; his Kalashnikov leaned against the wall beside him. I realized he was the same one who'd been following me.

"You said you didn't think anyone had been tailing me," I said to Slater.

"Oh," he said, barely acknowledging that I'd caught him in a lie. "Yeah, I asked him to follow you. For safety."

"Whose?"

"What do you mean? Yours."

He was standing at a minifridge and I went toward him, picking my way through the construction materials there, including the disassembled parts for several bunk beds and a couple of mattresses and—I was startled by what I saw in the corner.

They'd built a jail. A man was inside, curled on the floor, facing away from us. Blood stained the back of his collared shirt.

"Welcome to our first SSI construction," he said.

"Who is that?" I stared at the prisoner.

"Oh, good news," he said as he looked through some boxes in a corner. "We found out who set that fire during the ULCR meeting. Just like I said, he's an agent for the KGB."

"He's dead," I said.

"I don't think so. Not yet. The KGB knows where to find me if they want him back. So if he does die it's their fault, not mine. They paid him to start that fire. And one of my agents has dropped off the face of the Earth; I'm starting to think they're behind it now. An eye for an eye."

I felt nauseated. These were people, not pieces to move around on a chessboard. Slater had made me culpable in whatever he was going to do to that man—I couldn't help him. And he'd made Helene culpable. I thought of the time in North Carolina—*they're gonna get us even if they don't want us.* SSI was the vision she'd laid out for me there. I'd been focused on her ambition and her talent. But in practice, what she'd wanted, now with these men in charge, was ugly. "Ah. Here it is." He removed a small package from the fridge and pushed it into my hands. "Unwrap it."

I did. There was a syringe inside and a small vial of clear liquid.

"Marie, *you're* SQLR. You're what will help set SSI apart. I didn't want to lie to you about it, and Ross explained that we weren't. Not really. He told me that you came up with the idea that this was a blackmail job yourself. He said we were just letting you believe that, that it was easier to let *you* come up with the reason that you're out here. You'd always believe yourself over us. He's very smart." He squinted his eyes and tapped his temples with both hands. "Has a very tactical mind. And he's right: You convinced yourself that we'd brought you all this way for something as simple as a smear campaign."

That was all disorienting to hear. It made me question my motivations: I'd thought I'd gone out there to speak to him. To get answers. No, I decided. What he was saying wasn't true. Ross—through Slater—was gaslighting me. I hoped.

"I've been keeping tabs on you for years," he continued. "You were getting nowhere in the FBI. Not your fault, of course. They're not an organization that's capable of appreciating your talent. But we can. I believe that with a little grooming you could be an excellent assassin. You're cold and you're calculating, and by choice, you don't have many close social attachments. You're beautiful. And you're also lethal. You did all of the work you needed to do to get Thomas to let his guard down without ever really challenging me on it. You've insinuated yourself very well into an extremely challenging target's life; all that's left now is the easy part.

"Next time it won't take so long. You won't need the training wheels that we were. And it won't take nearly as much effort on your part. Thomas is an unusually difficult target—if I'd had my choice, I would've started you out with someone easier. Next time, I promise, one meeting and you're out. One and done. But this is where I was stationed."

Slater and Ross were both megalomaniacs, and greedy ones at that; I could finally see that clearly. They were doing all this for ideology in the sense that a quest for money and power were the guiding principles of imperialism. Saying as much would be dangerous—I was miles away from the city, and the base was crawling with soldiers. I chose to be cautious.

"Where is he? Thomas, I mean."

"The day after tomorrow he's going to Ghana for a meeting at Mole National Park. It's a wildlife refuge near Tamale. They're going to talk about wildlife preservation, mostly for the press, but really they're meeting to sign an agreement about sharing the hydroelectric dam in Ghana.

"There's a change in the government coming. That's inevitable. What we have some control over is how efficient it is. The station office is pumping hundreds of thousands of dollars into setting up an electoral system and putting Blaise Compaoré in power. But unless they're willing to commit to killing Thomas it'll backfire. He's been a political prisoner a few times now, and it's always galvanized support behind him when his adversaries put him in jail. He's too popular. As long as he's alive no one else can seize power. We at SSI see ourselves as supplementing the CIA's electoral system project. We're doing the work that they don't have the balls for."

"Who's paying you?"

"Who do you think? We're getting money from lots of sources. There are many people, and corporations, and a couple of governments who'll benefit from this service. We've reinvested some of that money into this base.

"Thomas's death is inevitable. What's not inevitable is the international community knowing that the United States is behind it. At least it doesn't have to be. If he's killed in a coup by the head of a political group we're giving money to, it'll be obvious that we're involved. But if there's no financial paper trail, if he's killed quietly, and all anyone can prove is that we were here trying to create an electoral system, that gives us plausible deniability. A bonus is if he dies in Ghana. That'll cast suspicion on Jerry Rawlings, which will damage his reputation."

I nodded. Jerry Rawlings had come to power in a coup and was Ghana's head of state. Of the two economies, Ghana's was substantially stronger; it was his government that the CIA had been caught spying on. Rawlings had several of those Ghanaian agents executed. And it occurred to me that Ross had been station chief in Ghana when all this was happening. "He needs to be reeled in too; he's a dangerous Communist. Two birds, one stone. You see?"

"I see," I said as I followed him toward the exit. I glanced back once at the dying man in the cell—he still hadn't moved—then stepped into the scalding daylight.

I knew it was risky, but I needed to call my father. I couldn't say for sure what was going to happen, and I wanted the chance to say good-bye. Slater dropped me back at the house, and I immediately went to the phone and dialed his number. I sat on the edge of the bed with the receiver. He picked up and I said, "It's me."

"Hello, Marie? That you? I'm so glad I answered! I thought—" Whatever he'd said was drowned out by a click and a quick succession of pops on the line.

"What did you say?" I asked.

"I thought you wouldn't be able to call."

Ross had told me to tell him that. He'd also said I could tell him that I'd be in West Africa, but give no specific information about the assignment.

"This is important."

"What was that? I can barely hear you."

"I'll call you right back. Okay?"

It could've been innocuous—just a poor-quality long distance call. But the noises I'd heard were also sometimes the symptoms of a wire-tap. I pulled a screwdriver out of my bag and unscrewed the faceplate on the phone jack in my room. Nothing. I unscrewed the receiver on my phone. Also nothing. When I dialed him back, the connection was much better. He said, "Sorry 'bout that. Something's been going on with my phone lately."

"Pop. I just wanted to hear your voice."

"You all right?"

"Yeah."

"No. I can tell when you're upset. What's going on?"

"I want to ask you something about Helene's funeral. Do you remember the group of her army friends?" After I described Daniel Slater there was a long pause—so long in fact that I thought we'd been disconnected—before he told me he did.

"Why are you thinking about him now?"

"He's the one who brought me out here."

"He is? Why'd he do that?"

"It's a long story," I said. "He told me about the accident. That he was in the car. Why'd you keep that from me?"

He exhaled into the phone. "It was all a long time ago."

"Pop."

"I didn't want to talk about him."

"You'd met him?"

"Yeah. You and Helene had some kind of fight before she deployed. You weren't talking to each other. So I called her. But I remember, I couldn't get an answer—her number had been changed. I tried to catch her at the base but I couldn't. I even called the police station in North Carolina, and they were no help. So finally I went down there. I went to her house, and I found out she'd moved. I went to the base, and one of her friends took pity on me and told me she was living with that guy, Daniel Slater."

"Did you find her?"

"Yes. I rang their bell and she answered the door. I asked her if we could go for lunch so we could talk. He came to the door then too, and she asked him for permission to go out with me. He said no.

"I've never been able to get that look she gave him out of my mind. I asked her to come back to New York with me but of course she said she couldn't go AWOL. He threw me out. But he still had the nerve to smile up in my face at the funeral."

"Is that why she stopped calling me? Do you think he was isolating her?"

"Yeah. A little bit." He asked, "What was your argument about? I know it was a long time ago."

"I don't *know*, Pop. That was the hardest thing about it."

"You were mad that she wasn't at your graduation. I remember that."

"She was being distant though. If I knew what I'd done to her, I could've apologized."

"Maybe it didn't have anything to do with you. Maybe she was pulling away from all her friends."

"Maybe," I said, even though it didn't quite seem true. She'd seemed so angry at *me* when we'd boxed that last time. Although I had criticized Slater. Maybe that was what set her off. "You should've told me about this back then."

"I was upset. I didn't like thinking about it."

"Why didn't you do anything else to help her?"

Emotion rose in his voice. "I stayed there for three or four days, just trying to get her to talk to me. After I got back to Queens, I kept on calling her. I called so much that he told me he'd call the cops if I kept it up. I told him go ahead. What else could I have done, kidnapped her? She was an adult."

"You could've told me."

"And what would you have done? Gone down there and busted his head open? You were a kid."

"Did you know they got married? When she got back to the country. That's what he says. But I have to say that doesn't make a whole lot of sense to me."

"Why not?"

"I don't know. Because if he didn't want her seeing her friends and family, by marrying him she was choosing him over all of us."

"Marie. Women do that all the time."

I thought for a moment. I wanted to think he wasn't the kind of person she could've loved, but everything suggested that he was. I didn't know what that meant about who *she* was.

"Marie? You still there?"

"Yeah, sorry. But how could he have been in the car? I remember him at the wake. He didn't have a mark on him."

"From what I remember his face was all bruised and scratched. I'm sure the rest of him was in bad shape too. You really don't remember that?"

I didn't, which scared me. I remembered the feeling of recognizing him, of holding on to him. I remembered him giving me the photo booth pictures. But hard as I tried, I couldn't conjure up an image of his face at either the wake or the funeral. The line started to hiss again. "He's a strange guy," Pop said. "Like his cheese has slipped off his cracker."

"Pop. Careful, all right? I have to go now. Be careful what you say on this line; someone might be able to hear you."

"What?"

"Get your phone fixed," I said as loudly as I could. I didn't know for certain that his phone was bugged, but if it was, Ross was certainly behind it.

There was a threat in that. He knew where my father was. If he ever felt like putting pressure on me, Pop would've been in danger.

23

I decided to go to Ghana to warn Thomas about what was happening. I'd failed to protect my sister from Slater's corrosion, but I could still protect Thomas. I was frightened by his swerve toward authoritarianism, but he represented revolution and change to millions of people. I couldn't let people like Slater and Ross extinguish that for the sake of greed and power.

It was a seven-hour journey, and Slater had assigned one of his agents to take me. I packed a few things into the backpack I'd brought, including a small bottle of Scotch, and slipped my service automatic in a holster under my shirt. The driver was late, so I waited on the patio. I was very anxious, so I poured a little Scotch into my coffee and drank it as I flipped through an old local paper. Earlier in the week, Thomas had spoken at the opening of an exhibition on Che Guevara in commemoration of Che's death twenty years earlier. A delegation from Cuba that included one of Che's sons had attended. Part of his speech was quoted in the paper, in which he'd told an anecdote from the Cuban Revolution.

The assault on the Moncada garrison had failed and the men who'd attempted it were about to be put to death. As the rebels were led out in front of the firing squad, one of Batista's officers tried to persuade the squad not to shoot them. He said to his fellow soldiers: "Stop, stop. You cannot kill ideas."

"And it's true," the speech continued. "No one man is the revolution. Not me, not Che. That it continues after us, that is how you'll know the work hasn't been meaningless."

All of that seemed ominous—it reminded me of something Fred Hampton had said before he was assassinated: *You can kill a revolutionary, but you can never kill the revolution.* Thomas must've known that. I thought it was a signal that he was giving up. That he could see what was coming and had resigned himself to it.

I was tense and quiet as we rode south, thinking about him, the way he used his power to pursue freedom for others. That was love for him. For me, that is goodness. Either way, I hope that you will share those values.

I arrived at Mole National Park in the late afternoon. My room had already been paid for, and the clerk gave me a key from one of the cubbyholes at his elbow. I crossed a grassy expanse in the direction of a row of two-story white bungalows, passing a dining room beneath a white roof with a series of peaks, like a child's drawing of a wave. There was a pool deck beside it, the savanna and the sky beyond, and through the tall windows I could see tourists at the tables.

I rounded the villa along a walkway studded with lampposts. My room was on the bottom floor of one of several two-story villas, in a block that had been reserved for the government meetings. Several armed guards stood at attention near one of the rooms on the second floor.

Just a few paces from my own door, I spotted a baboon sitting on the white railing. I knew the place was a wildlife refuge, but it was still a shock to see such a large primate in real life. I stopped. We stared at each other for a moment before I moved on, feeling like I'd been judged and found wanting. Alone in a relatively luxurious room, I put my bag down, took my gun and holster off.

Almost immediately, the phone rang. It was Ed Ross.

Slater had let it slip that he'd been keeping tabs on me for a long time, which meant that Ross had been manipulating me from the first time we met. I'd blamed Gold and Mr. Ali for my suspension, but had realized that Ross could easily have put pressure on Gold to sideline me for as long as he did, to cultivate that low point in my life that got me out here.

Ross was in my head then and he still is. When I first met him, he knew immediately to flatter my intelligence, which blinded me to some of the ways he was manipulating me. I'll never be certain about the extent to which he managed to do it. I don't know, for example, if I myself came to the conclusion that they wanted photos of Thomas and me for blackmail, or if Ross planted that idea. I'd assumed that was the case after I saw that surveillance van parked outside my building. And I let that slip to him. But had I just misinterpreted what I'd seen—was it a regular van? Or did he have a van parked there to lead me to that conclusion? In trying to follow his trail of clues, there are times when I think I've finally found him. I pounce. And then I realize it's only my own intellect that I've caught. My own capacity to overthink things.

"SQLR. Do you know what you're supposed to do?"

"Yes. Where is he?"

"On a tour."

"What?" I said, sounding incredulous.

"Well, it's a wildlife reserve. And he's gone to take a look at the elephants. I suggest you go and find him out on the trail. If you don't you could miss him."

"Is he alone?"

"I doubt it. Just get him to ask to come back to your room. Dan says you're good at that."

"I'll try."

"I have every faith that if you try you'll succeed. But I want to remind you of something. Slater thinks you're one of a kind, but that's
only because he's still in love with your sister. As far as I'm concerned,
you're expendable. If things don't go as I planned, I have no problem
with you disappearing out there. Which would be easy, because you're
very vulnerable right now. You're in a foreign country, with no contacts outside of the ones we've given you. Slater understands that. He's
accepted that if I have to make the call he'll do what he has to. Do you
understand?"

"Yes." He was saying that if I didn't kill Thomas he would tell Slater
to kill me, and the realization made my hands start to shake. "I'll do
what I was sent here for."

"Make sure you do."

I hung up. Then I slammed the receiver against the phone a few
times, relishing the plaintive, ghostly little rings. Needing to calm
down, I drank some Scotch.

From my window I could see that a crowd had already gathered on
the knoll outside and was being held at bay by several security guards.

A group of men came down the same stairs and a loud cheer went
up. I looked out the window and saw two men who were waving to the
crowd—they were obviously politicians. They had to cross the knoll to
get to the parking area. Most of the crowd followed, and so did a couple
of security guards. I realized it was because Jerry Rawlings, the Ghanaian president, was among them.

I walked across the knoll toward reception, and followed the front
desk clerk's directions to the trail. It began near a toolshed, where a
dozen or so green rubber boots were lined up on the patio. I followed a
series of blue trail markers through a wide-open savanna populated
with flat-topped syringa trees. Antelopes hopped through the tall grass.
Rustling in the underbrush beside the path proved to be a warthog
scurrying past.

I crested the top of the hill and looked down on a lovely sight. In the
valley below was a lake, and standing on the near bank was a pair of

elephants. Thomas was there with Sam and a man who must've been a tour guide—he was wearing a khaki shirt and pants.

"Thomas," I called as I approached. I saw Sam Kinda's hand go to the pistol at his hip.

"The American," he answered.

"It's Blaise," I said with my hands up, wary of Sam. "He's our most important ally in the country. He helped create the ULCR. The whole point of it is to prevent the reunification of the CNR at every turn and to put him in power. You can't trust him anymore."

Sam Kinda intervened between us. It had always been clear that he didn't like or trust me, but he'd never been so openly hostile. He said something to Thomas in Mooré and began to pat me down for a weapon, as the other men looked on. The guide had a gap between his front teeth and was also armed, carrying a rusted hunting rifle that must've been just for show; it couldn't possibly have stopped a charging elephant.

"That's enough, Sam," Thomas said.

"The CIA wants to install Blaise as president."

"I know," he said quietly. "There's not much that happens in my country that I don't know about. People have been warning me about Blaise's plans for months. At first I didn't want to believe it, but then . . . Did you listen to the speech I gave on the anniversary of the Political Orientation Speech?"

I nodded, remembering how much it had meant to Asalfo, the bar owner; how he'd gotten his radio fixed just so he could hear it.

"Blaise wrote the speech given by the young man who spoke first, Jonas Somé. He was attacking me through Jonas, pointing out where we diverged on certain policies. That was his way of publicly throwing down the gauntlet. Blaise is the vice president, but he's also the minister of defense—the highest-ranking member of the military in the country—so of course your CIA would approach him. In a way he's always been the enforcer, doing what he had to with force—with violence—in the shadows so I could create policies in the light."

"They're willing to kill you to make him president."

He inclined his head to signal he knew.

"Then have Compaoré arrested. Stop him."

"No. His ambitions have divided us, but he's still my brother." It was painful to see how resigned he was. How tired.

"Thomas. Listen to me. Your life is in very serious danger. Do you know who Daniel Slater is?" I said, then used his alias.

"Yes, he approached me a few years ago. He wanted my permission to build an American military base here—your government would give him a private contract to do it. I said no. But when Blaise is president he'll agree. And Daniel Slater will become a very rich man."

"He's a bad person, Thomas. I'm risking my life to tell you what he's up to so you'll prevent it."

"He's greedy, not bad."

The semantics made me furious. "He wants to kill you! That's what matters!"

"I'm not afraid of death," he said. "Only of not having done enough, of having failed out of laziness. I'm prepared to fight until the end against that. But I've already told myself either I'll finish up an old man somewhere in a library reading books, or I'll meet with a violent end, since we have so many enemies. Once you've accepted that reality it's just a question of time."

"It's selfish to martyr yourself. You have children." I was surprised by how angry I was. The elephant observed us for just a second before striding into the water. She stood there, not quite knee deep, as her baby paddled around beside her. She swung her trunk, lightly splashing him.

I started back up the trail. He called after me using my alias.

"Marie," I called back, correcting him.

I returned to the room, where I sat on the edge of the bed and thought. I'd risked my life for him for no reason. Someone rapped on the door and I went to open it. Thomas was standing there, winsome despite his exhaustion.

"How did you find me?"

"I asked at the front desk for the black American woman." He stepped into the room.

"What are you doing here?"

"That's a good question. I've been asking it of myself ever since I came to your house. I wish I knew why."

"Self-destruction," I said. "Loss will make you pursue it, and you're losing something very big. Something very powerful." I knew what I was saying to be true; after I lost my sister I completely fell apart.

He shook his head. "Maybe it's that I'd rather die quietly than by firing squad."

I realized then that he'd known even before I did what Ross and Slater had wanted from me. If it was obvious to him then maybe my blindness to it had been willful.

I leaned toward him and kissed his cheek. He seemed conflicted then as he had before—the theory I've since landed on was that he was equal parts attracted to and repelled by my Americanness. Then I felt him smile, I guess at the forwardness of it. He kissed me.

He began to unbutton my blouse. He had some trouble with the hook-and-eye closures and I looked up at him, charmed by his clumsiness, how it contradicted the confidence in his animated face at the podium that day in Harlem, how he'd looked as he held up the pistol in its holster.

I know it reflects a weird convention, to admit that I feel compelled to detail his violent death for you, but also like I should censor myself about our physical intimacy. So I'll limit myself to talking about afterward.

Once more he lay still. He put his head on my chest and listened to my heartbeat with a smile on his face. Rest was something he rarely afforded himself; he treated sleep like a chore. I was pleased—the most loving thing you could do for someone like your father was to allow him to be. And hope that he could find peace in a moment of quiet. Eventually, he got out of bed and began pulling his clothes on. I dressed too and we went outside.

I asked him to give me a ride with them back to Ouaga. "I don't want Slater to know it when I'm back."

He agreed. Sam, who'd been standing guard outside the room, said something. It must've been an objection because Thomas—momentarily revealing his old commanding self—answered in French: "We'll do what I say. I'm still the PF."

The three of us started north with Sam behind the wheel. It was quiet in the car and I rode for much of the way with my head resting against Thomas's shoulder.

"I don't see how he can betray you for the sake of greed," I said at one point.

"It's not just about greed. It's about ideology."

"For ideas? That's even worse."

"I don't agree. Blaise is a soldier, and a soldier without ideology is a criminal." He added: "Are you a soldier?"

"No, not really. Maybe I was once but not now. Not anymore."

"What did you believe in then?"

"Nothing much."

He searched my face before he spoke. "I don't believe you. I think you believe in a way the world should be."

It was flattering, but it wasn't true. I didn't have a guiding ideology until you were born. Now all I truly believe is that the world should be a place where you can thrive.

At dusk, we stopped at a gas station in a small town that was just on the other side of the border. Sam opened the driver's door and planted his feet in the red dust. Thomas leaped out of the car and went into the building across the road for some water. When he came out, it was with a small group following him at a respectful distance. The station was manned by two boys. It wasn't much more than a giant wood rack at the side of the road that held glass jars filled with amber gas, and a couple of dozen one-liter bottles that I'd first mistaken for water before realizing it looked too slick and had to be kerosene. The boys worked fast, filling the tank with adult efficiency.

A small crowd formed around Thomas as he approached the car. Sporadic whistles and voices increased into applause. He smiled and thanked everyone. I could feel how much they loved him. And why shouldn't they have? He'd touched lives and improved them. Even mine.

As he was opening the car door, a man approached with a little boy. "Please, PF. Please. This is my cousin's son. You're his hero."

The man hitched the boy up onto his hip. Thomas was exhausted, I knew he was, but I saw him gather himself. He spoke to the boy. "How are you doing, little brother? It's nice to meet you."

The boy shyly put his face against his cousin's neck.

"He's Sudanese," the man said. "He doesn't speak French yet."

"*As-salamu alaykum*, little brother," Thomas said.

The boy was overwhelmed but grinning as he lifted his face and turned to Thomas, repeating softly: "Bonjour. Bonjour, bonjour!"

Thomas got into the car and pulled the door closed. Eager faces crowded the open windows. Hands banged on the hood. Sam started the car and moved forward slowly through the cheering crowd. A few people managed to keep pace with us for a little while, and as we left them behind someone kicked off the chant: "We will win! We will win!"

24

When Sam pulled up in front of the house in Zone du Bois, I leaned over to kiss Thomas on the cheek. "Goodbye."

"Be careful," he said. I stepped out of the car.

In the house, I showered and dressed, put the gun in my holster. I wanted to move quickly, to take advantage of Slater believing I was still in Ghana. I pulled the black comforter from my bed, stuffed it and a few clothes into my backpack. I'd have to leave the rest behind. It was a little after three in the morning when I left on the bike. There was no moon; I still wasn't used to darkness like that. I cut the engine on the quiet boulevard and pushed the motorcycle toward Slater's street. I could barely make out the half-dozen homes that stood on Slater's cul-de-sac, all of them hidden behind mud-brick walls. The only light was from a floodlight mounted on the front of one of the larger homes, and the only sound the crickets stridulating in the trees.

I'd learned from Awa, the embassy secretary, that he lived in the first house on the street. It was hidden behind a wall topped with glass; other than that, there wasn't much to see. As I paced back and forth in front, trying to figure out the best spot over it, I heard a sound from the direction of the boulevard and pressed myself against the wall. A young man on a bicycle rode into the floodlight, where he stopped and waited. I hadn't been anticipating anyone else being on the street at that time of night. Although there wasn't much distance between us, he didn't notice me—I was totally hidden by the dark. A girl came out into the street. They talked for a while, standing close as they spoke, the boy straddling his bike, then she got on behind him, and they rode off back up the road.

I waited a few more minutes until my heart slowed. No one else appeared. I took the comforter from my bag and folded it up before taking a couple of practice runs toward the wall. On my first real try, I only managed to get two steps up the wall's smooth surface before sliding back down in what seemed to me like a very loud fashion. I waited, terrified that someone had heard me, but the night stayed quiet.

I started from farther back and ran at top speed toward the wall—then up it—draping the comforter on the sharp shards of glass on top and pulling myself over in the same motion. I dropped down into the yard. I looked around and froze—I'd come down too close to Slater's night guard. He was lying on the bench beside the gate, his hands sandwiched between his thighs, his plastic sandals tucked under the bench. I held my breath and watched him. Once I was sure he was still asleep, I moved forward as quietly as I could, tucking my comforter back into my bag. It was a compound-style home, and the only light was coming from the middle building, a kitchen illuminated by a fluorescent bulb, its door propped open. The building to the right was small, so I thought it must be a bathroom. I looked to the three buildings to the left; I had no way of knowing which one Slater was inside. I started with the first building. The door was unlocked. I cracked it open slowly and found a living room with a television and sofa. I glanced around quickly, but there wasn't much furniture to hide anything important inside.

The door to the second building was locked. That seemed more promising. I took out my tension wrench, giving thanks to my hours of living room practice. Once I'd picked the lock, I took out my flashlight—there was a desk against the far wall that I trapped in my beam of light; above it hung a busy gold and black tapestry. I went to the tapestry and lifted the edge to check for a wall safe. Nothing. But there were a number of items lined up along the wall behind the desk: a red crate filled with tall Coke bottles, a long metal crate containing Kalashnikovs, a few bottles of Slater's brand of Scotch, a carton of French cigarettes. A mailing envelope that I peeked inside. There was cash inside, which is why I took it. Later, I'd discover it also contained something else important: several sets of blueprints. I pulled the door closed.

The third building was his bedroom. Nicole was asleep in bed beside him, which I hadn't been expecting.

"Slater," I said, and then I kicked him awake. Although he was still drowsy, his eyes were open when I shot him.

25

Nicole was still screaming as I backed away from the bed. Something metal struck me on the back of the head and pain ripped through me. As I turned to face the guard, he hit me again.

I came to in the courtyard with a terrible headache. The guard was pointing my gun at me; it was obvious he'd never held one before. He was like my own night guard who was just a deterrent, not a trained security expert. I stood, and as I advanced on him he shouted for Nicole. His hands shook as he tried to pull the trigger, but I toppled him at the knees before he could. As we struggled for the gun, Nicole threw herself into the fray. I grabbed it, and pointing it at them both, I backed through the gate.

The sun was starting to rise. I started up the bike and sped out onto the boulevard, where I had to swerve to avoid a 4x4 filled with soldiers. Nicole must've called members of Compaoré's presidential guard. As the vehicle chased after me, I sped around the few other commuters on the road at that hour then veered sharply onto the quiet road I used to get to HDF. I accelerated. Went right over the plywood bridge, which fell into the sewer behind me, and turned into the light traffic flowing on that street. I glanced back and saw the 4x4 stopped at the sewer, the soldiers climbing out of the car.

I raced out of the city. I blew past the *péage,* despite the guard there waving for me to stop. Just a few miles out of the city the paved road ended abruptly. There was virtually no traffic. The savanna was red and flat and dotted with scraggly trees, the sky empty of clouds.

Sudden Kalashnikov fire startled me. The 4x4 was in my mirror, the driver signaling for me to stop. I panicked and veered away from the car tracks I'd been following. At Quantico I'd had a class on emergency vehicle operations, but my FBI training hadn't anticipated the reality of that moment. I sped across the bright landscape, thinking of nothing beyond outrunning the truck.

The XS1 was the nimbler vehicle. I mowed over errant scrub and sped around copses of anemic trees, putting more and more distance between us. It felt right speeding on the bike, like fast was the natural expression of the vehicle. I could no longer see the truck in my mirror, but still I kept on. When I finally glanced behind me and saw that I was alone, that they must've turned back, I let out a whoop, adrenaline buzzing through me.

I continued on, and passed into a barren pocket of land. I rode past a sight that was almost magical: The wind had managed to form a tiny dust storm. It swirled a foot above the soil, like a hovering tumbleweed. It was beautiful, and I thought of Helene, who would've insisted we stop and investigate. She'd always been so interested in the world.

About a mile farther, I slowed to a stop. My excitement quickly gave way to fear as I looked around. There was very little about the wide openness of the terrain that made any part of it distinct for me. I'd never been agoraphobic, but suddenly understood the condition: I felt a natural terror in that landscape. There was nowhere to hide if a large animal were to suddenly appear, no tree that was tall enough to get me out of danger were I to climb it.

I took out my compass and map, even though it wasn't particularly detailed, to make sure I was still headed south, in what I hoped was the direction of Pô, the city nearest the border. I thought that if I could reach it, I could get a ride across the border to the city of Tamale, where I could catch a bus down to the airport in Accra.

But I ran out of gas far too soon. I continued, pushing the XS1, aiming back toward the car tracks at what passed for the road; the bike was incredibly heavy, and it made my going excruciatingly slow. The sun on my skin was brutal, my back was soaked in sweat, the heat terrible. I realize as I write this that I should've been worried—or something—but I'd shut down. Ill with fatigue, I sat and allowed myself a ration of water.

The sun began setting—the impending darkness made my fear finally kick in. Although I was exhausted, I slept fitfully on the hard ground, waking up to the sound of small scurrying animals and intense starlight.

My mind kept returning to the story Thomas had told me in the car ride back to Ouaga. The tour guide I'd seen—Kwaku—was Ashanti, and in a mix of English and French he'd told the group a story about the lake his village was built beside, Lake Bosomtwe, which is considered sacred. I've told it to you before, but a gentler version.

A certain hunter was running through the forest after an antelope. He shot the antelope, which hit the ground (I'm reminded of my sister as I write this, the hoofs on her doe still moving). Thinking the animal was dead he approached it, but it suddenly leaped up and ran away. The hunter pressed after it, and when he came to a clearing, found that the antelope had run up onto the surface of a small pond. As he approached the pond, it got wider, and the hunter looked on, astonished at the way the body of water seemed to be protecting the antelope. As he watched the animal walk on water, he realized that it was in fact a spirit. Taking his inability to kill it as a good omen, he went home and told his wife that they would resettle closer to the banks of the pond. The hunter had good fortune there and other families started to settle nearby. Over time the pond grew bigger, and so did the settlement. It eventually became the village where Kwaku had grown up.

I'm not sure why I thought about that story so much. It must've been because it reminded me of Thomas.

I woke at dawn and looked out at the wide-open savanna. I was all alone. I started out, covering a few more miles before I had to stop. I could push the motorcycle no farther. Leaving it where it dropped, I crawled toward the paltry protection of a frail tree and lay on the ground underneath it. At one point—it couldn't have been later than midday—the sky suddenly grew dark and the wind picked up, causing dust to sting my exposed skin, blow into my face, and scorch my eyes. I reached for the helmet and put it on, grateful for the yellowed visor. My world was black-blue. Then, just as quickly as the storm arrived, it passed and the sky abruptly brightened. The sun returned with a vengeance. I was covered in red dust.

Hours slipped by, and my fear gave way to bland exhaustion. I drank the last of my water. It was oppressively quiet, almost mystically so, and disorientation inclined my thinking toward the magical. I thought I was going to die. If I ever were going to be spoken to by a burning bush, that would've been the moment. If an antelope spirit were going to lead me, it would've been then. But no divine magic struck.

Until I heard the rumble of an engine and looked up to watch a hazy spot on the horizon evolve into a lumbering truck. I waved. My heart lifted when it came toward me and stopped. A wiry driver jumped down from the cab, and as he came toward me he said something in a language I didn't speak.

"*Français?*" I said hoarsely, my voice cracked and dry. I tried to sit up.

"What happened?" he asked in French as he helped me to my feet. "Did you break down?"

I nodded.

He was stronger than he looked and easily lifted me into the cab. He reached over me toward the driver's seat and picked up a bag of water, which he put in my hand on the seat.

"Gas?" I said.

He shook his head. "The truck's diesel, but someone at the village will have some."

In the relative dark of the truck, my eyes took a long time to adjust. They hurt. In the cool, the sunburn on my shoulders, chest, and back seemed even more intense. He closed the cab door and I heard him wrestling my motorcycle up into the bed. I bit a corner off the bag and quickly sucked down all the water. Then he climbed up into his seat and started the truck. I closed my eyes and leaned weakly against the door. As he drove he asked: "It's a little early for the start of the harmattan. Did you cause the storm?" He laughed, evidently making some joke I didn't have the energy to understand.

"Is that a helmet or a mask?" he continued, playing with the rhyme, *casque* and *masque*.

"Don't worry," he said when I didn't respond, even though he himself sounded worried. "We'll be there soon."

He continued to chat idly to fill the space. He told me we were going to the village where he'd grown up. His uncle's younger wife was in labor, and he was going to take them to the maternity hospital in Koubri. "She's been asking to go to the doctor for a while; it's the first pregnancy that she's ever said that. But she'll be okay. You both will be."

We'd been driving for only twenty minutes before he stopped the truck. I opened my eyes. Squinting, I saw that we'd arrived at a village. It was closer than I was expecting, but I would never have been able to find it on my own—he'd been following landmarks that were too subtle for me.

He started driving again, slowly passing a few mud huts hunched in the savanna, then stopped in front of a compound where an older woman was sitting outside its mud wall beside a cooking fire, slicing eggplant on a large metal plate. The driver got out of the car and came around to help me out of the cab. Dizzy, I leaned on him heavily. There was a blue school nearby with a mural of Africa on the wall; three young teenagers were resting in the thin strip of shade that its roof created along the building's edge. As the driver got out of the truck he called out what must've been instructions to them, and one of the girls stood and took off running.

The woman greeted us as we went through the gap in the mud wall. We walked along a narrow corridor formed by the wall and the back of several huts in the compound, accompanied by a boy of three or four wearing just an oversized shirt. He ran along in front of us, glancing back at me occasionally, unable to hide his curiosity.

The driver helped me into one of the huts, which was dark and surprisingly cool. The floor was on an incline and I sat in the lower half. On the higher side a woman in labor lay in bed, her husband dabbing at her sweat-glistened face with a damp cloth, while a small, compact woman who must've been the midwife spoke quickly. The driver went over to them, pointed at me, and said something in Mooré to his uncle, who nodded once, apparently indifferent to my presence, before returning his attention to his wife.

There were two blue plastic lawn chairs stacked beside me near the doorway and a prayer rug along the wall that was piled with books. Above my head there was a ledge lined with kitchenware, one identical to a pot Helene had often used to make meals for us: white aluminum with that ubiquitous blue cornflower embossed on it.

I was loopy from heatstroke and nearly laughed then, absurdly, to be reminded of home when I'd never been so far away from it. The girl who'd taken off running behind the school now came into the hut with a *bidon* full of water on her head, poured some into a plastic tumbler, and handed it to me. I got a bandana from my backpack and wet it, pressed it against my forehead and the back of my neck. I rubbed my face with it to get the dust off. My shoulders were throbbing.

I asked the girl's name, but she only shook her head, smiled, and said something in Mooré. She left again, and I heard her speaking to someone outside, then a boy came in and squatted beside me.

He and the girl must've been siblings, maybe even twins: They had the same high foreheads and triangular eyebrows, a similar shape to their mouths. When he spoke to me in Mooré, he did so slowly, as if that would resolve the problem of my total ignorance of the language. He tried again: "Màm yuur la a Kamal." Pointing to himself, he repeated, "Kamal."

"Marie," I told him, the first time I'd used my real name in two weeks. I was surprised by my lapse into honesty.

"Marie. Bonjour."

Kamal was wearing a T-shirt similar to one I'd occasionally seen in Ouagadougou, a silk screen of Thomas's face. I pointed and gave him a thumbs-up. He nodded and said solemnly, "Nous vaincrons."

I gestured to the woman in the bed and asked, "Ta maman?"

He nodded, and when his mother let out a loud moan, Kamal's head snapped in her direction. He got up and went over to the bed, where he jockeyed with his father and the midwife for space. Finally, his father put an arm around him. Speaking gently, he pointed Kamal back to the doorway. Kamal crouched beside me again. Gesturing toward his mother he put his hand up with his palm out. "Cinq jours. Très difficile."

He pantomimed driving, then drew a cross in the air with his pointer finger. "Koubri. Lògtór yírì."

The truck driver had said the hospital was in Koubri, but I couldn't understand why Kamal was making a cross to represent it until I remembered that the Burkinabè Red Cross ran a busy hospital in Ouagadougou, near Zone du Bois, appropriately enough off the avenue de la Croix Rouge. There was a giant red cross on its roof.

The midwife poured water into a tumbler from the shelf above me and gave it with some pills to Kamal's mother. She then had her turn on her side and began massaging between her shoulder blades. I kept hearing the same word Kamal had used, *lògtór yírì*. Hospital. The only other word I recognized, because it sounded like English, was Pitocin.

The truck driver stuck his head through the doorway, having returned with a hose, a bottle filled with gas, and a big guy in his wake. I followed them outside, where I found that the XS1 was out of the truck bed. There was a tower of mattresses inside the truck, some of them wrapped in flimsy plastic.

The two men were having a serious conversation. The driver turned to me and said in French, "We're talking about the news. We will win."

"We will win," the other man repeated in thickly accented French. Their solemnness made my stomach flip.

"What news? About the PF?"

"He was attacked at a meeting last night."

"Is he dead?"

"Missing." He gave me an incredulous look. He must've been about to ask how I could've missed such big news before realizing I'd been in the desert.

I was so overcome that I pressed my face against his chest and started to cry. I'd never done something like that—crying on a stranger—in my entire life. He put his arms around me, comforting me as best he could. I was still too dehydrated to produce real tears, but wept until I couldn't anymore.

"Are you all right now?" the driver asked.

I nodded. The big guy said something, and the driver translated for him, "He wants to know where you're going."

"I'm trying to get to Tamale."

The driver translated, and the big guy asked another question. "Where are you from?"

"New York."

"New Yawk!" the big guy said to make me laugh. "Eh, fugged-aboutit."

I did laugh; I appreciated the gesture.

"I filled your tank," the driver said as he handed me the bottle.

"Thank you. You saved my life."

He shrugged it off, but it was true and I was very grateful. I took my damp passport from my back pocket, removed a few of the francs I'd tucked inside, and pressed the money on both men.

"The sun is going to set soon," he said. "You should stay here and leave in the morning. There are bandits on the roads at night."

"Have you ever been robbed?" I asked him.

"No."

"Have you ever seen any bandits?"

"No."

"I'll risk it." Although I was exhausted, with my temperature a bit lower, and some water in me, I was ready to get to the closest city with a hotel room as soon as I could.

The truck driver glanced over my shoulder. Behind me, Kamal's father was helping his wife toward the vehicle as Kamal's sister and several other children orbited the pair. The truck driver went over to help the woman up into the cab. I handed a few bills to Kamal's father, and thanked him for his hospitality; he absently tucked the money into his pocket, then climbed up into the cab, still too occupied by his own life's affairs to give mine much thought. I sat in the shade of the school roof and drank more water and rested for a few more hours.

Years later, while reading some book or criticism having to do with the African diaspora, I suddenly burst out laughing at what was a fairly dry piece of writing. Completely unexpectedly, I'd learned the truck driver's joke: he'd been pretending to have mistaken me for Oya, the Yoruba deity of wind. His job had made him worldly—they weren't myths that he would've heard in the small village where he'd grown up. And although the tradition has been transported to the Americas, through descendants of slaves, I grew up ignorant of it.

My mother named me Marie Madeleine, Mary Magdalene, even though I could never internalize her French Catholicism, her blue-eyed Jesus. I like Oya better. She makes more sense to me—presented as an Orisha with her own business to attend to, which is precisely what bonds her to Shango, her husband. What compels him to her.

People always used to ask me why I was a Fed, because it seemed to them that what I did for a living didn't line up with what they expected of me. In that way, it was shorthand for asking what I believe in, the question was a way of asking who I really was. The answer is here, in the way I feel stuck between these two legacies. And simultaneously like I should claim both and neither.

I was still fatigued when I went to my bike, kick-started it, and continued south. Being back on the bike was rejuvenating, and the farther

I went, the greener the landscape around me got. After I passed through Pô, it took another hour to get to the Burkina-Ghana border, and by that time, the sun had already set. In the beam of my headlight, I saw that the road on the other side of the border was paved and in much better condition than the dirt road I was on. A white arch spanned the border crossing, and on it was the hand-painted declaration: Welcome to Ghana, but the gate beneath it was incongruously locked. All of the commercial buildings crowded near the border were shuttered too. I'd arrived too late in the day to cross legally. Still, I was lucky to have made it at all.

I got off the bike, took out my flashlight, and pulled my gun from my holster, then went on foot into the forest behind the buildings. The air there was fresh and pleasant. I found that the trees weren't particularly dense—I could easily cross into Ghana on the motorcycle.

As I was turning back toward my bike, I heard one voice call to another and froze, picturing a group of bandits, or worse, soldiers. But as I kept listening, I realized how young the voices sounded. They belonged to children. I quickly put the gun away, feeling ill about even having it out in the first place.

I moved slowly back out of the forest. There were three boys in flip-flops, all of them pushing bicycles. Each had a wheeled red Coke crate tied to his bike. The glass bottles in the crates were filled with what I assumed was gas. They must've been smuggling it into Burkina from Ghana, where it was much cheaper. For all I knew they were the suppliers for the boys at the gas station where I'd stopped with Thomas. Thinking about him made tears well up in my eyes that I chased away.

"Hello," I said. "Bonsoir."

Two of the boys just stared at me, while the third broke into an instinctive run, and I called after him: "Gaz! Can I buy some gas?"

The boys looked at each other, and I realized then that the silence I was being confronted with wasn't one of incomprehension but astonishment. A strange foreign woman had suddenly appeared in the woods. "D'accord," the tallest boy finally said. He reached down, took a couple of Coke bottles from his red crate, and followed me in the direction of my motorcycle, where he poured the gas into my tank. I paid him much more than he'd asked for, and he disappeared back into the woods with his empty bottles. I put the motorcycle in neutral and pushed it through the trees in his wake. The forest spit me out on the road on the other side of the border. I was relieved, believing that Compaoré's guards wouldn't bother with trying to find me in Ghana. I continued toward the safety of Tamale.

26

I'm sure you'll look up your father. You'll find that, officially speaking, there's a lot of mystery surrounding his death.

Blaise Compaoré didn't make a public appearance until the third day after the coup. During a press conference, which I listened to on the radio at a hotel in Tamale, he denied the rumor that he'd issued the order for Thomas's assassination, claiming that he'd been home sick, but added that Thomas was becoming an authoritarian.

"It's unfortunate, but Thomas's presidency suffered severely from his penchant for adventurism and spontaneity when it came to economic, political, social, and cultural policies. He—"

"But where's his body, Blaise?" an unmiked reporter demanded loudly. "The president deserves to rest in dignity and peace!"

A few moments of overlapping voices and general commotion followed before Compaoré regained control and continued the press conference, further slandering Thomas as a leader, then ending with a general promise of improvement under his new regime.

Despite the press conference, I couldn't yet let myself believe that Thomas was dead. There'd been a report that he was being held in the military prison at the installation in Pô. I spent three days alone in my hotel room, alternating between dreading and hoping for more news about him.

The radio news did finally confirm that Thomas's body had been found buried in the cemetery in Dagnoën, a neighborhood not very far from Zone du Bois. After I heard, I switched the radio to music and turned it up as loud as it would go and let myself cry. I granted myself the freedom to suffer. I'm reluctant to describe those days in more than broad strokes. I will limit myself to saying that I have a capacity for profound anger and sadness and shame. Had anyone who knows me been there to witness the intensity of my sorrow, they would've thought I'd lost my mind.

You've likely never seen me like that. Almost no one has. It has never earned me anything to share my darker self with other people. The only anger I ever expose to the world is through implication, by suggesting that I'm on the brink of no longer being able to contain my fury. That is what a woman's strength looks like when it's palatable: like she is containing herself.

In my mind's eye, I can picture those thirteen mounds of soil. Thomas and his twelve colleagues had been buried unceremoniously— I'd read in the paper that to distinguish each grave there were only simple wood markers with a name painted on each. Rumor had it that it was only thanks to the initiative of the military prisoners who'd buried the bodies that the graves were marked at all.

I hated Ed Ross for forcing me to be complicit in Thomas's murder. He'd bound me to a ghost. Thinking about it now still causes a whirl-wind of heartbreak and anger to crash through me. I have to stop here.

Thomas was assassinated during a special cabinet meeting at the Coun-cil of Entente grounds in downtown Ouaga. My interpretation is that when Compaoré learned that SSI wouldn't be able to do what they'd promised, he gave the order for his fallback plan to seize power—an old-fashioned coup.

The council, a government office that employed a half-dozen people, was conceived as a meeting place to promote political alliance and understanding. On the afternoon of his death, Thomas and Sam were driven to the council in a black Peugeot. The two men waited briefly in the courtyard for a second car with three bodyguards and a driver to arrive, and when it did, Thomas, Sam, and a second bodyguard went into the council villa. The drivers and the other guards—all of them uniformed soldiers—waited with the cars in the courtyard.

Thomas and Sam went to a room at the back of the building where the six members of his special cabinet were already assembled and had been waiting for him for a half hour. The bodyguards took their posts in the hall. All of the cabinet members, including Thomas, were dressed in athletic clothes; they planned to attend a public exercise event after the meeting. Thomas was wearing red track pants and a T-shirt. He sat at the head of the U-shaped table and called the meeting to order.

As one of the members of the cabinet was talking about his recent trip to Cotonou, where he'd participated in a conference with the People's Revolutionary Party of Benin, he was interrupted by the sound of a car with a broken muffler outside. Then a volley of Kalashnikov fire exploded in the courtyard.

The gunfire brought faces to the first-floor windows. There were commandos in the courtyard. Terrified employees fled into the hall and up to the roof to hide.

The cabinet members took cover, all but Thomas, who stood. He was the only one in the meeting who was armed, his automatic pistol lying on the table in front of him. A second burst of gunfire sounded and a voice called, "Come out!"

"Restez-la, c'est moi qu'ils veulent," Thomas said calmly. *Stay here, it's me they want.* He told Sam and the second bodyguard not to follow him as he went down the hall. Thomas Sankara had his hands up as he walked out into the courtyard.

"I'm coming," he called to them as he approached the car.

Seven commandos—all of them under Blaise Compaoré's direction—were clumped together in the courtyard near the white Peugeot 504 they'd arrived in. Thomas knew these men, recognized all of them. Some had once been members of his presidential guard.

The two drivers had been shot to death and were lying in the shade of the neem trees planted along the border of the courtyard. A third soldier's body was crumpled near a moped. He had been shot in the chest and propelled off the vehicle. Letters and packages had spilled from the leather carrier bag slung from his chest and were blanketing the ground around him. The soldier had only been at the council grounds that day to deliver mail.

Thomas must've noticed the carnage in the courtyard too late. He was shot twice in the chest and died instantly. The commandos dedicated a few minutes to arguing about the best way to storm the building before heading inside. Sam and the bodyguard with him shot at the commandos when they entered into the hall; the commandos returned fire, hitting both men. Stepping over their bodies, the commandos went into the meeting room and ordered the cabinet members to stand. They did as they were told. They were marched down the hall and out into the courtyard, where they were summarily executed as the witnesses on the roof looked on in terror.

There was an eerie moment of performance after the assassinations for the witnesses who were close enough to hear the events unfolding. The commandos shot their guns in the air, pretending that the siege was an intense one, that they were justified in their slaughter. After the show they began to argue, again unable to agree about what to do with the bodies, and as they piled back into the Peugeot, they were still arguing. Finally, the engine started and the witnesses on the roof watched the car depart.

Then it was quiet. Bodies lay where they'd fallen in the courtyard. Minutes ticked by. The sound of scraping footsteps on the stairs up to the roof reached the witnesses, and the frightened group waited anxiously for whoever it was to appear.

It was Sam Kinda, miraculously resurrected. He'd been shot in the thigh. A tall man in a striped shirt ripped up Sam's jersey for a tourniquet and wrapped it around his thigh to slow the blood oozing from the bullet hole there.

The sun sank in the sky. Two trucks rumbled onto the grounds. Doors opened and slammed. The man in the striped shirt went to the edge of the roof to look out and reported back to the others that it looked like the men who'd arrived were convicts from the military prison—he thought that because of their uniforms. The convicts quickly loaded the bodies into one of the trucks, then sprayed down the bloody courtyard. Both trucks left the grounds, and it was once more quiet.

Quietly, bravely, the group of witnesses started down the stairs with Sam Kinda at the back, his arms slung around a pair of men. The employees scattered across the courtyard, heading to their cars and mopeds and into the night.

27

I was afraid to return to New York, where it would be too easy for Ross to find me if he cared to go looking. I spent a few weeks in Accra, then flew to London, mostly because there was an inexpensive direct flight there, and from London went to Paris. I wandered all three cities aimlessly, but always looking over my shoulder. It was a mild fall, and I liked to walk along Canal Saint-Martin or to sit at one of the cafés. It was there that I decided to resign from the bureau. The events of the previous few months had made it impossible to stay in denial: I couldn't enforce their laws anymore without questioning who they'd been designed to serve.

When I got sick in Paris, my first thought was that I'd contracted malaria in Ouagadougou. I went to a doctor there and learned I was six weeks pregnant. What was surprising was how much I suddenly wanted to be with my mother. I made the decision to fly to Martinique in an instant, before I'd even returned to my hotel from the doctor's office, and only began to second-guess the choice after I'd touched down.

I took my suitcase toward the weathered white farmhouse, a mirror of the approach the four of us would make five years later. On the porch I could hear the distant crash of the ocean, could see the sky and the road unspooling below me. It was empty of cars.

I called into the house, and although there was no answer, stepped inside. Through the slats of the plantation shutters in the living room I could see Agathe approaching; she came through the open back door and put a bowl of lemons down on the dining room table.

"Marie." She smiled and gently rested her hand on my shoulder in greeting. That was the extent of the affection we shared after years of separation. Luckily we've gotten a little better at being around each other since then.

"Are you hungry? I made lunch."

"No, thanks." It's terrible to have morning sickness on a plane; I was still reeling from it. The hum of an engine and the sound of tires on the rocky pavement came through the open doorway. I tensed and sped out onto the front porch, where I saw a car pulling into the space beside my own. A man in a white shirt stepped out, and I called to my mother. I pointed to the man who was walking in the direction of the barn and asked who he was.

"Nicolas. He's a farmhand."

"The road I came up is the only one that leads to the house, right?"

Mystified by the question, she hesitated for a moment before saying it was. I asked her to show me around, wanting to familiarize myself with the property so I wouldn't be taken by surprise by any unwelcome visitors.

She led me in the direction of the barn. She showed me a pair of small white buildings. One turned out to be a chicken coop, and the other was what had once been a detached kitchen. There was still an old icebox inside on the dirt floor. Chickens scooted across the brown grass around us as we went to the barn. She'd already stepped through the doorway, but I had to hang back because of a sudden surge of nausea.

"You're sick," she said.

"No." I took a paper napkin from my pocket and wiped my mouth. "Pregnant."

She beamed at me. "Can I hug you?" I hesitated before saying she could.

"Congratulations," she said as she put her arms around me. "I'm so happy for you."

"Don't worry. I'll be out of your way in a few days. I just . . ." I trailed off, unable to finish the sentence.

"Where will you go?"

"I'm not sure."

"Who's the father?" she asked.

"I don't want to talk about it."

"Is he going to help?"

"No. But I'll be fine."

She smiled and shook her head gently at what I recognize now was my naïveté. "You should stay here."

"I thought . . ."

"What?"

"That you wouldn't want a kid around." She let out a long, slow breath.

"That you don't like kids."

"I'm sure I'll like yours," she said.

"So I can stay?"

"I want you to."

I nodded. Although I couldn't admit it, I'd been hoping she would ask.

"I bet you're tired," she said. "I can show you the rest of the property some other time."

She was right; I was exhausted. I followed her back to the house, where she showed me to a bedroom, the one you've been sleeping in since we got here. It wasn't what I'd expected. The giant four-poster bed had ornately carved feet and was far too big for both the room and the rest of the furniture, its surreal effect akin to *Bedroom in Arles*. There was a photo on the bedside table of a woman in a stiff wig, who was smiling without showing her teeth. I asked my mother who she was and felt embarrassed when she told me that this was my grandmother. The second photo was of Helene—in it, she was milking a cow. I laughed and picked it up.

"She really liked milking," my mother said. "She was good at it too."

"She looks like she's having fun." I put the photo back. "I've always wondered why she didn't stay."

She cocked her head slightly as if the answer was obvious. "She wanted to go back to New York because that's where you were. She loved you, Marie."

"I know," I said unconvincingly.

"She was angry at me for leaving, and at your father for sending her down here. But never at you."

I shook my head. "She was angry at me too."

I was overwhelmed by sadness for my sister. It hadn't been her job to make sure I was okay. I wish she could've stayed in Martinique with the cows for a little longer. I wish she could've had a little more time to be a kid. I wish she could've had more time in general.

I wanted to hear more about Helene, but Agathe told me to get in bed, and as I undressed, she went to the kitchen. Returning with a cup of tea, my mother handed it to me before pulling the door behind her so I could rest.

JANUARY 1988

My ob-gyn was in Fort-de-France, thirty miles away. I'd gotten into a routine of taking the ferry there, traveling across the bright blue water from my mother's part of the island to the capital city. Before my appointment, I'd go to the strange and beautiful Schoelcher Library to leaf through the newspapers, even though there was rarely any news about Burkina Faso in the French press.

I would only be able to fully piece together what happened after the coup much later, after you were born and we'd moved back to the United States. There are African newspapers on microfiche in the New

York public library; from them I learned that Sam Kinda and a few of the other witnesses to the assassination had recognized the commandos and named them all to the police. The men weren't jailed—they were rewarded with positions as soldiers in Blaise Compaoré's presidential guard.

Compaoré quickly reversed all of the CNR's social programs and adopted austerity measures to pay back the IMF debt—precisely the kind of move that Thomas had condemned at the UN. The country continues to suffer badly under Compaoré's rule. While Thomas had augmented the budget by cutting government excess, Compaoré does it by cutting social services. He's also managed to accumulate massive personal wealth—enough so that he owns a private jet. Several of Compaoré's enemies were tried and executed; others disappeared. A journalist was assassinated. Thomas would've been outraged.

I still miss him every day. If I've been cagey about that, it's because I feel unentitled to that emotion. I wasn't his wife. In the aftermath of his death, I wasn't the one forced to flee the country with two small children. That wouldn't happen to me until much later.

I learned I was pregnant with twins at twelve weeks—after the ultrasound I closed myself in the doctor's bathroom and almost cried. I splashed water on my face, patted it dry. Walked over to La Savane, a park where groups of teenagers from a nearby high school were sitting on the cement benches, and people in business suits were already appearing from the surrounding offices for lunch.

In the park there was a statue of Josephine, the first empress of France, and I sat on the bench closest to it. I glanced up at Napoleon's first wife, the accidental symbolism not lost on me. There were food kiosks on the paving stone stretch in the center of the park, and I watched the people queuing up. I was happy, but also terrified. I felt sure I could raise a child by myself, but two was an overwhelming prospect. I must've looked worried, because a gray-haired man walked past my bench and told me to smile, adding, "It's too nice a day out to look so mean."

I nearly told him to kiss my ass—if only it were so easy to smile. To just put away the complex emotions swarming inside me. Instead I got up and walked slowly back to the ferry launch.

My mother was waiting for me in the parking lot on the other side. I went to the truck and found my aunt, Sido, sitting in the cab too, holding a package. She moved over so I could get in.

"You all right?" Agathe asked. "What did the doctor say?"

I told her I was fine, that the baby was fine. I'd insisted on going to the appointment alone, and it would be a few more weeks before I told her I was carrying twins. I instinctively keep secrets. These journals are a huge departure for me; I have never told anyone as much about myself as I've told you here. I hope you understand how much I love you, how because of that I think you deserve to know the truth about me.

Sido handed me the package. "This is for you."

"It came to the house today," Agathe said.

I opened it and pulled out a small stuffed elephant. I looked at the return address, which said Primary Consulting and nothing else. My stomach tightened. It was a threat: Ross knew where I was and knew I was expecting.

"That's cute," Sido said. "Who's it from?"

"An old friend."

A face appeared at the window next to me and I jumped, but it was just a hitchhiker. He said something to Agathe in Creole, a language it had never occurred to me that my own mother spoke before I'd heard her doing so with Nicolas, the farmhand. The teenager hopped into the truck bed. Sido lifted up a handful of my curls then let them drop back against my collar. "It's so long."

"It's the pregnancy hormones," my mother said as she started up the engine. "My hair grew fast too. Isn't she beautiful?"

"I bet you're sorry you didn't inherit your mother's good hair," she said to me.

"It's been sixty years. When are you going to let all this color struck nonsense go?" Agathe said, mixing French and English.

The two of them continued to bicker as she drove. My aunt thinks I don't have nice hair because it's not bone straight, which is a demon-

strably stupid thing to believe. I was too overwhelmed to bother arguing about it. It's not that I didn't care about their (oppressively
well-visited) argument, I just had other things preoccupying my attention, like abject terror.

And I was quiet because watching Agathe with her sister made me
sad; it reminded me of the many ways I didn't know her. I'd had a
mother who was mostly absent, who had parts of herself that were hidden from me. I hated how abandoned that had made me feel. I'm truly
sorry to do the same to you.

Agathe called my name. "You sure everything's all right?"

I wasn't, but I nodded and asked, "Can you drop me at the beach?"

"Sure."

Near the roundabout closest to our farm, Agathe stopped the truck
for the hitchhiker, who scrambled out of the car and called his thanks.
She took me past the farmhouse to the very end of the road, where I
climbed out and went to her window. "I'll walk back. See you in an
hour or so."

I crossed the narrow parking lot and passed beneath sea grape trees,
their leaves crunching underfoot, then stood for a second on the brown
sand, looking out at the ocean. The air smelled like a mix of the sweet
of the sugarcane being processed somewhere nearby, the salt of the
ocean, and the sour of cow dung. Now, the smell makes me nostalgic
for that time in my life. Overall I really enjoyed being pregnant.

I stripped down to my underwear and waded into the water. Turned
on my back and floated, looking up at the bright sky. Twins. Two different people! I thought of my sister—I was especially missing her that
day. I had a vision from a version of the future that would never exist:
Helene holding one of you to her chest, smiling down on you. I ached
for her then as acutely as I ever had.

I saw shapes in the clouds and described them to you. During my
pregnancy, I often talked to you while I was floating—it's a little silly
but I thought of it as a kind of sympathetic bonding because you were
doing the same.

A nearby splash made me stand abruptly and look around. The only other people in the water were a father and son. Talking to you made me feel good and peaceful, so I had let my guard down for just a moment, but I couldn't afford to do that. I felt at my most vulnerable when I was pregnant. I often stayed up at night hearing Ross's footsteps in the settling noises of the house.

I got out of the water and sat on the sand, looking out at the view. I can't bear Agathe's Catholicism, which gets more mystical with each passing day, but there are intangible things about this world in which I have faith. There are all kinds of soul mates, all kinds of bonds I've shared that seem like more than the products of chance. I had one with your father, whom I loved intensely despite everything that I am. I have one with Daniel Slater. Plot our trajectories. Picture us as bodies colliding with the fact of Helene's death, the trauma sending us on separate courses that share an exact intensity. I have one with Ed Ross, to whom I am now bound. I didn't hunt him down then because I was afraid that act would ruin your lives. But now he's forced my hand, and I have no other choice.

As a kid, I must've asked Agathe to tell me the story of my birth dozens of times—it appealed to the natural childhood inclination toward mythologizing my origins. I was born in the afternoon, at Brooklyn Jewish hospital in Crown Heights, which has since gone bankrupt and no longer exists. Your story's much more interesting.

You were born a little early. I'd started having contractions at night but didn't want to wake up my mother. I didn't sleep at all and was worried in the morning when I heard that the gas strike was still on. At the breakfast table Agathe told me I looked exhausted.

I remember that my water broke as I was still poking at my meal. I looked across the table at my mother and said, "I'm sorry."

"About what?" She didn't know that my water had broken. I didn't even know why I was apologizing, except that it was my body, and I felt I should've had some control over what was happening to it. I showered quickly and went to my bedroom, where I looked at myself in the mirror attached to the chest of drawers. My mother was right: I did look exhausted, my face covered in sweat. I put my hair up and began to put on makeup. Agathe eventually knocked on my door and said: "Marie. Let's go."

I ignored her. It wasn't that I cared so much about my appearance. I just wanted to get one thing, even if it was small, under my control. It was terrifying to lose command over my own body, the only thing that, through all that had happened, I'd remained convinced I could depend on. Labor made me understand that too was an illusion; it was like a trapdoor opening beneath my feet. I can laugh about it now, almost, but at the time it was terrifying. I don't think I've ever been so scared, and it wasn't the kind of thing I could express to my mother just then.

Instead I reached for my mascara and unscrewed the cap, my hands shaking. She came over, put her hands on my shoulders, and spun me around so that I was looking into her face. "That's enough now. We have to go."

She picked up my overnight bag and led me out to the truck where she helped me into the cab. As she started the engine, both of us looked at the dash—the gas gauge flitted up then dropped down below the last bar. The gas strike had taken us by surprise, so we hadn't had a chance to fill up the tank.

"Shit," she said.

We coasted down our hill and out onto the road. The roads were very well maintained, leagues better than any street in Ouagadougou. I'd never seen them so empty. Agathe parceled out acceleration very carefully as she drove. When we rolled into the relatively flat stretch in Le Lamentin, nearly ten miles from the hospital, the lights on the dash started to flash. Agathe pulled over to the side of the road.

"Shit," she said again.

I was breathing in and out as deeply as I could, focusing on a spot in front of me. A parallelogram of reflected sunlight fell across it. A fly buzzed in, bounced between the dashboard and the window, flew out.

"It's the twenty-second of July," my mother said. "I hope they come today.

"You want to know why?" she said. I didn't answer.

"If they do their birthday will be Mary Magdalene's memorial day," she said.

"Agathe," I gasped. "Please."

"What?"

"Just shut up. Please."

We waited in silence. Eventually I heard the sound of a car and looked up. It was approaching from the wrong direction, but Agathe was out of the truck anyway, standing in the middle of the road. "Please! It's an emergency!"

The driver stopped, and I watched as she spoke to him, then came back to the truck and helped me down. The driver was out seeing to an emergency of his own that he wouldn't elaborate on. Still he was kind enough to go out of his way to take us to the hospital.

There is such goofy humor in a newborn's seeming bonelessness. I remember laughing at it through chattering teeth when the doctor flopped William onto me. Tommy, you arrived soon after, with the umbilical cord wrapped around your neck so tightly that your face was blue.

I looked down to Agathe's hand nervously squeezing my stirruped foot, only vaguely registering how surreal it was not to be able to feel it.

"Is he okay?" I asked. The doctor didn't answer right away, and I asked again, my voice pitched a little higher.

He said, "We're gonna see."

Once he'd cut away the cord, Thomas, you immediately began to cry, and the doctor finally said, "Yes. Yes, he's all right."

The nurse took you away quick, Tommy, to clean you up. Everything was too quick. The placentas came out. I started feeling like I was looking at the room through gauze and knew I was going to pass out.

The doctor had been too fast to look away. He was distracted, talking to one of his medical students. I called my mother's name, told her something was wrong.

"Marie?" She took my hand and called to the doctor. "She says there's something the matter."

He glanced over and shook his head—too quick to dismiss me—right before the blood pressure monitor began to sound. He hurried over. "That's too much blood."

The last thing I remember was that he called for a shot of Pitocin. Thinking about it now reminds me of Kamal's mother. I still think sometimes about how scared she must've been. I don't even know if she lived.

The hospital where you were born wasn't a great one, but at least they kept me alive. I do think your birth was the closest I've come to dying, edging out the time I spent in the desert and even that night the man came to our house in Connecticut.

I woke up again to the doctor standing beside my bed with a startling amount of blood down the front of his blue gown. My first thought was a panicked one, my mind disordered because I'd been unconscious. I thought he'd been attacked before I realized it was my blood.

"Marie," the doctor said. "Marie. Can you focus on me?" I nodded, still feeling woozy.

"You had a postpartum hemorrhage," he said.

I'd looked to my mother. She'd been crying and that scared me more than knowing I'd passed out. I wanted to put my arms around her, but they were too heavy for me to lift. I asked her, "How long was I out?"

"A few minutes." She took my hand and squeezed it.

"Shit," I said, and she smiled.

I could feel my strength and lucidity coursing back. Once I was strong enough, the nurse rested you on my chest, one in the crook of each arm. I looked down, exhausted and happy. I started to cry. I'd never felt such violent love. Like in that one episode of that cartoon I shouldn't let you watch (I'll confess now that I like it too) where the main characters fall into a black hole, explode, and are reassembled anew. Love like that.

You spent the first two years of your lives here, and Agathe worked hard to support us and to help me take care of you. Pop came down for a visit when you were about a month old. The bell rang, and as I crossed the living room I smelled my mother cooking *accras de morue*. My mother knew he loved codfish cakes, as my grandfather had.

Pop was standing on the porch waiting to be invited inside like a ghoul in a story. As soon as he put his suitcase down he was hugging me as tight as he could. My mother came out of the kitchen, wiping her hands on her apron.

"Hello, Bill," she said in English.

"Agathe." He nodded at her. "You look like you're doing okay."

"Thank you. You also look as if you are doing well."

I smiled at their strained formality. It was so endearing that I nearly wept; then again, my emotions had been running near the surface since you were born.

Pop went over and looked down at the two of you lying in your bassinets. "You want to hold one?" I asked as I joined him.

"I better not. Not yet." He added, "Jim sends his regards, by the way."

"Tell him I said hello." My life had changed too much for me to stay angry at Mr. Ali.

"Bill. Hold one of your grandsons," Agathe said. "You won't drop him. Just go wash your hands first."

He went into the kitchen and did as she'd told him. When he returned, she gestured to the sofa. "Sit."

She put William in Pop's arms. He held you awkwardly to his chest and looked down. "Well, hello there. Hello."

After a few moments of bonding with him, William, you began to cry.

"He's hungry." I took you from Pop.

The crying woke up Thomas, who began to cry too. It would take me awhile to get used to the way you'd cry in stereo. Before you were born I understood that having twins would be difficult, but not in the way that it was. I expected to be tired and I was. I expected to be frustrated and guilty about your crying and I was. What I didn't expect was the way you challenged my approach to things.

I hate to lose, for example, and every time I couldn't get you to stop crying it felt like a loss. For the sake of my sanity I had to stop approaching my life in that way.

After I'd fed you, Agathe said in French, "Marie, maybe you can take your father over to the beach. Leave the boys here for a little while. I'll be fine." She turned to Pop and added in English, "The beach isn't very far. Do you still like to swim?"

He smiled. "Sure do. Did I ever tell you I learned at the Harlem Y?"

"Yes," Agathe said. I heard her exasperation and understood it—I knew she'd heard the story of how he'd learned to swim dozens of times.

I also understood that Pop wanted to tell it because he was nervous and wanted to fill the silence with something reliable. He started to tell the story and surprised us both with a detail I'd never heard before—that he swam nude in the pool.

My mother made a muffled noise—when I looked over, I saw her laughing into her hand. I started to laugh too.

"What?" Agathe said to him. "I never heard that before. It's true?" He nodded.

"But why?"

"Well, the old swimsuits were wool. The fibers used to get stuck in the filters."

It made sense, but it was also so bizarre that the explanation made us laugh harder. My father looked pleased, but maybe also unsure why we thought what he'd said was funny, which in itself was funny too.

I was happy. I thought of the last time I could remember our family laughing like that. The four of us were at Jones Beach, Helene and me wearing yellow T-shirts over our suits, which Agathe insisted on so we wouldn't get lost in the crowd. I don't remember what Pop said, only that same placid, pleased but confused look on his face, Helene with her legs crossed and a smile on hers, and Agathe with her hand clapped over her mouth, laughing until she had tears in her eyes.

While I was pregnant, I had a fantasy that the three of us could live happily forever in an anonymous suburb. That is where I thought you'd be safest, so after two years with your grandmother that I'll be forever grateful for, I took you back to the United States. And for a little while it worked. We lived on a cul-de-sac, in a quintessentially suburban town. Before the night that man broke that life apart, you were learning how to ride a bike with training wheels. We had a dog and family dinners. We looked like a good family—by that I mean a family constructed by the good version of myself I present to the world. I guess it was naïve of me to believe that fantasy would last.

I've spent the last few days on the phone with the lawyer who prepared my will. I've included a note here for your grandmother: instructions on how she and your grandfather should provide for you if anything happens to me. I've invested some money for you in mutual funds and have left you the two buildings in Brooklyn. I used the cash Ross had given me as a down payment on the brownstone across the street. Geneva sold it to me for criminally below market value because she was getting too old to take care of it and was giving me a deal because she liked my grandfather.

Pop has since admitted that my grandfather was right to leave me the brownstone. He would've sold it, not expanded it into a sizable inheritance like I have done. I felt vindicated by that. I've asked him to manage the buildings until you're of age. I'm glad that I can provide for you, but haunted by the poor decisions I've made that mean I might not see you grow up.

Although I've left you some money, that isn't a signal that I hope you'll spend your lives in pursuit of more of it. I want to give you power and agency, of which you'll have dangerously little without money. But for you, for black American boys, the middle class can't help guarantee your safety. Maybe you'll help change things.

28

After you two fell asleep, Robbie and I went out on the back porch with some wine and a few other items. I gave him a plane ticket and the first installment of the cash I'd promised him for his help.

"Are you scared?" he asked me.

"Only of leaving my kids orphans."

"I won't let that happen. I'll keep you safe."

I smiled at him, even though he couldn't promise that, and began to explain how we'd get started. I believed that SSI had won three contracts in the last five years to build American military bases in Africa. They'd started in Burkina Faso and moved on to Ivory Coast, having used the connection between Compaoré and his father-in-law, the Ivorian president, Felix Houphouët-Boigny, to smooth the way. I told Robbie where I thought SSI had moved on to from there, a guess based on the coordinates printed on those blueprints of Slater's and news from that country.

I always read the news with an eye toward finding hints about what

Ross was up to, and I'd picture him out there, catalyzing political skirmishes in West Africa and making a fortune from it.

"Marie, can I ask you something?" Robbie said. "I never understood why you became a Fed. With Helene it made sense, but——"

"I felt like I owed her something. It's hard to explain. And I think there's something else to it that I never wanted to let myself admit."

"What's that?"

"Maybe I was a Fed for as long as I was so that if I ever had to, I could safely elevate myself above the law."

Which isn't to say I had the intention of being dirty. I'm just describing something that lived in one of the corners of myself that I rarely shone light upon. I wasn't the only person I knew to have those impulses. Our neighbor Matt Testaverde had run around with Robbie when we were teenagers and was, by my estimation, the same brand of petty criminal. Matt's whiteness had saved him from any real repercussions though—while Robbie was languishing in jail, Matt was attending City College. He'd eventually gone to law school and, last I heard, had become a defense attorney for only the shadiest clients—men who paid him in cash to make their legal problems go away.

I doubt Matt would explain it in the same way I just did, but I can't help but see a connecting line. His interest in the law also reflects a belief that it isn't equitably applied and therefore that he shouldn't be held to its discretion. I might be cynical, but he's even more so, because he's willing to game the system for the right price.

This outlook may be a product of growing up in the seventies. Although I was *good*, even I wasn't immune to the rallying cry around me that the system was broken, and the ample evidence piling up to confirm it.

Yesterday I got the photos of us from that afternoon at the beach developed. As I was shuffling through them, I noticed one in which Tommy looked like an older boy. It was just a tricky angle, but I suddenly felt the pressure of time. I imagined you as adolescents, then men. There's something about the act of writing to you in the future that makes me, I don't know, strangely nostalgic for the present. For the time I have with you now. I realize that doesn't make much sense. I'll put the photos with these journals.

I made breakfast with your grandmother this morning, and while the three of you were eating, I went to the living room to find Robbie. He was packing for our flight this afternoon. I'd told him the details about where we were headed the night before and what exactly I believed Ross was up to out there. Now he looked up at me and asked me a question he'd clearly been turning over in his mind since we'd spoken. "But why are they building military bases in the middle of nowhere?"

"Strategically it's not. This base is just one in the network he's planned. If he manages to build dozens from east to west, think of how much more quickly our military could mobilize against the Russians, against terrorism. Against war in the Middle East."

"They're trying to garrison the continent," he said.

"Yes."

"And our government's letting them do that privately?"

"Of course. Think about it. Our government would prefer it that way. They gain the military advantage of bases in Africa without the liability of having to be directly responsible for their construction."

"We should burn down the one you saw," he said.

I shook my head. "It's too much risk. And there are soldiers living there. I don't want to hurt anyone innocent."

"Nobody out there's innocent. They're expanding the American empire. Invading."

"That's not the fight I want to have," I said, my voice rising. I turned toward the kitchen, wanting to make sure you couldn't hear me. I knew what he was saying. These men who'd been chosen to defend American interests abroad were so dysfunctional that it threw the whole undertaking into question. They were so fallible, they were agents of a bloated, broken bureaucracy, and yet they were obliged to treat the expanse between Burkina and Burundi as their own dominion. But I couldn't fight that ideology, not through flat-out warfare.

"It's about more than you, though," he said.

"You're right. It's about raising my kids."

He exhaled slowly, clearly frustrated with me. I didn't care. There have been a lot of men in this world who have tried to shape it by getting it to conform to their own ideology. My own beliefs are too inconsistent and contradictory to expect them to change the world by having other people conform to them. I want something else. I wanted to form you into agents of change—that's the way I want to fight. If I'm not around to raise you, know that's what I want for you. Reading this may tell you why I believe you can be of service to other people.

I left him and went out to the barn, taking with me a cup of coffee, the local newspaper, and this notebook. Nicolas was bent over the complicated-looking milking machinery. I called his name over the noise of the lowing cows and gears, to wish him good morning, and he waved back, his hand covered in grease. His exchanges with me in French were always as brief as they were voluble with Agathe in Creole.

I went to the back of the barn, where I slid open one of the tall doors and sat in a chair looking out onto the pasture. The day was perfect.

There were lemon trees behind the farmhouse, and tall palms, and mango trees with bursting, star-shaped fronds. Beyond them, dense-looking jungle and mountains jutted up into the sky, the tallest of them wreathed in clouds. As a child I'd spent a lot of time trying to picture the place Agathe left us for. It had never occurred to me to imagine mountains. If you have to stay here because something happens to me, I think you'll be happy.

I picked up the paper. The news there was mostly concerned with the statue of Josephine in La Savane. It had been beheaded, in protest of the fact that Josephine had encouraged Napoleon to reinstate slavery on the island. The vandals had also splattered it with red paint and written on the base in Creole: *Respé ba Matinik*. Respect Martinique.

I just heard your voices in the barn; you came down the corridor to find me. There's a calf in the pen closest to where I'm sitting, and, William, you slunk by, as far on the other side of the corridor as possible, obviously terrified. Thomas, you stopped to pet it on the nose and laughed when it licked you. "His tongue! It's rough!"

William, you threw yourself across my lap. I kissed your forehead and asked, "You don't like that cow, huh?"

You shook your head. "Maman, let's pretend . . ."

"Hmmm?"

"Let's pretend to be alligators and get Tommy," you whispered loudly.

I agreed and said I would come play in just a second. You both ran out into the pasture. William, you take up space in the world like I'd expect a little boy to do, but, Thomas, you are like a little adult sometimes. So composed. You look like me, but I hope you'll *be* like your father. I'm finished telling you all that I have to. I have tried to offer you the truth in these pages. If something happens to me, at least you'll have that.

I hate that I have to leave you. Going to find Ross, having to do him violence, might take me away from the most revolutionary work I could do. Raising you to be better than me, in hope that you will make the world better. That you will remake it in your image—into a place that deserves you. Anyone can burn down a military barrack; my commitment to you is where real change begins.

I love you. I hope you grow into men who are the best parts of your father and me. I hope that if you're called to resist injustice you'll have the courage to do so. I hope you'll love fiercely and freely. In those ways I hope you'll be good Americans.

ACKNOWLEDGEMENTS

There were many people who were crucial to the production of this book:

The most important are Caitlin McKenna and Kristina Moore, without whom I wouldn't have published it.

Caitlin, thank you for your patience and for sticking your neck out for me. You've helped me grow as a writer, and for that I'm very grateful.

Kristina, had you not asked me to consider writing this novel, I likely would not have done it. Thank you too for being an excellent reader for me.

Arielle Angel and Gabe Levinson, thank you for your feedback. You both gave me insights that proved immensely helpful.

Sam Ross, thank you for letting me borrow your last name.

Justin Mugits, thank you for being the most generous and loyal person I have ever met.

Jean-Éric Boulin, thank you for correcting and editing my French and for your unwavering support.

Paul Beatty, thank you for your advice and for picking up the lunch tab way more than you should.

John Freeman, thank you for your dedication to diversity in books, your compassion, and for giving my fiction a shot.

Linda Perry, thank you for believing I could write novels before I did, and never once wavering in your support for me.

Coleman Collins and Eric Osborne, thank you for being early readers.

Cédric and Nicole Protière, Ousmane Barra, Ouépia Korabié, and Samir Ouedraogo, thank you for showing me around Ouagadougou.

Nathaniel Sasson, thank you for always being able to make me laugh.

Thomas Pico, thank you for being my closest friend for more than fifteen years now, and for being the only person I want to turn to when writing (as it so often does) makes me want to yank out my hair.

David Ebershoff, thank you for acquiring my book.

Laurence Wilkinson, thank you for your support and assistance on my research trip to Martinique.

Elsie Wilkinson, thank you for sharing your memories with me.

Nicole Perry and Osaze Perry-Porter, thank you for the joy that I've shared with you both and for being two of my favorite people.

Bianca O'Brien, thank you for being a sister and a friend I was lucky enough to choose.

Gilda Millar, thank you for your help and thoughtful answers on my research trip to Martinique.

Sara Nović, thank you for blazing the trail.

Bruno Jaffré, Ernest Harsch, Sennen Andriamirado, and Pathfinder Press, thank you for all of your research.

Norbert Zongo, thank you for your courage.

John Phillips, thank you just because.

And to my grandfather, former deputy police commissioner for community affairs, William E. Perry, thank you for inspiring me.

Bringing a book from manuscript to what you are reading is a team effort.

Dialogue Books would like to thank everyone at Little, Brown who helped to publish *American Spy* in the UK.

Editorial
Sharmaine Lovegrove
Simon Osunsade
Thalia Proctor

Contracts
Anniina Vuori

Sales
Hannah Methuen
Rachael Hum
Viki Cheung
Barbara Ronan
Sinead White

Design
Helen Bergh
Ellen Rockell

Production
Nick Ross
Narges Nojoumi
Mike Young

Publicity
Millie Seaward

Marketing
Jonny Keyworth
Hillary Tisman